Primal Ties
In The Company of Wolves

By Dwight Tusing

"I AM NOT WHAT HAPPENED TO ME, I AM
WHAT I CHOOSE TO BECOME"

CARL JUNG

For Dawn and George

CONTENTS

ACKNOWLEDGMENTS

I would like to first thank Dawn and George, who make up my pack and let Dawn know that her support was amazing as she never questioned getting this book published. I would also like to thank John Brown for being my editor and beta reader. After writing this book and starting on the second book in this series, I often walked in Neil Summers store to ask questions about anything from artists to editors. He was always willing to help and never questioned anything, so thank you Neil for always helping. He did introduce me to Rowena Mina, who I am very fortunate to have met. She is a true artist in every aspect and helped me with creating a great cover. I also want to thank Chris Harlow for filling in the blanks on all things nontraditional. This book has been a journey for me and allowed me to see the good in myself and others. I wanted to have something at the beginning of the book to let people know about this journey but couldn't find what I was looking for until I found a list of famous quotes. After reading the list, I decided to have a quote from Carl Jung as part of this book. I think this is a lesson for us all, so whatever may have happened in your life, never let it define you and whatever you decide to be, make the decision to be something great. I sincerely hope you enjoy reading this book as much as I enjoy presenting it to you. Thanks for reading

CHAPTER ONE

Aaron Braun stands proudly at a field he has just plowed; he switches his gaze from the large horse in front of him to his two boys as he removes the large black hat that, shielded him from the sun most of the day, then wipes the sweat from his head and a long beard that the Mennonites are recognized for in the area.

"Unhitch Sampson from the plow Joshua and you can help if you want, Liam."

" Okay papa, Liam, you hold on to Sampson while I unhitch the plow" Liam walks in front of the large animal, attempting to grab his head but is unable as he is only eight and his short stature makes it hard for the young boy to complete his duties. Joshua easily unhitches the horse from the plow, as he has done so many times. He is ten years older than his younger brother and considerably taller, standing six feet and two inches with very little body fat, life on the farm had a way of keeping those who choose a simpler life in shape. The elder brother has his father's height and build but has his mother's green eyes and high cheekbones, but Liam is a smaller version of his mother with his blonde hair and soft smile. The elder brother stands up after completing his assigned task and walks to the front of the horse, easily grabbing the reins.

"Let me help you, Liam" Aaron looks at his two boys stroking the large animal while Joshua helps his younger brother.

"Walk Sampson a little before you get him settled

for the evening, wipe him down good, and make sure he gets plenty of grain."

Liam runs down the hill to the whitewashed barn yelling that he will feed the large animal. This is 1911 in Virginia, but it could have easily been 1811 as the Braun family are Mennonites and do not believe in anything of convenience, no running water, no electricity, just a simple life avoiding anything that "the English" has to offer. Aaron and Joshua walk down the small hill from the field that had just been plowed. The Braun family primarily plants crops to make a living but also makes furniture. It's the end of April, so the weather is perfect for this type of endeavor. The two men walk past the large garden and smokehouse that is currently full of cured hog meat and enter the stall; the horse follows without hesitation walking to the bucket hanging on a wooden post. Joshua returns with a bucket of water and begins to gently wipe the horse down as his father walks over to the container, looking down at his younger son, who is standing proudly at the bucket of grain.

"I think you may have given Sampson a little too much, let him eat half the bucket and then give him some hay, we don't want him to get sick."

Aaron walks over to his other son, who appears to be doing everything to avoid eye contact with his father. The elder Mennonite grabs another cloth from the bucket and begins wiping the horse down from the other side, after checking on the other two horses that resides in the large barn.

"You know, Sampson, Delilah, and Goliath appear to be content on the farm, don't they, Joshua?" Aaron hangs his hat on a nearby hook revealing his thinning gray hair as he talks to his son.

"I guess, papa" Joshua continues to wipe the horse down as he answers the question.

"You know, none of them seem to care what the neighbors are doing or what's going on in town." Aaron looks to the large area at the center of the barn where his woodworking shop is located before continuing his statement, "he appears to be happy on the farm and doesn't need to take a week out of his life to go see what the English are doing."

Joshua looks to his father "If you don't want me to go to Harrisonburg for Rumspringa, I will not go and stay here, papa."

Aaron looks to the ground with his hands on his hips. "No, it's our way; you will go and waste your time with the English."

Joshua and Liam complete their tasks in the barn and start walking to the back of the house with their father lagging behind; Aaron is in good shape for a man approaching fifty, but plowing all day would make anyone tired.

In her late thirties, an attractive young woman enters the small porch where her sons are cleaning their hands in the large white washbasin to greet the trio. Aaron soon enters with his hands cleaned from the old hand pump that sits outside the porch area.

"And brush yourself off before you sit at the table," The woman instructs her two boys, stroking the younger son's blonde hair as he runs past her after brushing himself off. Sarah married when she returned from Rumspringa nineteen years ago. The woman is younger than her husband and is very attractive with her green eyes and blonde hair. Arranged marriages are not uncommon for this community. Aaron didn't have time for such things when he was younger, his father died when he was seventeen, and his mother died from influenza a short time later. Aaron enters the kitchen and takes a seat at the head of the large oak table that he built years ago. The woman looks to her husband as she removes the bread from the wood oven that sits in the kitchen.

"You look tired Aaron; you could have finished planting in two days, and not do it all in one day." The woman places her hand on her husband's shoulder while sitting the newly sliced bread on the table. Aaron leans back in the chair and looks up to his wife, Sarah loves her husband and is very happy to be married, despite the obvious age difference.

"The sooner we get seeds in the ground, the sooner we can see about getting a second crop this year."

"Well, it's not worth killing yourself over" she returns to the oven and removes a large plate of meat. Sarah proceeds to lay a plate of food in front of her two boys and her husband, adjusting her simple gray dress before sitting down. The family lowers their head and prays before consuming the food as they do at every meal.

"This is very good Sarah, another fine meal" Aaron reaches over, placing his hand on his wife's forearm while complimenting her.

"It's good, mama" Liam rests on his calves in his chair, and continues to chew while speaking to his mother.

"Sit correctly when you're at the table, and don't speak with your mouth full" Sarah smiles at the youngest son, then looks to her eldest son. "Are you excited about visiting Harrisonburg for Rumspringa?" Joshua nods, but doesn't say anything, fearing it will start another argument.

"The English have nothing to offer but damnation if you ask me, and I think it's a waste of time to go find that out" Aaron points his fork at his oldest son as he speaks.

Sarah gets up, looking at her husband as she removes the empty plate sitting in front of him. "He needs to sow some oats, and I hope he has a good time" Aaron shakes his head and grumbles as he exits the kitchen. Liam turns and notices his father reaching for the pipe that sits on the mantle above the fireplace. Smoking is the only sin that the Mennonite man allows for himself and has no worries about this simple vice, considering what he has witnessed from others in the community.

"I want to light the pipe" the youngest son rushes to his papa, fearing that he will miss out, not realizing that his father always waits for him.

Joshua remains in the kitchen to help his mother clean up. After the dishes have been cleaned and put away, he takes the large white pan outside and empties the dirty water as he does every evening. His mother greets him at the side of the house and asks the young man to join her on the large bench that sits just outside the side door, and looks to the horizon while her son takes a seat beside her. "We'll need to light the lamps before too long" Sarah leans in and bumps her son's shoulder playfully, who is looking down quietly, tapping the empty pan on his shin.

"Why doesn't papa want me to go?" Joshua said

7

"He's just afraid that you might stay with the English" Sarah pulls out a stick of store-bought candy from her apron and gives it to her son while placing a finger over her mouth. "I got this from Charlotte while we were quilting one day, don't tell anyone" The young man takes the bright red stick from his mother's hand.

"Did you ever think about leaving and not coming back?" The young mother looks into her son's eyes, proud of the man sitting beside her. Both sons look like their mother, but Joshua has matured into an attractive young man.

"I think everyone thinks about what might have been, and about roads not taken, but every time I look at you and your brother, I know God chose the right path for me." Sarah strokes her son's shoulders, lightly grazing his hair as she offers her words of comfort. "And I know he will pick the right path for you."

The next day Joshua gets out of bed as he does every morning, making sure he doesn't hit his head on the low ceiling in his upstairs bedroom and begins packing clothes for his trip. He takes his time as he folds the clothes that his mother made for him, before placing them in the large flour sack, and checks to see that the money that he saved over the years is hidden before closing the large white sack with a piece of rope. The eager young man rushes down the stairs to the kitchen, where his parents are drinking their morning coffee.

"You look overdressed to work on the farm" Aaron raises his cup and takes another sip of coffee after he speaks. Joshua begins to say something but is interrupted by his mother.

"Please go and wait on the porch, Joshua" Sarah crosses her arms and waits for her son to leave before continuing, then looks to her husband sitting across from her. "You need to calm down Aaron, and please speak to your son before you turn him loose in the city," the blonde-haired woman looks down at her cup as her eyes fill with tears. "What happens if he doesn't come back because he's afraid of you and not because of what the English have to offer?"

Aaron looks at his son standing on the front porch, and places his empty cup on the large wooden table that he made years ago. "I'll say something when I take him into town," he leans in and kisses his wife on her forehead. "I know he's a good man, but I'm not ready to let him go."

The city isn't far, but the Braun's only go to town once a month. This isn't uncommon as most members of the Mennonite community try to avoid the English whenever possible. Joshua is excited to go to town most of the time, but nothing is said or discussed on this trip until the two reach the city limits. Aaron pulls the brake on the buggy, signaling an end to the trip, then reaches out and removes the large black hat from his son's head. "You don't want to wear this into town, son" Aaron struggles to find words as his son starts to step down from the buggy. "Joshua, wait.... I know that I've been hard on you, but I want you to know that I hope you are happy whatever path you choose. I would miss you, but I know that you will be a good man regardless of where you end up."

Joshua looks to his father with a nervous smile. "I know our ways better than the English, and I will not learn that much in a week" the young man exits the buggy, with his bag of clothes in hand, and looks up at his father. "And

I'll do my best to avoid temptation and damnation as much as possible" Aaron looks down and laughs.

"I'll pick you up in a week, enjoy yourself son."

Joshua looks as the horse-drawn buggy fades in the distance before walking into the city. Joshua is familiar with this part of town as his father does business with the feed mill but has never ventured past the hardware store in his travels. He walks slowly down the street, looking at the various buildings as he makes his way to the hotel at the center of the city, where he was told to stay by his parents. He enters the hotel to find a man standing behind the counter and Joshua cannot help but notice the high collar and large mustache on the gentleman. Both are forbidden in his culture, and the young man cannot help but stare for a moment at the dapper middle-aged man.

"Three dollars a day to be paid daily, the bathroom is on the first floor, and sheets are changed weekly. How long will you be staying?" the innkeeper presents his logbook to be signed as he asks his question.

"I'll be staying this week, but may leave sooner depending on things" Joshua signs the logbook, and then removes some money from his bag for the innkeeper. He begins walking up the polished wooden steps, but stops to see the lobby before continuing up the stairs to his room. Joshua enters his room, tossing the sack on the bed as he looks around, noticing the large bed and wash station. He goes to the window, facing the street, to admire the view from the upstairs window. Joshua looks outside for several minutes at the various buildings within his view from the small window, including the large courthouse in the center of town. The young man turns back to the room but is unable to find what he is looking for. He eventually flips the mattress, exposing the steel springs, and places a letter that holds his money within the circular steel rings. After returning the mattress back to its original location, Joshua makes his way downstairs and heads for the front door.

"If you need a good place to eat, we have a nice dining area and some of the best food around," the innkeeper smiles and waves as Joshua exits the door to start his tour of the city. He soon finds himself standing at the front of a store. The young man looks quietly, admiring the stonework that surrounds the large glass windows, before noticing items that sit on the small platform for passersby to see. He enters the store and immediately heads to the polished glass counter that holds various watches and other items. "*Maybe papa was right; what am I doing here?*" Joshua does not see anything he wants, but his thoughts are soon interrupted by a less than friendly voice.

"Can I help you?" Joshua stares at the older woman in front of him, still trying to get his thoughts, but before he can respond, the woman asks a second question. "Do you want anything or not?"

Joshua takes another look, but doesn't find anything to buy, and is about to leave before noticing the large selection of candy that sits on the other side of the counter. He looks to the unpleasant woman and points to the various colored sticks that line the shelf in front of him. "I would like one of each stick, please" the woman grabs a bag and begins filling it. Joshua waits patiently but then notices a rectangular item for sale with a confused look.

"It's chocolate, what's the problem? You've never seen a candy bar before?" The woman remains motionless as Joshua tells her that he would like two bars of chocolate. After completing his purchase, he takes a stroll through the store, looking at the brightly colored clothing, laughing to himself. "*Who would wear something like that?*"Joshua pulls the candy bar from his bag and is looking intensely at it while exiting the store. He continues to look at the writing on the simple brown paper wrapper that covers his newly purchased bar of chocolate, but is interrupted by a nicer female voice.

"Excuse me" Joshua looks up to see the most beautiful woman he has ever seen. "You almost bumped into me" The young woman smiles, as the young man stands quietly with his mouth open, looking at the contour of her face and black hair tied in a bun. "Chocolate will melt before too long in this weather. Are you new to the area?" Joshua nods as the young woman reaches up and gently closes his mouth before turning his head to one side. "Your build and facial features look German to me."

"I live a few miles down the road, but I don't get in the city that often" Joshua looks at the woman's form-fitting dress that compliments her figure, and his face soon turns red, alerting her to his embarrassment. She briefly looks down and smiles at her admirer's discomfort but doesn't say anything as the young man attempts to hide his embarrassment.

"Then you will need a tour guide, my name is Anna. What should I call you?"

"My name is Joshua" the young man continues to adjust his pants as he answers her question. Anna reaches out, grabs her escort's arm, and begins touring the city with her new friend. Hours pass as the couple walks, while eating the chocolate and talking. The day ends quicker than Joshua wants, as all his time is spent walking with this beautiful woman. He feels at ease with Anna and tells her everything about his upbringing, Rumspringa, and his father's view of things. He spends his remaining days telling her everything about the Ordnung, while Anna tells her escort what the outside world has to offer, without judging and acting ignorant when Joshua adjusts his trousers. His time was coming to an end, and a decision needed to be made about the future. The last day of his trip ends in front of the hotel, the dark-haired beauty looks at the shy young man and smiles. She understands the decision he needs to make, and the enormous stress he is under. Anna leans in, kissing him on the cheek.

"We should eat together this evening, say around six?" Joshua is silent, ashamed that he doesn't have a watch. In his world, you wake up and start the day when the sun comes up, and the day ends when the sun goes down. Anna reaches out and strokes the young man's back realizing his situation.

"You know, I'm always late, so how about I stop by when I'm making my way to the dining room?" Joshua smiles and nods eagerly.

"I'm sorry, I don't have a watch." The young woman reaches out, gently patting his flat stomach.

"Never apologize sweetie, it makes you look weak." The young man returns to his room with a pitcher of water, and soon finds himself standing in front of the mirror in his best clothes, clean from top to bottom. Joshua tries to sit patiently on the bed but finds himself frequently opening the door, fearing she will not come. After what seems like an eternity, he opens the door to find Anna standing in his doorway. The young woman removed the bun from her hair, allowing it to fall perfectly down her sculptured shoulders, complimenting her face perfectly, and her dress was more conservative than what she wore earlier but did little to hide her beauty. Joshua stammers, trying to find words.

"You are the most beautiful woman I have ever seen." Anna smiles at the young man, who is still in awe of her, and struggles at times to speak.

"Thank you Joshua, that's nice of you to say. Shall we go to the dining room?"

The two enter the dining area and sit down at the far corner of the room. A waiter approaches the table, alerting them to the specials before presenting menus. Joshua is too busy admiring the lights that shine brightly on the intricate red designs on the walls, but soon returns to staring at Anna, who points to the menus. "Do you want to look at the menu or order one of the specials?" Joshua picks up the menu and struggles as he looks at the words. Reading is secondary in his world, his mother has taught him the basics of reading, writing, and mathematics, but his father has little use for those things and frequently has his sons learning what he feels are more essential skills, like carpentry and farming. His dinner companion is quick to realize her date's confusion and reaches out, pulling Joshua to her.

"Would you permit me to order for us this time, my love?" Joshua looks up from his menu and smiles nervously. Anna looks to the impatient waiter standing with his pencil and pad in his hand "I will have water with lemon, and he will have a Coca- Cola" then looks at the menu briefly before finishing her order "I will have a steak very rare, and my friend will have the fried oysters with fried potatoes and a salad" the well-dressed gentleman groans as he writes then turns to Joshua.

"What's your problem? Are you slow or something?" Anna looks at the waiter with eyes that seem to look through him. Her voice deepens as she glares at the arrogant gentleman with the look of a predator.

"He's fine, and that's all for now" she continues to glare at the attendant, who swallows and stumbles backward as he leaves the table. The stunning woman closes her eyes briefly before looking at a proud Joshua.

"At night, we only have oil lamps and it's amazing to have this much light after the sun goes down." The young man looks around the room, making sure that no one is listening, "I'm not very good at reading, but I didn't mean to embarrass you" Anna leans into her dinner companion, completely engaged in the young man.

"It takes a lot to embarrass me, but I have to ask, are you returning to your family at the end of your trip?" Joshua sighs as he looks into her deep blue eyes pausing briefly to admire the stunning woman sitting with him.

"As exciting as this is, it's not me, I have a good life, I can go back home and papa said he will give me two cows to give Mr. Yoder for his daughter's hand in marriage, after I get baptized. Her name is Susanna" Anna sits back in her chair and tilts her head slightly.

"Does this Susanna know that she is being auctioned off for a life of servitude, and the highest bidder is offering two cows?" Joshua looks at Anna, ready to defend his way of life.

"Well, that's how it's done where I come from. Susanna will make a good wife. She's pretty... not as pretty as you... I mean, she has smaller...no, I mean you have bigger" the young man is abruptly interrupted by Anna while stumbling through his explanation.

"I have bigger what, Joshua?" Anna smiles as she teases her dinner companion, who has placed his hands out from his chest, still struggling to find the right words

"What I meant to say is yours are bigger and nicer," Joshua continues holding his hands out from his chest while explaining the differences between Suzanna and Anna "Your backside is also bigger and nicer...." The young man finally lowers his hands with a look of desperation.

Anna, still amused at her dinner companion's awkwardness, continues to tease him. "So you're saying I have a big ass?"

"I think your ass is perfect, I think you're perfect and someone I could start a new life with." Joshua stops mid-sentence, realizing what he has just revealed. Anna reaches out and holds his hand before speaking.

"I would not make any life decisions based on a few days" Anna is interrupted by the waiter bringing the food and refilling the now empty glasses. Joshua looks at the food in front of him, not knowing what to make of the entrée, Anna offers an explanation to what she has ordered "It's oysters, I thought you may want to try something new, and thank you for the compliments, for what it's worth Susanna would be fortunate to end up with someone like you, I think you are a very handsome man." Anna waits as Joshua takes a bite of his food, nodding his approval as he chews. The evening continues and Anna tells Joshua that she is also from a rigid religious community.

"I'm originally from a strict Quaker community and I know what it's like to walk away from the only thing you know." Anna looks to her dinner companion and continues, "but there's nothing wrong with wanting more; it's our choice most of the time" she stops briefly, lost in thought "but sometimes not" Joshua looks to Anna, imagining a life with her but is reluctant to say anything. The dark-haired beauty snaps out of her trance "as long as we make the best of our situation, that's all we can hope for" the couple is interrupted before the young man can respond.

"We have apple pie if anyone is interested" the waiter looks at the table as Joshua acknowledges that he would like a piece and soon returns with the pie. He also informs them that they can pay the innkeeper after placing the check on the table. Anna laughs as her date chews.

"Not a fan of the pie?" Anna says

Joshua swallows and looks down at the half-eaten pastry. "It's not mama's pie," Anna smiles as the two exit the dining area and make their way to his room upstairs.

Joshua unlocks the door and turns to Anna, not quite sure what to do next. The stunning woman leans in, kissing her shy date passionately, exploring his mouth with her tongue. The inexperienced young man looks into her deep blue eyes as she unbuttons his trousers, smiling lovingly at him as she runs the tip of her finger across his manhood. Joshua stumbles into the room and falls on the bed as Anna approaches, kissing him softly. The stunning woman steps back and removes her clothes, revealing her perfect body before joining him on the bed. Normally when she is recruiting members for the pack, she convinces the potential member to join willingly, but it was different with Joshua, and she couldn't explain the attraction she has to this young man, but she was certain that she needed to bring him into manhood before he joined the pack. The gorgeous woman takes charge but gives herself to Joshua lovingly, making sure she submits to him when needed and allowing him to be a man. The two lovers spend the night connecting. Anna has a sharpened sense of who will be a powerful wolf, and everything was telling her that this man is going to be strong, maybe this is what drew her to the inexperienced Mennonite man, but deep down, she knows it's more. Anna continues to lie on top of him until she hears his breath deepen. The dark-haired beauty strokes his hair gently while he sleeps; she has been a werewolf for many years and has never been that concerned about those that does not live long after they change. The weak need to be weeded out for the benefit of the pack, but this is different; he's pure and will need to harden if he has any hope of survival. She looks down at her lover sleeping, and her eyes begin to tear as she turns his head to one side. Anna leans down and kisses his neck gently before biting into him, allowing her blood to mingle with his. Joshua attempts to get up but soon collapses as blood drips from the side of his neck. After dressing, Anna cleans the injured young man's wound, pausing to look down at him before leaving. She doesn't immediately leave and sits beside him for several minutes. She was protective of him as soon as she saw him, but now that she has shared his bed, the need to protect him was stronger than before. Anna rises from the bed and turns to Joshua before exiting the door. "You're a wolf among the sheep now."

Joshua awakens to the light coming in from the window and rises from the bed looking around for Anna, who is nowhere to be found. "*I guess it wasn't meant to be, time to go home and put this past me*" is the only thought running through his head before getting dressed. The heartbroken young man sits on the bed, lost in his thoughts, as he stares out the window. Joshua stands and begins gathering his things but stops when he notices a large bruise on his neck, unsure how he received the injury. After making his way downstairs, he approaches the innkeeper. "How much do I owe you?"The innkeeper explains that his bill had been paid in full with instructions not to disturb the room.

"I realize she paid for additional days but no refunds" Joshua looks at the innkeeper, confused.

"Did she say where she was going?" The innkeeper nods his head back and forth, offering no explanation. "An attractive woman stopped in and paid your bill but she wasn't a guest, now listen, this is a nice hotel and I don't judge, but if all you want to do is stay upstairs, fornicate and get drunk, you can leave."

Joshua exits the hotel, still confused about the missing days, but those thoughts soon fade as he realizes his parents thinks he stayed with the English. He looks around, aware that his father will not be there to meet him at the town limits. Joshua sighs as he starts the walk home and the paved roads soon change to dirt and open fields. All he could think about was Anna and his future with Susanna as he walked. The sun was starting to disappear for the day as Joshua approaches the house. He soon notices that the lamps are not lit but can see everything clearly despite the fading sunlight. After taking a brief tour of the farm, he enters the house and is overwhelmed by a sweet metallic odor that he never noticed before. The young man lights up the oil lamps in the house, while waiting for someone to answer his calls. As light fills the kitchen, Joshua notices scratches on the walls and what appears to be blood on the floor. He follows the blood out to the front of the house only to find more scratches. Joshua places his hand up to his mouth, yelling one last time, hoping for someone to answer. He begins stroking the small amount of stubble on his chin, fearing the worst.

Early the next morning, Joshua loads wood in the stove and starts a fire to make coffee; loading the stove wasn't new to him but drinking coffee was. The young man cuts himself a piece of pie that his mother obviously made for his return. He takes a bite and smiles *"That's what pie is supposed to taste like"* after finishing his second cup of coffee, Joshua goes outside to start tending the farm still hoping that his family will return. He approaches the barn to tend to the animals but is met with some very frightened horses, and his attempts to calm the animals down are unsuccessful as the horses continue to kick and bellow in fear. After releasing the animals to the field, he continues his tour of the abandoned farm. Joshua soon notices dust rising from the dirt road that leads to the property. He walks to greet the horse and buggy but soon notices four other buggies following. The open area in front of the house fills as all the passengers soon gather around Joshua, who immediately notices these are the elders of the community, including Mr. Yoder, who owned the adjoining farm, and is Susanna's father. He also notices the Mutza suits and begins to worry, as it's never a good sign to wear such things on a weekday.

Bishop Landes is the first to approach the young man, who stands awaiting an explanation. "We thought we lost you, but when Levi saw the lights on, we knew you had returned to us, please sit down son, we have much to discuss." Joshua sits down as instructed, almost in tears, realizing why the elders have visited. The Bishop continues to offer an explanation "understand that our Lord and Savior has a plan for all of us as he knows best." The church leader takes a deep breath before continuing, "He decided to call your family home while you were gone," Joshua attempts to steady himself but is caught by Mr. Yoder, who keeps him from collapsing.

"It was an animal attack son, we buried what was left of them up on the hill" Mr. Yoder continues to hold the young man adding some comments.

"We would've waited, but everyone thought you stayed with the English" the rest of the group offers condolences, and takes turn praying with the distraught young man. Mrs. Yoder is the last to approach him.

"I put some sauerkraut and dumplings on the table for you honey, Mrs. Miller also fried up some sausage, and there's a plate of bacon for you to eat on." The large woman looks to her husband" he cannot stay here; you can still see some of the...." She stops abruptly, attempting to hold back tears, before continuing. Mrs. Yoder has held this young man as a baby and grieves for him more than anyone. "We need to clean the house up better Levi" she stands up and adjusts her black bonnet before continuing, "I'm taking him with us." With some help, Joshua stands up, still being held by Mr. Yoder but struggles to find words as he's still in shock.

"Thank you for the food, but this is my home, and I will stay here" the rest of the group assures the young man that he's not alone. The Bishop continues to deliver his message, but the house is empty again after a few hours.

Joshua continues to perform his daily tasks, assisted by the community, which supplies all the support and food that anyone would need, but after a few weeks, things start to settle and get as normal as possible. Joshua visits his family daily and sits with them at the gravesite for hours. He placed a bonnet and black hats on the simple wood crosses that serve as a marker for his loved ones. It is late afternoon when he stops for the day as most daily tasks are performed early morning. Joshua sits on the porch, lost in his thoughts, staring at his father's pocket watch that he finally decided to carry. He was never allowed to hold the watch and feels like he is being disrespectful for picking it up, "*Maybe God has a plan for us like the Bishop preached, but maybe Anna was out there somewhere waiting to give him another path.*" His thoughts are soon interrupted by a knocking sound as two cars pull up and park at the porch. Joshua has seen a vehicle a few times in the city, when he goes to the hardware store with his father, but has never been this close to a car before. A well-dressed man exits the vehicle; he isn't a large man by any means, compared to the local farmers who endure a simpler way of life, but is obviously in good shape. The well-dressed man places a fedora on his head, complimenting his black vest and pants nicely. The black-haired gentleman pulls up the sleeves of his white shirt before approaching Joshua. The young man gets up from his chair and places the watch in his pocket before meeting the black-haired man at the bottom of the steps. Joshua is unable to see the other two individuals in the car in front of him but turns to see three men exit the other car, including two black men. The well-dressed man places his hand on Joshua's shoulder, speaking to him like a long-lost friend.

"You must be Joshua, allow me to introduce myself, I'm John Bennett, and the two darker fellows are James and Henry. The larger blond-haired gentleman is Bram, or Bull if you prefer" Joshua looks at the three men; the two black men were not as well dressed as John but had a neat appearance and looked similar to each other as both were slim and muscular, the large blonde man wore a simple white long-sleeved shirt that did little to hid his large muscular arms, and stood proudly sporting new hair growth on his face. Joshua looks at the three men before turning to John.

"What do you want with me?" The well-dressed man smiles with a devilish grin.

"I understand that you had a bit of bad luck, and I want to help," Joshua reluctantly replies to the bold gentleman standing beside him.

"This place is not for sale!" John leans against the car facing Joshua.

"I have no interest in buying anything, my friend," the suave, charismatic man opens his arms, tilting his head slightly, "but I know about loss, you're at a crossroads Joshua, wondering if this is it." The well-dressed man stands up and begins escorting him away from the vehicles, "I'm here to tell you it's not." John waves his hand across the horizon "I want you to picture an endless supply of women, no money worries and friends that'll die for you." Joshua remains quiet, all his life he has been told the devil never appears as an enemy, but as a friend, and this guy has evil written all over him. After being directed to join everyone, a rather intimidating man exits the car, his hair is also black and has a similar build as John's, but his eyes are cold and lacked emotion. John turns to Joshua. "That's Michael, don't worry, he's harmless" the driver nods and politely says hello with a faint Irish accent. John slaps the young man on his back, "and you already know…." Joshua stands stunned as Anna exits the car smiling softly, the love-struck young man steps to her, but is interrupted by the other four men introducing themselves. John walks with his back to the others, whispering to the stunning beauty, "fix this or we'll have to throw him in the car and get moving" Anna shoves John back as her face turns red.

"We wouldn't be in this situation if you didn't kill his entire family" the dark-haired beauty shakes her head as she continues to whisper. "Dammit John, if you would've let me stay with him a few more days, he would have left and never came back," Anna points to the barn and leans into John. "These people don't talk to anyone that isn't like them and no one would have come looking for him." She turns, looking to the young man standing with the others "he's just a baby John, but you better hope he doesn't find out what happened, he's gonna be a strong one." The well-dressed leader looks to the woman standing beside him, unfazed by her comments.

"My way is faster, and I don't like loose ends, so fix this, or I will." John said

Anna grabs Joshua's hand and begins walking away from the house, instructing him to be quiet. After the pair is away from the others, Joshua stops and looks at Anna. "Why did you leave? I would have stayed with the English for you." Anna interrupts the young man as the two reach the top of the hill.

"You must never tell anyone about what we shared; John is a very dangerous man and would not understand." Joshua looks at the three graves a few feet from them.

"I can't leave, someone needs to tend the farm" the young man doesn't look up as he continues to stare at the ground in front of them. "They buried some body parts of papa and Liam" He looks to the woman standing beside him with tears in his eyes. "Mama was the only one that wasn't ripped apart." Anna moves to the front of Joshua, standing between him and the gravesite. She reaches up and holds his head in her hands.

"Things are different and you will need our protection, please believe me that in time everyone in this area will be in danger if you stay" Anna leans in and kisses him. "You need to trust me," she pulls the grieving young man to her, holding him tightly. "Just keep them in your heart" Joshua looks down into Anna's deep blue eyes and nods as tears continue to flow down his face, he would follow her anywhere, but the only woman he ever had sex with showing up, with a crew of questionable men, weeks after his family died, leaves him with a lot of questions. Most people in the valley view the Mennonites as simple but simple doesn't mean ignorant and this doesn't feel right to Joshua.

"I gave you my heart and was willing to leave it all for you, but I never..." the sandy haired young man swallows hard before he continues."Knew it would come at such a high price" Joshua's jaw tightens as he looks to the gorgeous woman. "Did you or those guys have anything to do with this? Would you have spared them if I wasn't so selfish?" Joshua begins to make a fist and tremble, worried that he may have been the reason his family was gone. Anna leans in and kisses him passionately.

"I don't share a bed with just anyone, I made love to you because I wanted to" Anna begins stroking the young Mennonites chest. "There is nothing wrong with enjoying sex or wanting something more, and being with me did not end your parents' life." The dark haired beauty's fingertips continue to stroke the young man's chest as she speaks, "If you introduced me to your parents and told them that you were leaving with me. Then showed them how happy you are, what would they do?" Joshua stares blankly into her eyes confused and unsure what to do next but Anna is aware of the situation. She needs to get him to come willingly, or John will beat him and throw him in the car. She knows how it feels to be beaten by the Alpha wolf until he gets what he wants, but she senses a powerful wolf in the young man standing in front of her, and intimidating him before he realizes what he is may ruin any chance he has to grow into the man he needs to be to survive.

"They would be sad to see me go but happy that I found someone like you" the young man turns to look at his family's graves. "I guess this way I can leave knowing their not worried about me"

Anna wraps her arms around the Mennonite man and holds him for a few moments before turning to the gravesite. "Do you want me to help you gather your things, maybe take a hat as your Papa wore?"

Joshua looks to the ground. "Papa said that um..." he swallows hard before continuing, "That people will make fun of me if I wear a hat." Joshua continues to stare at the three graves in front of him."They died thinking I left them," Anna turns and whispers to Joshua.

"They know you came back," Anna steps back and looks up at the large man with a soft smile, "and no one will ever make fun of you around me, sweetie."

John looks up to see the pair walking down the hill, then looks to Michael. "You, me, and those two will drive to the house we found" James looks around then turns to

John.

"Why not stay here? It's isolated" John turns his attention to the crew standing around him.

"It's also open, and there's a lot of people coming and going" John looks up at the house. "As a matter of fact, burn it down, burn it all down after we leave." He takes a few steps to greet the approaching couple "everything okay? Can we go now?" Anna nods as she guides Joshua to the car, who stops before entering the car.

"We need to tell Mr. Yoder that we're leaving so he can tend to the farm," John immediately responds, pointing to the pair leaning on the other car.

"They'll take care of everything, we got this" John walks to the passenger door and waits until everyone is seated. He looks to the remaining men. "Make sure everything is on fire before you leave, no loose ends"

CHAPTER TWO

Joshua stares out the window for most of the ride, unsure if he made the right choice. The car eventually turns to a dirt path, almost unseen from all the brush and branches enveloping the path. The car emerges to a small clearing and an abandoned cabin; the structure was still upright but has seen better days. Moss coated the side of the cabin where sunlight was able to reach and bowed weathered boards covered the rest of the house. He walks slowly to the cabin, trying to decide if leaving the farm was the right thing to do, but with his family gone, Anna is all he has. John leans on a post holding up the rusted roof of the front porch and waits for Joshua, while the other two enter the run-down shack. He places his hand on the new member's shoulder with a grin. The grieving young man takes a long look at the man standing beside him. His grin wasn't comforting but was the look of someone hiding bad intentions and was someone not to be trusted. Joshua sits down on the weathered chair as instructed while John begins his speech "No running water and you can either take your chances in the outhouse or take a walk in the woods, but you're used to that, aren't you?" Joshua nods cautiously but remains silent as his first impression of John hasn't changed. "I understand that you're not sure about all this, but years from now, you'll look back realizing that this was the day your life started."

"I was told people would be in danger if I stayed, want to tell me about that before I start walking back home?" Joshua looks at the dark-haired man defiantly. "I've also been warned about people like you my entire life" John points to Joshua and smiles.

"That fire is what you need, and I know what the bible says about how man is supposed to struggle," John shrugs his shoulders as he puts his hands in his pockets. "It has a lot of writing about how being happy is a sin, but I refuse to believe that." The well-dressed leader stands up with his hands still in his pockets, "I'm not the one who'll hurt you, but everyone else will, including those bible thumping hypocrites in Dayton." John pulls out a pocket watch and presents it to Joshua. "My father gave me this watch before we left England, that was in 1775, I was apprenticed at a shipyard in New York and was around twenty when I was turned from some pissed off slaves, we all have a story my friend, and most of us didn't start out from anywhere good." Joshua continues to stay guarded as he listens to John telling him about his life in England and his life as a werewolf. He ends his speech proclaiming himself as the leader of the pack.

"So you're the boss, and you're..." The newcomer begins to struggle to count the years in his head. John places his watch back in his pocket.

"I'm 156 years old and the Alpha of this pack, Anna's almost as old as me and I think she's around 125 years old. She's the sub alpha but don't let the blue eyes and that body fool you my friend, she can be one tough bitch when she needs to be." Joshua frowns, shaking his head in disbelief.

"Let's say I believe you; where do I fit in all this?" Joshua stands up and looks at John, still unsure if he believes the crafty man. The two men survey the woods in silence for a few moments before the question is answered.

"Michael's the Beta, I turned him in Boston, I think he's Irish, and that was around the 1840's" John laughs softly before continuing. "He was a nasty one before he was turned and wouldn't have made it without me. Bram is the Delta; I turned that big Swede in Philly around 1850, big arms but no brains."

Joshua remains cautious but starts to believe what he is hearing as John has honed his skills, and can be very persuasive. "What about the two black men?"

"You mean James and Henry?" John turns and smiles at his newest pack member. "Bram and Michael got caught screwing some slaves in North Carolina and got shot; I think that was around 1860, so I had to clean the fucking mess up, and those two showed up a few weeks later." John kicks the dirt in front of him "they're brothers, Henry's older, but James is the better soldier." Joshua sighs a bit as his leader continues with his sales pitch "we never stay in one place for very long, it's in our nature to roam." John puts a hand on his newest member's shoulder "It's not as bad as it sounds; we take what we want, fuck who we want and move on. When you change, we'll see where you fit in. Anna has a good eye for talent, so time will tell, but make no mistake, you will turn in a few cycles." The pack leader continues to speak to his newest member in a calm tone, almost hypnotic at times. "I don't know how much you know about our kind, but transforming is painful until you get used to it. Your hips will shift, and your legs will extend just like a dog's leg, but your knees will bend. You will pack on some muscle when you grow your fur, your jaw will break and extend out, and all your teeth will sharpen, your feet will flatten, and your fingernails will extend and be extremely sharp." The pack leader leans in, getting closer to the stunned young man "we run as a pack on all fours, but I always run in front." Joshua falls back against the cabin trying to get a handle on what he has just heard. He looks to John, noticing his brown eyes has turned to a deeper shade of yellow, almost amber, "you will come to call us family, or you will not make it. Anna seems to be the only one you listen to, so ask her about all this while you follow her around with a hard-on, and about these while, you're at it" John points to his eyes with an arrogant look.

Anna and Michael stand in the one-room cabin listening to the conversation outside. "I don't know why you turned him, I'm not that damned impressed" the Beta walks to the other pack member, getting uncomfortably close to her. "And if he can't pull his weight and starts dragging the pack down, I'll kill him and let him join the rest of his family." Anna shoves the second in command back with a defiant stare.

"He's going to need time to adjust" Michael is aware that Anna isn't afraid of him but is quick to respond.

"He has until his first full moon to get adjusted, or bad things may happen to poor little Joshua, and screw you if you don't like it bitch." Michael points his finger at Anna but is surprised when she grabs him by the crotch and begins to squeeze.

"I've seen you after you change back, and you don't have enough between your legs that interest me little boy," Anna tightens her grip, making Michael visibly uncomfortable. "And if you try and harm Joshua in any way, I will rip this little dick off and eat it" Michael backs up slowly with his hands up.

"No problem Anna, just looking out for things, no need to get pissed" Anna releases her grip and gently pats his manhood before removing her hand. John enters the room, followed by Joshua, who remains outside the door.

"Knock it off you two, Michael, get away from Anna before she kicks your ass" John walks over, shoving Michael to the side as he looks at Anna. "I've told him about a few things, but you need to work with him, start with the colors." John turns to Michael as he points to the doorway where Joshua is standing, "and he's off-limits until I say so, got it?"

Anna walks over, grabbing Joshua's hand leading him outside "Let's go for a walk" they walk through the woods, and Joshua listens to her every word. He is hesitant to believe anything John tells him, but Anna is different. She explains the pack rankings and how the color of your hair after you turn determines your strength.

"So black is the most powerful, and lighter gray werewolves are weaker than darker gray's? I guess a pure white wolf is the weakest of all" Joshua said.

Anna stops to face Joshua, placing her hands on his chest as she looks up into his eyes. "Blacks are rare, and a pure white wolf is the one that will lead us all, but it's only a legend, I know your struggling with this, but you need to move on or John will kill you." Joshua grabs Anna and kisses her passionately while trying to lift her skirt; she hesitates and pushes his hands away.

"No, Joshua, we can't do this" Anna said.

Joshua looks deep into her eyes, "Being with you is the only thing keeping me going, I need you, or I'm not going to make it." Anna turns away from Joshua, trying to avoid eye contact; no one has affected her like this in several years. She tilts her head and offers no resistance when he attempts to lift her skirt a second time. The dark-haired beauty closes her eyes as she feels him kiss her neck, moaning quietly when she feels his shaft pressing into her beautiful backside. She leans over as if in a trance and gasps, struggling to accommodate the large shaft inside her. Joshua does his best to be gentle but soon feels her body shake as he moves his hips back and forth. Anna reaches out, placing her palms on the tree in front of her, not sure if she is shaking due to her approaching orgasm of how forcefully she is being penetrated, but soon feels her lover's hands move from her hips to her breasts as he releases. Anna remains quiet as Joshua grunts filling her with more of his essence, allowing him to remain inside her. The young man rises and looks down at the gorgeous woman in front of him, whispering, "I love you."

Anna stands up and adjusts her skirt before turning around "I'm pretty sure I'm the only woman that you've been with." She reaches up and runs her fingers through the young man's hair "a hundred years from now, you won't feel this way my love" Joshua is visibly upset, hoping she would proclaim her love to him.

"I will feel this way regardless of how many women I'm with" Joshua lowers his head. "Was any of it real?" Anna smiles, leaning in to kiss the broad chest in front of her.

"I don't know why I'm so attracted to you, but what we're doing is dangerous" Anna said.

"We could leave if you honestly cared about me, but you don't love me at all, do you?" Anna explains to the love-struck young man that John would find them regardless of where they go and that he has eyes everywhere. Joshua looks down, upset and love-struck, as

the lovers make their way back to the cabin. The beautiful
woman continues to walk but stops when the young man
leans over and returns with a shiny blue gemstone;
mountain quartz is not uncommon to find in the area but
has little value. He hands it to her and smiles. "I don't have
much, but I'll love you for the rest of my life," Anna looks
at the rock in her hand but is reluctant to say anything.
Joshua will be a very powerful werewolf, and guiding him
into manhood was needed, but having him fall in love was
not part of her plan. The beautiful woman is also concerned
that if John smells his scent on her, he will kill them both as
the leader has no tolerance of her being with anyone else.

"I know you would, honey" she places the rock in
her pocket as the two emerge from the woods to find the
pack standing around a fire, including the three that were
driving the other car. John looks up briefly at them and
points to a bag of lemons and a stack of steaks on the hood
of the car.

"Show him what to do with the lemons and feed
him some red meat" John looks to Joshua, who is standing
beside Anna. "After she gets done with you, go kill a deer
and skin it, those few steaks will not feed all of us" Joshua
looks at the men surrounding the fire with a confused look
on his face. Joshua smells the same metallic odor that he
had smelled previously at the family farm.

"What am I going to hunt with?"

Everyone standing around the fire laughs except
John, who doesn't look up from the fire. "Fix this Anna, or
I may have to find us something to eat, understand?"

Anna takes Joshua and the lemons inside to the
open area of the abandoned shack; she grabs a pail and

begins pulling the dull green handle of the water pump that sits on top of the counter of the small kitchen area until the bucket is almost full, and then tosses the sliced lemons in the metal container. Joshua steps back, covering his mouth and nose. "What kind of lemons are they? My nose and mouth are burning."

"Lemons help dull our senses, you will need to be trained on how to use them, or you will go crazy in a few years." After placing lemons in the bucket, she points to the stack of steaks, "and we only eat cooked meat in public to avoid suspicion. It's only browned to give the appearance of cooked meat" the newest werewolf looks out the dirt-covered window behind his trainer.

"I like my meat cooked" Joshua stands defiantly with his arms crossed. "I don't eat raw meat" Anna reaches out and grabs the startled young man slamming him on the deteriorating wooden counter behind her.

"In time, the rain will be so loud you'll pray for it to stop and the raw meat will stop you from getting too aggressive." The beautiful trainer looks down at Joshua with a final warning, "and if you start to go crazy from the noise and aggressive from the hunger, I'll have to kill you, and I don't want to do that." She looks up to see John standing at the door entrance smiling.

"I see his training's going well, don't worry about the deer, the boys decided to kill something." John walks a bit closer, looking down at Joshua. "Tonight after the sun goes down, I want you to go take a very long walk in the woods; it's some of the best training you can get" John looks up to Anna and smiles. "Glad to have you back, baby," and kisses the stunning woman before leaving. Joshua gets up from the table, refusing to look at Anna as he rushes out of the room.

He walks outside to find the others eating a deer with their face and upper torso covered in blood; the metallic odor had left and was replaced by a musky smell. John instructs Joshua to remove his shirt before tossing him a piece of meat. He removes his shirt, exposing his flat stomach and toned body, before reluctantly eating the bloodied meal that he was given. James walks over in front of Joshua, looking him up and down. "Damned if our boy ain't ripped," then turns to the others. "He may be able to give Bull a run for his money" Bull stands proudly, glaring at Joshua.

"Anytime, pup" he begins walking to the new pack member but stops when Anna exits the front door shaking her head. "This isn't over, pup" is all that is said as he walks away.

Anna looks at the large Swedish man. "It better be Bram."

Bull walks off, mumbling in his native language.

That night, the others gather around the large open area of the cabin sitting on various makeshift chairs, playing poker. John picks up a bottle turning it upward.

"So you found this in one of the cabinets? This is good bourbon." Michael accepts the bottle from John taking a drink as he looks over at Joshua.

"Does your kind play poker, or is that also not allowed in your little rulebook?" Joshua shakes his head, ignoring the overbearing Beta as he walks out the door. Michael looks to the female werewolf continuing to speak in his Boston, Irish accent. "Aren't you going to take your puppy for a walk? He'll probably get lost" Anna gets up from her chair as Michael stands up to meet her. "Anytime bitch"

John stands up with yellow eyes getting between the arguing pack members, "If you ever talk to her that way, I'll rip your head off" he then looks to Anna standing on his opposite side. "Still, you need to quit being so damned overprotective of him" the pack leader grabs the bottle, taking another drink. "Joshua's family, he may be new, but it's obvious that he is going to be powerful, and yes, the pack may change, but we're still family." He sits the bottle down beside the pile of cards on the table. "When we change, it's all instinct, and how long we've been turned doesn't matter." John looks around the table at his pack. "If anyone tries to hurt him in his current form, they will answer to me and if they fight him after we change for pack ranking, don't come crying to me when it's over."

Joshua walks outside to get away from the others, with thoughts racing through his head about his family and Anna. Does she even care about him or is he being used to be part of her and John's pack. Regardless of her age, she knows how to use her looks, and a simple farm boy could never get a woman like her. His father warned him that the English offered nothing but damnation and so far he was right, but he could never tell his papa this or anything. He also realizes that his family was killed by wild animals, and he is keeping company with a group of people that claims they turn into wolves, and this sends a chill up his spine as he fears they may have killed everyone close to him, but did Anna know anything? Does she actually care about him or is she just screwing him to keep him obedient? The sandy haired farmer is startled when he hears a voice coming from the shadows behind him.

"You need to forget about what you can see and start with what you can hear and smell. Close your eyes and start using your other senses first." Joshua immediately recognizes Henry's voice, but is unable to respond before he is given further instructions, "just try it."

Joshua does as he is told and hears nothing at first but his trainers' voice is almost hypnotic and he is told to clear his mind, and focus. The new werewolf clears his mind and soon opens himself up to the sounds and smells of the night. He starts to laugh softly, "I hear something over there," and points to the right of where he is standing.

"Looks like a possum and it's a far piece away from us, not bad, you'll get better in time." Joshua opens his eyes, looking to his new friend. Henry hasn't been as eager to show dominance as the others have.

"Why aren't you with the others" his eyes adjust to the darkness as promised, and he can clearly see his trainer.

"I've never been much of a drinker, so I guard the pack, from things outside and at times, from things inside the pack." The black man turns to the young man with a raised brow "understand?"

Joshua looked confused and worried at the same time. "No, not really" was all he could say, unconvincingly.

"You need to get over Anna, I understand, I really do, she looks the way she does and I don't think you've had that much experience with someone like her." Henry places his hand on the newest member's shoulder "it's not gonna end anywhere good," Joshua nods his head up and down while looking around enjoying his developing senses.

"Why are you nice to me?" Joshua doesn't wait for a

response and continues to vent, "no one other than Anna has been nice, there's something about John that I don't trust and don't get me started on Michael." Henry continues training the young man as the two walks in the darkness.

"You remind me of papa, I'm older than James, but it doesn't seem to matter when you get as old as we are, mama and papa were slaves, papa always read the bible to us, and when I asked what do we have to be thankful for, he would always say that God has a plan for us and we shouldn't judge." Joshua laughs softly.

"I've heard something like that too Henry, your papa sounds like a good man to have that kind of faith."

"James and I were alive to see slavery abolished, but papa was hanged after he was caught reading when we were young, and mama was shot after she got pregnant with a white man's baby, both died as slaves." Henry's eyes begin to water as he reflects, "the fact that she was being raped weekly didn't seem to matter. John showed up after Michael got shot and killed everyone, James and I was bit by one of them." Henry pulls his shirt to the side, showing his friend his scar "been like this ever since." Joshua looks at his trainer's scar and runs his fingers across the bite mark on his neck.

"So John took you in when he found out you were like him?" Henry nods.

"John got turned from killing a slave in New York on the docks and doesn't have much use for a black man, he was going to kill us and move on, but Anna convinced him to let us join the pack." Henry stretches a bit as he looks around for one last time "but trust me if things get too weird with you and Anna, he'll kill you both." Joshua yawns and soon finds a spot on the ground under the front porch. Henry sleeps in the grass outside while the others find a comfortable spot in the cars. The new werewolf has slept on the floor of the barn at his home, helping to birth calves in the fields at times, so sleeping on a hard surface isn't anything new, but the sound of Anna and John having sex was all he could focus on tonight.

The next day Joshua wakes up from his makeshift bed by the shock of Michael throwing him in front of the cabin.

"Since you are the newest member of the pack, take your worthless ass out there and find us something to eat." Michael points to the woods as he kicks dirt onto the newest member of the pack. The sleepy young man walks past the others, refusing to look up. John nods at Anna to help him. It doesn't take long for her to find him, but the new wolf is quiet as he stares at the ground in the woods. Joshua eventually looks at the stunning young woman with a look of confusion and rage.

"Did you and John have fun last night?" The distraught young man grits his teeth, not realizing that Anna has no choice, and refusing the leader can be dangerous for her. "I have no Mama, no Papa, and no Anna," Joshua's voice begins to deepen as the whites of his eyes turn yellow and fangs appear in his mouth.

"Joshua sweetie, you need to calm down and focus" Anna speaks softly and nurturing, aware of what an inexperienced wolf can do with this much power this early. She also realizes that his brief transformation this far away from the full moon means Joshua will be a full black at some point. It also explains her unusual attraction to him. "Just calm down and focus, remember what Henry taught you about using your hearing and your nose more than your sight. Joshua looks to Anna as his hair begins to darken.

"I DON'T WANNA CALM DOWN!" Joshua's chest expands as his breath begins to deepen, and he soon finds himself unable to speak. He roars at Anna, who reaches up and kisses him passionately.

"Please calm down for me...please" Anna continues to stroke him as he calms down and stops turning, the new werewolf looks around as the sounds of the forest are alive. He hears and smells everything around him and can detect the slightest movement around him. Joshua places his hands over his ears and as promised, everything begins to overwhelm him, and he soon feels himself turning again but stops when his beautiful trainer reaches out and places his hand on her chest.

"Just stop and focus, listen to our heartbeats" Joshua closes his eyes and soon hears the beating of their hearts. "Now remove our heartbeats and listen, just listen." Anna continues to speak softly as Joshua hears a strong heartbeat in the distance and begins running through the forest, leaping down on a deer, snapping the large buck's neck on impact. Joshua stands over the deer with his head lowered and growls as Anna approaches the young man and presents him with a knife.

"We need to drain the blood and remove the organs to make things lighter for us to carry, but keep the heart." Anna still speaks softly while keeping an eye on him while he cuts into the deer.

The other pack members wait patiently while John discusses other transportation plans with his second in command. Michael looks to John, voicing his opinion that the cars were obtained up north and that getting another set wasn't needed. Both men agree as Michael looks to the woods throwing his hands up. "That is if we don't starve waiting for that dumbass to get something, I'm telling you John, she messed up this time."

John sighs as he is also beginning to question Anna's decision, but turns to see Joshua dragging a deer from the woods. The new pack member approaches the men, tossing the deer in front of them. A low growl escapes Joshua as he looks to the others with the eyes of a predator. John laughs and points to the new werewolf with pride.

"There he is, that's what I've been waiting for!" The proud leader looks to the others, barely able to contain his excitement. "Someone hang it and let it drain out a little more, he did his part," Anna walks over and stands beside Joshua, stroking his back, keeping him calm.

Henry and Bram hang the deer as James looks at the pack's newest member nodding his head. "Damn, that's one badass wolf," then turns to the second in command. "Call him a dumbass now, Michael."

Anna reluctantly leaves Joshua to speak to John. "We need to talk" the two leaders walk into the cabin to discuss Joshua's transformation. The female mentor continues to keep an eye on her pupil as she talks to the male Alpha "he damned near fully changed out there, and we don't change until four days John." The dark-haired beauty begins pacing the floor, "only a black can do that, but I've never heard of someone being that strong the first time they change."

John remains quiet until Anna finishes her rant, "How did you calm him down? And why did you calm him

down anyway? He's not gonna hurt anything around here."
The pack leader walks up to her and kisses her on the
cheek. "Joshua may be a dark gray at best, and it's normal
for a new wolf to change out of cycle" Anna stands with
her arms crossed and turns to John.

"If you really want to know, I kissed him and
stroked his manhood," The pack leader laughs, putting his
arm around her.

"Well, that would certainly calm me down, this is a
good thing for us, and we may have a Beta to lead another
pack." John stands in front of the female Alpha, placing
both hands on her shoulders "for now, we may have a new
Delta and Bull will have some growing pains." Anna
remains quiet as she continues to look out the dust-coated
window, hiding her concern. "He trust's you, so keeping
him on a short leash should not be a problem."

Joshua stands in the woods, fascinated at the smells
and sounds of the forest that surround him. His training
with Henry ends, but the meetings continue, as he is the
only voice of reason at times, and does a good job putting
things in perspective. The two have developed a friendship
as both are not as aggressive as the others. Henry decided
to follow his father's example and accepted his previous life
as a slave and the injustice of that time in his life. This has
allowed the former slave to educate himself; Henry speaks
English, French, and Spanish fluently and reads anything
he can get. His brother hasn't accepted the horrible things
done to him and his family in his past life, and is a bit more
aggressive than his older brother. Anna also asked Henry
to look out for their student.

"Tonight's the night, Bull take James and Joshua
about 10 miles down the road to park the vehicle. Pack

some clothes for us, and if you happen to find some clothes along the way, having a few extra wouldn't be a bad idea" John turns and leaves after instructing the three men.

Bull instructs Joshua to get in the car with a thick Swedish accent. The two head down the road, with James following behind, and are soon pulling into a dirt driveway. Bull looks at Joshua and points to the clothesline beside a small house at the end of the dirt path. "Get the clothes" the young man looks confused, so Bram repeats his command. "Go get the clothes, pup."

Joshua is hesitant to get out of the car but does as he is told. The nervous thief begins removing the clothes from the line. He turns to make a quick exit but is startled to see the owner of the garments looking at him. The petite middle-aged woman crosses her arms as she confronts the thief attempting to steal the clothes.

"What are you doing? If you need some clothes, just take a pair of pants and a shirt." The middle-aged housewife turns to enter the house. "We don't have much, but let me get you some bread or somethi…."

Suddenly, the woman strikes the ground hard, Joshua looks down at the woman whose face is now coated in blood as she attempts to get up, but is kicked back to the ground, and now lays unconscious between the two men. Joshua looks to Bram, who is obviously irritated.

"Quit screwing around, I didn't tell you to talk to this useless bitch, I said get the clothes" Bram said.

Joshua stands shaking his head, "She was going to help us, why hurt people when there's no need?"

Bram steps over the woman getting uncomfortably

close to Joshua, who doesn't move. "Do you think you're the only one who's been turned by Anna? They didn't make it, and neither are you, puppy. Now get in the damned car!"

Joshua looks at the end of the driveway to see James sitting in the other car, shrugging his shoulders, but says very little when he gets in the back seat. Bram soon joins them after hiding the car behind some weeds. James looks to the distraught young man in the backseat.

"Don't worry, we may not remember that much when changed, but the alpha remembers everything, even when turned." The former slave begins backing the car up, "so don't worry, we'll find our way here."

Nothing is said after the three men return, and everyone can feel the excitement. After a few hours, the sky turns orange; alerting everyone that night is approaching. Joshua looks around and begins noticing the sound of the forest has increased and his sight getting better, but this time isn't overwhelming like before. The sky begins to darken and the new pack member finds it hard to concentrate, and starts to tremble, alerting everyone to his condition. John nods at Anna instructing her to stay back as he walks slowly to the new wolf.

"Just go with it Joshua, embrace what you're feeling" the pack leader continues to coach the sweat-covered young man, who is now shaking uncontrollably. "The first time is special, Anna and I will look out for you, and we're nowhere near any towns or open areas, so we have everything covered."

John points to the others devouring another deer and instructs Joshua to eat. The new pack member walks up and begins eating at the carcass but is soon interrupted by

Bram, who attempts to shove him away. Joshua shoves the large man backward and growls, exposing his sharpening teeth. Bram attempts to show dominance a second time but is unable to move the emerging wolf standing defiantly and snarling at the stunned pack. John walks slowly up to the confused young man reminding everyone to keep calm.

"Just calm down, there's enough for everyone" John motions for Anna to come over and stay with Joshua. "Watch him, it's a little early for him to change, but your right, he's gonna be a strong one."

Anna rubs his shoulders, speaking gently as he eats; he could easily kill someone within the pack as no one knows how strong he will be. "You need to undress and put your clothes in the car, I undress out of everyone's sight, but we have some time yet." The dark-haired beauty remains with the young man as he jerks and struggles to breathe" Shhh, just relax."

Joshua attempts to do as he has been told but is unable to unbutton his shirt as his hands are trembling. Anna assists in removing his shirt, looking into his eyes that are now yellow. She places her hand on his sweat-covered chest, telling him to calm down before assisting him in removing his belt. Joshua's nose begins to point upward, and his lips curl as he growls at Anna, displaying claws that are emerging from his fingertips. The rest of the pack begins to transform except John, who steps toward the young man but stops when Anna shakes her head. "He would never hurt me, but I need everyone to stay back." The female Alpha begins to unbutton her top as she is also starting to change, "I'm right here sweetie, I'm not going to leave you." Joshua shakes, looking up to the darkened sky as his screams soon change to a roar. Anna finishes getting undressed while continuing to console him. "Don't fight it, just turn, it hurts because you're fighting it" he steps back as his height grows. Joshua looks down as his legs lengthen and his knees begin to protrude outward. His jaw and nose extend from his face displaying his sharpened teeth as hair begins covering his entire body.

John looks to the others who have changed and makes sure everyone is okay but shifts his gaze to Joshua, who is now covered in light gray fur. John shakes his head in disappointment. "I thought he would be stronger, but I'll take it" Joshua's hair ripples, turning darker and darker until only a small amount of dark gray can be seen within the black fur that now coats the new werewolf. John smiles at Joshua's hair color before changing.

Joshua succumbs to his primal nature enjoying his newly heightened senses. He notices every sound and smell and can see all the creatures in the woods clearly, including the pack, despite the low light. The creatures that hid in the shadows can be seen moving around but can also be tracked by smell. The new werewolf soon finds himself being thrown against a tree, before he can fully adjust to his new anatomy. Joshua rises from the ground, still stunned but is struck again by a large fur-covered fist. He looks to see Bram preparing to attack again but slices into his attacker's chest with his claws before the Delta can continue with his assault. The bloodied werewolf attempts to escape, realizing his mistake, but the new, darker werewolf continues his attack and leaps on top of Bram digging his claws into the Delta's back, slamming him to the ground. His upbringing no longer hinders Joshua, this is as primal as it gets, and he has held in so much for the last few weeks. He grabs the beaten werewolf by the back of the head, and begins slamming him to the ground wildly.

Michael attempts to stop him from killing Bram but soon finds himself looking up at Joshua, who has grown even larger and towers over the others, including John. The Beta attempts to stop the overgrown wolf but is easily tossed to the side. Joshua turns around to continue his attack to see John standing between him and Bram, growling as he points to the woods, before leading the pack. Everyone drops to the ground and runs on all fours, moving to their assigned places, including Joshua, who now runs in front of an injured Bram. The pack runs as one unit, and for the first time, the new werewolf forgets about his family and Anna as they run through the forest.

The next morning, Joshua wakes up in a small clearing completely nude. He stands up to find the others dressed, including Anna, and sees the others grinning. Michael tosses some clothes on the ground beside him smirking arrogantly.

"Happy to see us stud?" Michael said.

Joshua looks down to see his manhood protruding outward and turns beet red as he rushes to get dressed, attempting to hide his erection. He stretches; hoping to reduce the swelling in his pants, but soon realizes his back is extremely sore. He turns to John, who is approaching him, grinning, "Is a sore back normal?"

John laughs, "It is when you get thrown through a tree, but you should see the other guy." He points to a bruised Bram, who has blood staining the front and back of his shirt, "you're lucky he didn't kill you and next time, I may let him." John wraps his arm around Joshua, "A dark gray his first time out, you're gonna be a strong one." He turns to the others, pointing to his newest member proudly, "he even had some black streaks in his fur."

The entire pack gathers around the car and John proudly instructs Joshua to get in the car's driver's seat that he and Anna will be riding in. "That's your seat, Joshua" the young man stands dumbfounded.

"I don't know how to use this thing."

John laughs, still beaming with pride, "Today, you learn, the strongest always rides with me and my Anna." He places his fingers on Joshua's chest, "and you are a very strong member of this pack, my boy."

The remaining pack members laugh at the struggling driver, while Michael sits beside Joshua, cursing as he attempts to instruct him. After watching the car leave, Bram looks to the other two werewolves with a disgruntled look "This is bullshit, I always drive."

Henry looks at Bram, unconcerned with the large man's situation. "I'm guessing it's because you got your ass kicked last night, and it looks like our boy has got some sharp claws, so you might want to get used to this." Henry walks over, placing his hand on the large Swedes shoulder, smiling "he damned near kicked Michael's ass his first time, so you may not be the only one to drop in rank."

James nods his head at his brother's statement before adding his thoughts, "But if your next question is what's next, from what I just saw, we gotta get that boy laid." James looks to his other two pack members laughing "and from what I just saw, she is gonna be one sore little lady tomorrow."

Joshua soon returns, grinding gears, and stops short in front of the waiting pack members. Henry sits beside his friend as the others get in the back seat, then looks to the nervous driver sitting behind the wheel laughing, telling him that he might as well get used to being the driver as Bram sits in the back seat, obviously upset about his new position.

The four men return to the cabin and find the car packed up, John strolls over to meet the returning members of his surrogate family, "I didn't hear as many gears grinding this time." The pack leader points to the other car, "but I need Joshua to ride with us." After the remaining items are placed in the other vehicle, the leader looks to the crew standing around him "I think it's time for fun, food, and booze." John looks to his newest member smiling, "and get our new Delta laid tonight." Everyone laughs and begins to pile in the cars. Anna gets in the backseat patting Joshua on the chest as he opens the door for her. John steps into the backseat but is stopped by Henry.

"Are you sure this is a good idea?" The black man points to the other car where his brother is sitting. "Me and James aren't exactly welcome most places, and given what happened last time."

John interrupts the cautious black man "You worry too much" the pack leader gets in the car beside Anna, and then leans out the window of the closed door. "You may consider finding a wrapper for that sword of yours tonight as well" John looks to Michael, waiting at the steering wheel. "Find us a place to let the guys burn off some steam."

That evening the pack finds themselves entering a large dirt parking lot with a large sign, alerting passersby of nightly entertainment, food and drink, lit proudly on top of the run-down tavern. The pack exits the car and begins walking to the dull red door. A large overweight man in overhauls meets them before they can enter and points to the two black men. "Everyone can come in except those two."

John doesn't respond but pulls out a large roll of money, handing the owner a twenty-dollar bill. "My mates and I are going to eat lots of steaks, drink large amounts of alcohol, and then these fine healthy lads are going to ruin some women for other men," John points to Henry and James, who remain quiet, "including those two." The irate leader then lifts the large man off the ground with one arm. "Now you can take this twenty dollar bill, or I can take whatever I want, including the women, and keep my money." Joshua steps forward but stops when he looks to Henry, who nods briefly, instructing him not to interfere. Nothing else is said as the scared business owner sits the crew at a table, then returns with steaks. John scans the room while the crew eats; the dimly lit bar is no different than the others they have visited. A long bar extends the length of the establishment with various signs covering the walls. After looking around the pack leader notices an attractive waitress at the bar and motions for her to join them. The petite auburn-haired beauty walks over to the well-dressed leader, who presents her with a twenty-dollar bill, "keep it coming, and if you would like to make some more money." The stunned waitress looks as John places another twenty-dollar bill in her hand and points to Joshua "take that young man home with you and let him screw you blind the entire night." The attractive waitress places the money in her pocket and returns with two jugs of cider, then walks to the naïve young man and strokes his light brown hair.

"Easy money, I would've taken you home with me anyway," she instructs Joshua to pull his chair back and sit on his lap, kissing him before looking to the others. "I'll take good care of him" Joshua begins to shift in his chair as the softness of her well-rounded bottom caresses him, the young woman turns to Joshua and strokes his flat stomach. "It feels like you're gonna take care of me too," then pats the bulge running down his leg before getting up "I get off work at 12:30, then we can take care of that." Everyone laughs as John raises his glass.

"I told you I would get you laid tonight" the arrogant leader slams the glass down on the thick wooden table proclaiming proudly. "We take care of our own my boy," Anna looks to Joshua and smiles at his obvious anxiety.

"Joshua, the only thing that can kill you is silver or losing your head" Anna grabs her glass and lifts it in the air." "So here's to our Joshua and the red-haired little thing that's gonna wake up sore tomorrow." Anna takes a drink, allowing John to kiss her neck before continuing "and don't worry about getting anyone pregnant, your baby-making days are over, so enjoy yourself."

The next morning, Joshua walks out of the small rundown apartment behind the bar to find Michael and James waiting for him. He turns, not quite sure what to say to the red-haired beauty standing in the doorway "Thank you Jenny," seemed appropriate. Joshua stands nervously, looking at the woman that had made love to him the previous night, and spent most of the morning listening to him tell her about his parents, life on the farm, and his love for Anna. The young woman leans up and kisses him softly.

"Take care of yourself Josh," the inexperienced young man smiles, looking down at the woman as he holds her gently. She leans in and pulls Joshua close, whispering, "If she can't see what a catch you are, she's not worth it, honey." Joshua begins walking to the car and turns to Jenny one last time. The red-haired beauty blows him a final kiss, "I'm here if you need me sweetie," as he gets in the back of the car, still half asleep, despite the fact that it was mid-afternoon.

"There's a man that just got laid, you may give me a run for my money one day." James turns back around after teasing the embarrassed new Delta, then looks to Michael, sitting quietly and looking pissed off as usual.

"Can we go now? John wants to talk about our next move, but there's no rush, he was still screwing Anna when we left to get you." Joshua nods his head, hiding his frustration about Anna being with John. He has no right to feel this way, and understands he has no claim to the woman that took his virginity. Jenny is a smart, exciting young woman that genuinely cares about him, and Joshua would have a good life with her, but he doesn't love her like he loves Anna. A chill runs down the new pack member's spine as he realizes that a lifetime of yearning for a woman he can't have is all that's waiting for him.

Michael pulls into the small gravel parking lot of a small hotel just outside of Lexington. Henry and Bram walk out to meet the newcomers, and everyone soon starts teasing Joshua. John and Anna exit the door of the motel room and join the rest of the pack. John immediately looks to his new werewolf with concern.

"Always look presentable, tuck in your shirt and settle your hair." He turns to Anna while Joshua does his best to accommodate the pack leader. "Get him some other clothes, a haircut and a shave."

Joshua soon finds himself in a barber's chair; Anna ignores the stares of the other men, spending her time talking to Henry, who has joined them as a chaperone more than a driver. The well-groomed young man gets out of the chair and heads outside with his two companions. Anna walks in front of him, smiling as she looks him up and down. The simple handmade pants and shirt has been replaced with a nicer button-down shirt, black pants, and jacket. The suspenders have also been replaced with a leather belt that matched his shoes. "That's better" the raven-haired beauty runs her fingers lightly through Joshua's hair that is now combed to one side. "I don't think you'll have any trouble finding your own women now" Joshua nods, still unsure what to do or say around the woman that he has fallen in love with. The three stroll to the car that is parked just outside the salon.

"Where does John get all his money? Why do we move around so much? And why do we always stay in a run-down shack in the middle of nowhere?" Joshua said. Henry turns to Anna, sitting across from him, waiting for her to respond.

"Older werewolves are a bit more aggressive and aren't known for taking no as an answer if they want something. It's also best for everyone if we change in the woods and not on Main Street." Anna shifts with her back to the door so she can see both men. "As for John, it's best not to ask where the money comes from; that's another reason we don't stay in one place for long." Joshua looks down as he tries to get used to his new attire.

"Jenny really liked me" he then looks up into her eyes that always seem to look into his soul. "It's not like anybody else wants me" Anna sighs and shakes her head as

Henry starts the car, then points to the row of horses and buggies that line the street.

"John also likes to show off and take what he wants without paying for it," Henry pulls out and begins the short drive back to the parking lot. "Like this car or anything else he wants, including women," Joshua continues to ask questions about John not buying cars or property, the answers don't make sense to him, but everyone is silent when the car pulls up to the others.

"Better, now you look like a winner and not a farmhand" after John has voiced his approval, Anna and Joshua join him in the other car. The new Delta looks to Michael, asking him where they are headed.

"Don't fucking worry about it" is the only answer given.

The pack takes their time enjoying the various towns they visit and for the next few weeks, they stay in motel rooms. Joshua has a hard time adjusting to a life without purpose, his former way of life had him getting up before sunrise and working all day, but the others are drinking and fornicating most days. The new pack member is quick to find something to do as the only alternative is to sit in the room and listen to John and Anna have sex. A few days before the full moon, the pack finds themselves in Charleston, West Virginia, in a small diner. Michael looks to John and tells him that a really large plot of woods is outside of town and it shouldn't be a problem finding somewhere to stay. The pack leader instructs Michael to find a place with lots of room to run away from people and take Joshua. After a while, the two werewolves find themselves walking to a cabin, a far piece away from any roads or houses, Michael looks around as they approach the modest wood structure. The cabin is just like the other one with its warped weathered boards and rusted steel roof. "We were here a few years ago, this is perfect."

The pair enters the cabin to find an old man standing in the doorway. The elderly gentleman is obviously down on his luck, and his dirty appearance made his situation even more apparent. The vagrant looks at the two men, raises his hands, and shakes nervously. "I don't want any trouble. I been here about a year now, got no money or nowhere to go."

Michael looks to Joshua "Handle it"

Joshua looks at the old man then looks to the senior werewolf, "We can find somewhere else to stay." The two begin to argue, and the young werewolf stands his ground, fearing what will happen to the elderly gentleman. Michael finally walks over, snaps the stranger's neck without remorse, and then turns to Joshua in disgust.

"How do you think this works? The pack comes first, and I'm getting tired of you being a pussy." Both men begin to argue again with Joshua looking around for something, Michael places his hands on his hips, reaching his limit with the young werewolf, and explodes when asked if a shovel was available. "I promise you there won't be enough of him to bury in a few days" Joshua picks up the old man and carries him out the door, but falls to the ground after the Beta shoves him. He rises from the ground and looks at the senior werewolf.

"Killing is wrong, and the last time I checked, thou shalt not kill is one of the Ten Commandments." The elder werewolf grabs him but soon steps back when a growling Joshua's eyes turn yellow.

"Just go get the other's pup," Michael repeats his command louder "go get the other fucking members of our pack, and by the way, you didn't seem to have any trouble killing that woman the last time your eyes were that yellow."

Joshua is very quiet, holding back tears as he drives Anna and John, with the other car following close behind. Killing is wrong and one of the core beliefs of his religion. He pulls the car up to a small grassy area off the road to find a scruffy man dressed in flannel standing in the clearing. John gets out of the car and walks directly to the stranger, extending his hand. "Hello Samuel, it's been a long time."

The man sighs as he removes his cap. "Dammit John, we got a good thing here, and your gonna do what you always do, Show up, kill things, fuck what you don't kill, then leave."

John looks to the irritated man, explaining to him that the full moon is in a few days and there are plenty of woods for everyone. The man in flannel voices his obvious disapproval as he walks away.

"This isn't over John and if you're here when the full moon comes, it's gonna be a problem. The big bad John doesn't scare us" Samuel said.

John turns to the others after the man walks away and tells them to unpack the car. Joshua remains silent as he gathers up the items and begins carrying them to the cabin. Anna approaches the young werewolf, visibly concerned. "Are you okay? Don't worry about Samuel, it may be nothing." The dark-haired beauty speaks softly as Joshua begins to break down.

"I killed someone, I took a life" Michael looks to the distraught young man, grinning.

"You also killed the husband, killed the whole family, and it won't be the last, you fucking hypocrite." Anna wraps her arms around the young man, holding him as she looks across the room to the pack leader.

"Dammit, John, he didn't kill anyone" she continues to rub Joshua's broad shoulders after mouthing her disapproval, but is unable to calm him down. The grieving werewolf continues to mumble about going to hell and being evil as he holds her tightly. John approaches the pair instructing Anna to leave but the dark-haired beauty refuses to leave and moves to the side.

"Killing is needed at times, you know God also allowed you to become a werewolf, and put you in those people's path. How do you know that God didn't want you to kill them? You spent most of your days living a life of inconvenience, and for what? Where did it get you? If the Almighty didn't want this woman to die, he would've had us set up camp elsewhere." John slaps the young man on the shoulder. "I can see you're a bit gob smacked over this but buck up, lad."

Anna briefly tends to the distraught young man before heading outside to confront Michael. She finds the arrogant second in command standing proudly just outside the cabin door. "Why did you lie to him, you son of a bitch" Michael throws her back into the cabin and leans over, grabbing her throat.

"Because I don't answer to you bitch, the only reason you're still around is that you're only good for one thing." A surprised look appears on Michaels's face as he is thrown against the wooden wall behind him, shaking the house. No one moves as Joshua steps closer to the Beta, snarling at the second in command. Anna looks up to see her protector breathing heavily, with his eyes yellow and his teeth sharpening, Anna immediately runs to him.

"I'm okay, just calm down" Joshua runs out of the house and into the woods before anyone can reach him. His teeth has recessed, and his eyes are no longer amber, but the young man remains in the woods, sitting on a large rock, thinking about what had just been revealed to him. Maybe John was right; he spent most of his life dedicated to his faith, only to end up killing, and for all intents remained with the English and is not a practicing Mennonite anymore.

"Maybe I'm just evil at heart" A soft voice interrupts as he talks to himself.

"No you're not," Joshua turns to see Anna standing behind him and asks how she found him so quickly. The dark-haired beauty walks up to him, pulling his head to her chest before answering.

"I know your scent sweetie," Anna kisses her protector gently, "so I guess you're stuck with me." The gorgeous woman lifts his head, looking into his green eyes "are you okay? You gave us quite a scare." Joshua lays his head back on her chest.

"Well, I just found out that I'm an evil person. Michael just killed that old man, he didn't care, and that's gonna be me one day" Joshua said

She continues to stroke the young man's hair speaking softly, "You are a decent man, and being a werewolf doesn't change that." Joshua stands up towering over her and Anna looks up at the large man, placing her hands on his broad chest "I also know your heart."

Joshua leans in and kisses her passionately but doesn't ask as he kisses her neck. Anna is quiet as she undresses, and then wraps her legs around his waist, allowing him inside her. This time was different, more forceful and aggressive than in the past. This time she is making love to her man, and she is his woman. Anna begins to tighten around his exploding member and feels her womb fill with seed. Joshua is gentle and would never hurt her, not like John, who frequently slaps her and treats her like a piece of property. The dark-haired beauty rests her head on his shoulder, feeling his heartbeat against her chest. The two hold each other as Joshua is unable to let her go, but eventually lowers her to the ground. Anna looks up into his green eyes, realizing that she is looking at the man she loves.

John gathers the pack and tells them that tomorrow night is the full moon, and goes on to say that Samuel and the rest of his inbred morons will be back. The next day the pack sits in the cabin eating the remains of a deer they killed. Michael looks to the window, "Sun's starting to go down." John instructs everyone to get undressed, and go outside so Anna can remove her clothes in private. The pack members leave the building to find Samuel and four others waiting for them.

"Damn John, what did you think was going to happen tonight?" Samuel looks to his other pack members laughing at the six men standing on the porch.

"We undress, so we don't ruin our clothes, something that you all probably wouldn't understand as you dress in dirty flannel." The leader of the Bennett pack continues to taunt in his British accent "I assumed that you're used to seeing a man's penis since you probably spend most of the day screwing each other"

Sam looks at John, enraged at his statement, "Why wait for the moon to get full? We can finish this right now, asshole." John steps forward and begins walking toward the leader, transforming in front of him. Sam turns to run but is easily struck down by John, who bites into him then drops his lifeless body to the ground.

One of the pack members raises a shotgun, pointing it at John. Joshua leaps across the banister and tackles the unkempt long-haired man, but the shotgun goes off before anyone can react. The other barrel erupts into the new Delta's foot and Joshua feels a sharp pain running up his leg and looks down to see steam rising up from his foot. Anna runs out the door to check on the injured wolf. John soon joins the pack, huddled around the wounded man, after killing the remaining attackers. Anna holds Joshua, unconcerned about being nude in front of the others, screaming to an approaching John, who rushes to Joshua after getting a knife from one of the cars. The pack leader rubs the blood from the injured man's foot and ankle, noticing dark blue streaks running up his leg.

Michael gives Anna a stick and nods, everyone steps back as Joshua begins to tremble and change. John begins digging into the young man's growing foot "He's a dead man if he changes now," then instructs the others to change, including Anna, who looks at him nodding defiantly.

"I'm not leaving him" the beautiful woman's hand trembles as she holds him to her bare stomach, clenching her teeth in pain as John performed the surgery. After the last pellet is removed, John looks at her and nods, everyone changes and begins to run through the forest. Joshua stumbles a bit as he runs but manages to stay with the pack. This could be dangerous as the silver had weakened him, but even in his present condition, the dark-haired wolf could hold his own against most attackers.

The next morning, Joshua wakes up in a field behind the cabin and attempts to stand up, but soon realizes that his leg is swollen. John soon approaches an injured Joshua with a concerned look. "Easy Josh, easy" the Alpha looks at his pack member's leg, which is still bruised from the gunshot wound. "I think we got it, but you're lucky" the leader hands Joshua his new clothes and nods, "I saw you protect the pack, well done." The injured werewolf struggles, but gets up from the ground and down the embankment with some help from Bram. He looks around at the dead bodies; two were dismembered by John the previous night, but the others remain intact.

"You want to bury people so damned much, so have at it" the Beta looks to the confused werewolf and places the grey, weathered handle of the implement in his hand. "It's to cut the heads off, not dig a hole, dumbass," Michael storms off when he notices John approaching, with a stern look on his face. Anna helps Joshua sit on a wobbly broken chair, doing her best to steady the injured man. James also assists by taking the axe and returning to the corpses.

"You were lucky you got shot in the foot, you would have died if any silver reached your heart," Joshua nods at Anna but soon turns to see the remaining attackers heads removed. John walks up and pours some kerosene on the dismembered bodies. This is a typical werewolf burial, cutting the heads off is to ensure that no one returns to fight another day, and the fire is symbolic as it will not burn hot enough to turn anyone to ash. Joshua looks into Anna's eyes silently as the two lovers worry that they may be witnessing what awaits them.

CHAPTER THREE

Joshua gathers items from the house and places them in the car, it was 1955, and two Chevrolet Bel Airs have replaced the Model T cars. The former Mennonite has lived through prohibition, two world wars, and the depression in his sixty-two years. Henry does a good job of keeping him informed on current events and teaching him how to read. He and Anna have attempted to stop being intimate but have been unsuccessful as the attraction is too much. Joshua tells the stunning woman that he loves her often, but she never tells him about her feelings. John suspects at times, but his ego has saved them up to now. The pack leader's arrogance has also helped hide the fact that the Delta is now full black.

The smell of burning flesh fills the air from the bodies that lay smoldering from the previous night's fight. Anna comes out and struggles to place her items in the back of the car. She looks to Joshua, laughing at the limited space. "I don't think it's gonna fit" Joshua looks around to be sure no one can hear him, then turns and smiles.

"Love me?" The gorgeous woman leans in and kisses him quickly. She almost told him the words he yearns to hear after they snuck off and made love a few weeks ago.

"Maybe," a playful grin appears on her face as the two lovers shove the remaining items in the trunk of the car. Joshua notices stains on her shirt with a concerned look.

"I thought our kind didn't get sick, did you throw

64

up again?" Anna whispers, assuring him that it's nothing but is less than convincing. Joshua looks into the doe-eyed beauty and gently caresses her hair, still out of view from the others.

"I'm always bloated and a little sick after we make love" Anna slams the car lid, still smiling at the young man as she shrugs her shoulders." And since fiddling with yourself is a sin and you refuse to be with anyone but me." The two laugh but are soon interrupted by John.

"How long does it take to load the cars? You took longer to pack up than it took to burn the bodies" John said.

Joshua points to the other car that the pack had been using "The red one is not going to make it, so we put everything in this car."

John looks around a bit and points to the rusted Hudson Hornet sitting to the side of the isolated cabin. "Take that car until we find another one."

Joshua, Henry, and James pile into the Hudson; Bram insists on riding with John, so the recognized Delta rides in the other car. This arrangement is okay with Joshua as these two men have come to be his closest friends, even covering for him at times. Joshua gets in the back while the two brothers get in the front and begin arguing, James shakes his head as Henry adjusts the radio.

"Is that the only thing you can find? I'm tired of this song" the cars drive through town and start heading to West Virginia. Joshua looks at the sign that thanks them for visiting the fine town of Marietta, Ohio, ignoring the two brothers bickering back and forth about the music playing on the radio, but are soon interrupted by a flashing red light that sits on top of the local police car. James pulls over and is soon looking up at an overweight policeman staring down at him. The large man leans in and surveys the interior of the car as he chews on his tobacco. He turns his head and spits before standing upright and addressing the three men in the car.

"Any reason that two black boys are driving Mr. Murray's car?" The police officer doesn't wait for an answer as he pulls the gun from his holster. "So why don't everyone get out of the car while I decide if you three resisted arrest or not," the policeman turns to notice the flashing light on his car has dimmed before turning back to the men sitting in the stolen car, but is unable to speak as the bones in his neck are crushed from John's grip, and soon falls to the ground with a broken neck. The annoyed leader tosses the dead officer into the tall grass and is silent as he walks to the other car.

"Damn, he's in a bad mood, and he didn't even offer to pay the guy off." James looks to his brother and then looks to Joshua in the rearview mirror.

Henry turns to address the men in the car. "Something's got him pissed, and it's never good when he gets like this" James looks to see if anyone is coming before pulling onto the road.

"I don't think Anna's been giving him any lately" he looks at the rearview mirror at Joshua. "Probably because you've been hitting it a lot," Joshua remains quiet, but the two brothers have known about his feeling for Anna for years. Henry looks to his brother with a concerned look.

"That's never been an issue before, and If John wants Anna, he'll just keep slapping her until he gets what he wants or take it anyway." The reserved passenger turns to the Delta in the back seat. "This is different, just stay out of his way for a few weeks and pray he hasn't found out about you two" James agrees with his brother but only nods as he drives the car.

A few hours later, the cars are parked at a small store in Oilville Virginia, the Hudson had been replaced with a Ford Fairlane, but the crew huddles around the Chevy Bel- Air as John tells them about an abandoned cabin that sits isolated a few miles down the road. Joshua walks into the store behind Michael and Bram. He looks to the counter and smiles at the stick candy that lines the front of the counter. The sandy-haired former farm boy picks up the jar and smiles as he wipes the dust off the lid. Anna enters the store and looks at Joshua. "Are you okay?"

Joshua doesn't look up from the jar but simply answers Anna with, "I'm fine."

The two are soon interrupted by the sound of a young girl crying. The pair walks to the back of the store to find a balding middle-aged man struggling to get up from the floor, his head bleeding as he pleads with the two men standing over him.

"Please leave us alone, we don't want any trouble, just take what you want."

Bram laughs as he grabs the young girl attempting to help her father and begins rubbing her chest "What if I want this pretty little piece of ass? Is that okay dad?" The young girl continues to cry as Michael kicks the man lying on the ground, repeatedly.

"We'll need something to do tonight, so let's take

her with us" Michael laughs as he turns to see Joshua and Anna standing in front of the bleeding store owner. Joshua steps forward and attempts to diffuse the situation.

"Leave her alone" is all that is said as the young girl continues to beg the two men to let her go. Michael grabs the girl and shoves her to the ground on her knees.

"Maybe we'll have her take care of us right here and save me the trouble of breaking her fucking neck later, you gonna stop me, choirboy?" Anna begins to speak, but is interrupted by Michael "and don't start with me bitch" who shoves her to the ground as he glares at the two-pack members. Joshua leans over and helps the beautiful woman up as Anna steadies herself on her protector's arm. The Beta soon notices her weakened state and moves closer, but Joshua quickly glares at the arrogant second in command with yellow eyes.

"Leave her alone Michael," the argument is soon interrupted by John, who immediately looks at Joshua.

"This is great, just fucking great; I suspected you were a black for some time now." Anna steps in to console the leader, telling him about attacking the store owner and his daughter. "They're just cattle Anna, we're superior, or have you forgotten that?" He looks to the others standing around him. "So kill em, eat em or fuck em, it's okay with me" John looks at the whimpering girl standing over her father and begins commenting on her appearance. Anna steps in, attempting to console the frustrated leader.

"We can work this out, I know Joshua's black, but that doesn't mean he's not one of us." Anna walks closer "but John, we need to be more discrete; we can't start raping and kidnapping in public like this." John turns to his lover, in truth, she has been refusing to be intimate with him, but he has been hesitant to beat her as he has in the past. John looks down and hits the doe-eyed beauty with his fist.

"And now this," the leader points at the three men standing across from him, instructing them to ride with him. He looks to Henry shaking his head, attempting to hide his rage, "and you can drive these two in the other car." John gets in the car and drives off, leaving the three-pack members behind. Joshua looks at Anna sitting in the back seat quietly.

"We can drop Henry off and keep driving" Joshua said.

Henry solemnly looks at Joshua, "His reach is more than just us, and he would find you my brother." Anna nods but says nothing as the car heads down the road. Joshua grabs the beautiful woman's hand and kisses it.

"I love you" Anna looks at him, and gently strokes his face, but still refuses to tell him how she feels, hoping that not saying those words will protect him.

The Ford pulls up at the cabin that the pack visits often, to find everyone but John leaning around the other car. James looks to his brother and instructs him to step aside as Michael presents a shotgun, shooting Joshua across his legs, then points the other barrel of the gun to Anna, also shooting her legs. John walks down the steps of the cabin and joins the others, without looking at the two injured werewolves on the ground. He points to the large leather pouch, instructing Bram and James to wrap a chain around Joshua's neck. They do as instructed, dragging him to a tree while his neck sizzles from the silver chain and pellets in his legs. Anna struggles to get up as John walks up and hits her with his fist, knocking her back to the ground.

"I'll get to you later" the pack leader walks calmly to the car, picking up the shotgun before turning to Joshua. "I remember when flintlocks were the only game in town, but someone improved on that." The arrogant gentleman taps the gun in his hand, "they created something, made it better than before." John begins to speak, but is interrupted by Anna, asking him if he's crazy. The pack leader walks over and strikes the bottom end of the gun down on her face, repeatedly. "Shut up bitch" and takes a deep breath before walking to the car. He grabs a pair of gloves and slowly places them on his hands as he continues speaking. "But the only thing some people want to do is take" John turns to Joshua, who is now tied to a tree with a silver chain, "you took my Anna, several times, from what I heard, and now you want to take my pack." Anna looks down, her face is bloodied and swollen, but she still looks up, barely able to see, begging her former lover.

"We can leave and never come back and you'll never see us again." Anna said

John looks to Anna with no remorse or emotion, but continues to address the man that is currently chained to the tree in front of him. "Did this whore ever tell you her story after you two snuck off and fucked each other?" The psychotic leader leans against the hood of the car in front of the large leather pouch "since she likes to hump puppies so damned much," Anna continues to beg but is ignored. " You see, that fine Quaker ass was too much for the religious leaders to pass up, so they made her leave" John looks briefly at the beautiful woman crawling on the ground, "after they took turns screwing that fine ass of hers." The others lower their heads and are quiet, unnerved at what they are witnessing. "But after the third one took his turn with no resistance, that's just her being the whore she is. She tried to call it rape, but we know better... don't we whore." Anna whimpers and cries, as Michael walks over and kicks her to the ground. The gorgeous woman immediately wraps her arms around her midsection as she falls to the ground. Henry begins walking to help the tortured couple, but is soon stopped by his brother.

"This is wrong James, its mama and papa all over again." James tilts his head to his brother and whispers.

"Shut up unless you want to join those two" is all that James has to offer his brother as he continues holding his arm.

John unties the pouch lying on the hood of the car, removing an arrow with a very large tip on the end. "You know the Swiss may have their watches and Germans may have their beer, but the Blackfoot Indians know how to process silver better than anyone I know." The pack leader appears mesmerized by the arrow in his hand as he continues his speech. "You see, the silver is from a river coming out of a mountain and it's as pure as you can get." The leader walks over to Joshua," 99.9 percent pure, you ungrateful son of a bitch" then shoves the arrow in the young man's shoulder.

Joshua grits his teeth, fighting the pain "You killed mama and papa," struggling to speak as the silver chain continues to burn his throat; "you didn't leave enough of my family to bury."

"You're right; I killed your papa, ate your brother,

and fucked your mama." The demented man leans into the former Delta "repeatedly, but don't worry, she got a good shagging before I killed her." John reaches out as another arrow is placed in his hand "stay with me Joshua, I have a few more things I want you to think about while you die chained to that tree." John looks around at his pack proudly before stabbing Joshua in the leg with another arrow "that's where they got me,"   John walks to Anna and kicks her in her midsection.

"Not the stomach, please, not in the belly" John begins dragging the helpless woman to a near-dead Joshua. She looks up at Joshua with tears running down her swollen face. "I love you, you're the only man I've ever loved, and I don't regret one moment that we shared." John kicks Anna in the stomach before grabbing her by her hair, "Please don't hurt the baby! Please." The entire pack stands confused about what they are witnessing as John pulls Anna's head back. The pack leader reaches out for another arrow but Michael hesitates and looks to his leader.

"Is she carrying the blood baby? Boss, that's the pureblood" the Beta's concerns are ignored as John asks for the arrow a second time.

"That little bastard growing in her belly is the last thing you or anyone else should be worried about." Anna reaches up, trying to get on her feet as she continues begging.

"Not my baby, please" the beautiful woman looks around at a stunned pack desperately looking for someone to help." "Not the baby, don't kill my baby" the expectant mother begins choking on her tears as she begs for someone to help. The pack stands ashamed at what they are seeing, and for not helping as they are afraid of what

John would do to them.

"Looks a little bigger in the belly, don't she old boy?" The arrogant leader continues taunting. "You're supposed to be a big bad black wolf but never heard both heartbeats" the dark-haired beauty grabs her hair when John pulls her head back.

Joshua looks into Anna's eyes that are beginning to swell shut, struggling to speak as the chain is now embedded in his neck. "You'll be a good mama," the young man smiles softly at the woman he loves, "and you were never a whore." Anna looks to her soul mate, with tears running down her swollen face and mouths the words.

"*I Love You*"

John raises his arrow and looks to Joshua "Say goodbye to this dead...pregnant...useless ...bitch" the entire pack looks to the ground as John shoves the arrow in her chest, and cringes at the sound she makes as her lifeless body falls to the ground. The pack leader walks over to Joshua, who can barely speak. "Any last words? You know you're the reason she's dead" Joshua struggles to breathe, but leaves John with a final thought.

"God will avenge us" the arrogant leader leans into the dying werewolf.

"Be sure and ask about that after you die" John pulls up Joshua's head and looks into his eyes that are now coated in white. "There's only room in front of the pack for one wolf" John leans in and whispers in the dying man's ear "no one takes what's mine, you worthless bastard." Michael walks over and looks to his leader, stunned at what he had just witnessed.

"We should...cut the heads off and burn em,' and you may want to say a few words, I mean, damn John." The leader looks to his second in command and tosses Anna down the embankment into the tall weeds.

"Bears gotta eat, and hell is the only place that whore and ungrateful son of a bitch are headed." James approaches John cautiously as he avoids looking at Joshua.

"What did he say to you before he died?" John looks the dead man up and down, admiring his work as he answers.

"He said God will avenge him" John looks over at the steam still rising from Joshua's body, "let me know if he shows up."

Henry and James get in the Ford and wait quietly, avoiding looking at one another. Henry looks to his friend hanging on the tree.

"He deserved better than this and she did to, did John tell you what he said?" Henry said.

James begins driving down the road as he answers, "He said God will avenge him." The older brother looks out the window, visibly upset over his friend's death. Joshua was one of the few decent people he knew and never looked at the two black men as anything but a friend, and Anna was a protector for the entire pack. "But no one showed up to save them, including us, Henry."

Henry looks down at the floorboard holding back tears, "I have no doubt that Joshua is with Anna now, and at peace." He looks up at his brother and sighs, "but if anyone finds out she was carrying the white wolf, everyone will be out to get us." The two brother's look at each other for a moment before Henry continues "we watched something beautiful die, and hell is the only thing waiting for us after today."

James looks intently at the road in front of him. "He was dead the first time he messed with Anna, but for a short time," James swallows, holding back tears. "She was happy" Henry begins adjusting the radio, lost in his thoughts.

"If Joshua was the soul of this pack, Anna was the heart" Henry finally finds a radio station and sits back in the bench seat. "John has lived without a soul for years, but he always had his heart beside him" The elder brother looks out the window at the passing scenery. "Bigger wolves will be coming after today, my brother, and no one lives very long without a heart."

CHAPTER FOUR

Joshua briefly opens his eyes to find himself lying on a worn, tattered mattress in the run-down cabin, covered in sweat. His eyes scan the dust-covered rafters and broken glass from the windows on the dirt-coated floor before noticing that his clothes have been removed, and his injuries have been bandaged with his shirt, which has been ripped into smaller pieces. He soon realizes that he cannot speak due to the silver chain that was tied around his neck, and a sharp pain erupts from his swollen shoulder and leg. He sits back, noticing the dark blue veins all over his body from the silver and the arrows on the floor with his blood dried on them. Drifting off to sleep, he is interrupted by the door opening and a woman entering the room with a handful of clothes. His sight is still foggy, so he attempts to get up again, but this time he is assisted by the woman who gently helps him sit upright.

"Be careful, sweetheart," the woman places a mason jar of water to his lips, "drink some water."

Joshua looks at the blonde woman sitting beside him dressed in jeans and a flannel shirt in shock as he recognizes a voice that he thought he would never hear again.

"Mama?" Joshua said.

The young woman reaches for the clothes that she piled in the corner while holding her son. "I found some campers a few miles from here, he looks to be about your size, I left what few dollars I had and...."

The blonde Mennonite woman escaped after she

changed and went back to the farm the next morning, but had to steal some clothes as everything was burned to the ground. Sarah is interrupted by her son, who grabs her hands and asks how she is alive. She goes on to tell her son that she didn't lose her head and woke up a few days before the full moon, covered in lime and buried alive. She noticed the graves for Aaron and Liam, but no grave for her oldest son.

"I thought you were with the English, but after a few years, I realized that you were like me, I've been looking, but you and the others move around so much" Sarah said.

Joshua looks down at the ground, barely speaking above a whisper due to his injuries. "They burned it all down?"

Sarah hugs her son, helps him sit up, and looks into his eyes that are as green as her own. "We are together and alive, God has blessed us with this moment and with each other." She removes the pocket watch from her pocket and places it in his hands. Joshua looks down at the watch that was once his papa's and tears begin to fill his eyes. He collapses in her arms and begins crying uncontrollably as his mother rocks him back and forth "I know my dear."

Joshua composes himself and tells his mother about life with the pack and his love for Anna. He has to stop frequently as the silver running through his veins has weakened him, and can only whisper, but stops after telling her about the baby. Nothing is said as his mother wipes the sweat off her son and helps him get dressed, not sure how to respond. After tending to her son, she asks if he can walk.

"Barely, but I'll manage. Did you help Anna?" Joshua said.

Sarah explains to her son that she walked here, and the smell of blood and silver was what brought her to him.

"I didn't see anyone else, but you have been moaning about Anna and a baby when you started to wake up, I didn't look for anyone else" Sarah said.

Sarah assists her son as he hobbles out to the tree where he was chained, and looks down the bank. He notices a spot where blood is gathered and mentions that Anna may have been dragged. The injured man tries to get to the area where Anna was thrown, but is pulled back by his mother.

"You've been unconscious for days and you barely survived with my help, sweetie. I am sorry, but she's dead." Joshua continues to survey the area, refusing to believe the love of his life was gone. The young man turns to his mother, still struggling to talk.

"She's pregnant mama, and needs us" Sarah steadies her son and finally convinces him to leave with her.

"You can't help anyone in this condition, Richmond's the closest town and we should head in that direction." Joshua attempts to point but is soon reminded about his shoulder injury.

"What direction did John go?" Sarah leans Joshua against a tree and gathers what few items they have. The blonde-haired woman looks to the man standing in front of her that was only a boy when he left for Rumspringa. She also lost everything to John Bennett, but her commitment is taking care of her son, not killing the men who raped her.

"We need to get you healed up before we do anything else" the two start walking slowly down the road to Richmond, but do not get far before a car pulls up beside them. Sarah steadies her son against the car and looks into the middle-aged man sitting behind the wheel. After a brief conversation, the car speeds off, knocking Joshua to the ground.

"What was that all about?" Joshua said.

Sarah sits down beside her son, who is in obvious pain "He wanted to fornicate with me for a ride," Sarah places her hand over her eyes as she continues, "Including using my…mouth."

Joshua turns his head and looks down the road "I really didn't need to know any of that." He turns to his mother, who looks at him with a concerned look on her face.

"You don't look good" she reaches out and strokes her son's hair; Joshua is a foot taller and one hundred pounds heavier than her, but all she saw was her little boy. "Your face looks hollow, and your bruises are getting bigger around your neck." Sarah steadies her son, putting on a brave face, as she had done so many years ago for her family. A rusted-up station wagon pulls up in front of them and parks. A scruffy-looking man in his forties gets out of the car and approaches the stranded duo sitting beside the road. He looked to be in shape for a man of his age and his loose-fitting green trousers and polo shirt, which loosely hung on him, did little to hide his muscular physique as he stood upright in front of the stranded pair, refusing to slouch. He looks to the couple with a perplexing look on his face, as he removes the tweed Jaxon hat on his head.

"You two need some help?" The unkempt gentleman leans over and his hair falls forward, forming a mane around his head, as he takes a closer look at the injured young man. "He doesn't look so good," then turns his attention to Sarah, who has been holding her son upright. "It's the flu, isn't it? Lots and lots of flu around."

Sarah turns to the man and scowls, "Let me guess, you'll give us a ride if I put something of yours in my mouth?" The messy man stands up and adjusts his hair before placing his hat back to its previous location.

The gentleman doesn't respond to Sarah's question and adjusts his hair before helping Joshua up from the ground. "This kid doesn't look so good, and his neck looks nasty" the pair settle in the back of the car as the stranger gets in the car and looks in his rearview mirror, "hold on."

Sarah turns as she hears the back hatch open, after searching through all the clutter, he returns with a mason jar of water and two leather bags. The middle-aged man unscrews the jar, pouring some powder in the jar as he twirls the mixture, until the powder starts dissolving and, in a very gruff, bold manner, looks at the two in the back seat. "Boil your water, I always keep boiled water around, I've seen more dead bodies from unclean water than you can imagine, this water's boiled." The man hands Joshua the mixture, who can barely hold the jar. Sarah grabs the jar and assists her son in drinking the liquid.

The man turns to face the pair in the back of his car "That must be some nasty flu." He then tosses a leather pouch in the backseat that land with a thud, "Bull Scrotum!"

"What?" Sarah screws the lid on the jar, looking

confused.

The man points to the pouch, "That pouch is bull scrotum, and it's some tough stuff, put some of the goo on his neck." The middle-aged man rubs his unshaven neck as he instructs Sarah, "How did that happen? You two into some weird stuff?" Sarah gently rubs the salve on her son's neck and wounded shoulder as he collapses on her. She reaches down and unbuttons his loose-fitting jeans, and begins rubbing the salve on his thigh.

The man turns, starts the car and introduces himself as Lyle before driving down the road. "I'm headed to Richmond, any particular place I can drop you two off?"

Sarah holds her son, fighting tears, as she rocks him back and forth "He's just tired, but he'll be okay, he just needs to rest." She composes herself "I would appreciate it if you could drop us off in the Jackson Ward area, are you a salesman, Mr. Lyle?"

The man looks in the rearview mirror, looking confused at Sarah, "Have you ever been to the Jackson Ward area of Richmond? He doesn't look so good, and a pretty thing like you may not do well in that part of town." Sarah assures the man that she knows what she is doing as the man continues to talk," and it's Lyle, just Lyle, I was in management but never sales. I do cook sometimes, I make a pretty good moussaka, and I make baklava that will melt in your mouth." The man places his fingers to his mouth and kisses his fingers, explaining his culinary skills. After a short trip, the car pulls up at a cross-section of the Jackson Ward district. Lyle gets out and looks around at the run-down buildings noticing people on the street staring at him as he helps Joshua out of the car. Sarah gets out and steadies her son as she hands Lyle the bag of salve. Lyle smiles as he refuses the bag.

"You keep it and make sure it doesn't dry on those burns, keep the cuts wet" he reaches in the front seat and hands Sarah the bag of powder. "Keep feeding him the tea, you can't mix too much of it, but use it wisely, it's hard to get at times." Lyle steadies the two against the brick wall that stands at the side of the street where he parked. He reaches in his pocket and pulls out a roll of money, and hands it to Sarah, "take this" she hesitantly accepts the money and apologizes, but is interrupted. "Helping others is the only thing that separates us from the animals, my love." Sarah looks into her benefactor's eyes and swallows as she senses an aura of power from Lyle that she hadn't noticed before, his accent and darkened skin alerted the blonde woman that he wasn't local, but this was different, his eyes had the look of both predator and protector. Sarah smiles and kisses him softly on the cheek.

"God bless you, Lyle" the scruffy man smiles and shrugs his shoulders, looking upward.

"I hope so, maybe he will one day," he lowers his head and focuses on the pair in front of him. "Grey eyes are never a good sign beautiful, but he's lucky to have you." The man looks around "are you sure you want me to leave you two here?" Sarah smiles at Lyle and assures him that they're okay and, after a brief protest from Lyle, begins helping him down the street, and nods her head as the rusted station wagon drives past them.

Sarah doesn't go far before she walks up and begins banging on a large weathered green door. A very handsome black man dressed in jeans and a long-sleeved t-shirt opens the door and helps Sarah get her son inside. He instructs the two to go in the back, as he walks past the run-down table and chairs that sit in front of the large wooden bar, which can easily be seen from the large glass windows on both sides of the door. Opening a small door at the back of the kitchen, he lays Joshua down on a small cot. The man turns and holds Sarah by her shoulders as he leans in and kisses her. "I thought I lost you, it's been months since you called." Sarah falls into the handsome black man and begins crying.

"Look what they did to my Joshua Spencer, just look," the man holds his companion, before unbuttoning the injured man's shirt to see the burns on his neck, and the large gash on his shoulder.

"I assume he's one of us" she nods her head up and down, acknowledging that Joshua is a werewolf. "Looks like he was held with a silver chain, but what cut him like that?" Sarah exits the room and returns with a glass of water, taking a small drink before answering.

"It was an arrow with a large arrowhead that looks like this" she sits the glass down and forms a triangle with her thumbs and fingers. "He also had one in his hip, and I had to cut the pellets out of his legs," Sarah begins to rock back and forth, attempting to hold back tears.

"It sounds like a devil's tail; this has John Bennett written all over it." Spencer turns and wraps his arms around his lover, attempting to console her with his deep baritone voice. "Baby, that's a lot of silver and he may not make it through the night."

Sarah presents her fingers and then points to the leather pouches "The man that drove us here said to use the salve and drink the tea; the salve did heal my fingertips." She smiles as she grabs a chair and sits it at her son's bedside, stroking his stomach. "He just needs to rest, that's all" the distraught mother turns and looks up at her lover, "I'm not leaving him this time Spencer, not again."

"Baby, getting raped and left for dead is not leaving him," Spencer assists Sarah in undressing Joshua, but stops abruptly as the smell from Joshua is almost too much to stand. "What's that smell?" He reaches down, rubbing his fingers across the goo covering the injured man's legs, and jerks his hand back, looking stunned as his fingers begin to sizzle and smoke. "It's drawing the silver out of him; who gave you this?"

"Lyle gave us this stuff and told me to keep giving him the tea and don't let the cuts dry" Spencer grabs the pouch of tea and smells.

"I smell some tea, some things I don't recognize, but the salve appears to be made out of the same stuff," he looks to Sarah and hands her the pouches. "This is some old, powerful medicine, I've heard stories and legends about this, but even the oldest of our kind doesn't know anything like this." He goes to the kitchen and brings back a tin of coffee, and begins sprinkling it around the room. "John has eyes everywhere, but if anyone like us gets a whiff of him in his condition, he's finished."

Sarah gets some water and rags from the kitchen, while Spencer brings some clothes and sits them down on the stool he has been sitting on, he turns and looks to the beautiful woman sitting beside her injured son. "I've missed you" is all that is said before he locks the door behind him. Sarah continues to aid her son and strokes his head as he continues to mumble about Anna, John, and the baby in his sleep. Sarah looks down and notices his fingernails turning black as his chest begins to broaden. She raises his upper lip and notices his teeth sharpening, not knowing what to do; she leans in and kisses his forehead.

"It's okay, I'm here and you're safe," Sarah continues stroking her son, being careful not to disturb the pinkish bluish salve that's healing her son. She looks down, noticing his eyes had opened and appeared to be healing, despite still being cloudy. Joshua rises from his bed, attempting to get up. He bares his claws and begins to growl but stops as he realizes that it's his mother.

"Gotta…save Anna ... and my baby" Sarah continues to stroke her son, assuring him that everyone is okay as he lies back down and goes to sleep. Early the next morning, Sarah wakes up on the cot, to the sound of Joshua and Spencer laughing. She exits the small room and runs to hug her son, laying her head on his shoulder. Spencer pulls out a chair and presents her with breakfast, leaning in to kiss her as she takes a seat beside him. Sarah reluctantly kisses him back and eats her breakfast as she avoids looking at Joshua.

"So, you two are together?" Sarah looks up and nervously nods her head at the question she had just been asked.

"I had no one when I changed, and everyone was dead," I roamed around and had to fight off every man I met as all they wanted to do was fornicate with me." Sarah smiles nervously, waiting for a response from her son. "All I ever knew was our former way of life, I was told about this place, and that's where I met Spencer, he saved me and is always a gentleman." Joshua gets up from his chair and struggles to reach his mother, but hugs her tightly when he reaches her. He reaches out with his free hand offering it to Spencer. Who smiles and shakes his hand.

"Thank you for helping my mother and for everything" Joshua returns to his chair, then goes on to tell them about life with John, falling in love with Anna, and finding out he was a black Lycan. He stops for a moment before revealing that she was pregnant when she was killed. Spencer gets up from his chair and refills the coffee cups. He returns the tin coffee pot back to the stove before responding.

"Anna was the only good thing about that pack, and killing her would be hard to explain, but if anyone finds out she was killed carrying the pureblood," Spencer pauses before finishing his sentence, "everyone will be out to get him and his pack."

Joshua looks down at his coffee, lost in his thoughts. "I could have used someone that's been around longer than mama or me to help with all this, but Anna and John was old werewolves, so I don't see anyone coming much older."

Spencer sits down beside Sarah and points to the leather pouches on the countertop. "I'm not so sure that you didn't already meet an elder; I never met the guy that sold me this place, but I got it for next to nothing, and I think his name was Lyle. I also hear things from time to time about an older wolf showing up, taking care of things, and moving on." Spencer wraps his arm around Sarah and pulls her to him, "but when I say elder, I mean old country elder, hundreds, thousands of years old, and not the kind of people you want upset." Joshua attempts to stand but falls back in his chair, his breathing still labored.

"You are still very sick my friend, but if you could turn, it may completely heal you." Spencer looks at the door where Joshua had spent the previous night. "Come with me" he walks over to a large shelf that sits in the backroom and pulls the cabinet out, exposing another door. He takes Joshua and his mother down a flight of steps and flicks a switch, illuminating a room with limestone walls. Joshua looks around, noticing several corridors and the large iron chains bolted to the floor in concrete, "this used to be part of the Underground Railroad."

"How did you find this place?" Joshua asked the question but was sure he knew the answer.

"This is where I escaped when I was a slave; I lost my wife and both my children getting here, so I went up north, and the first thing I did was join the union army." Sarah walks over and wraps her arms around Spencer as he continues his story. "I bought the place a few years after the war ended, your mother and I use it when we change, we're only dark grays, but it should hold you, even though you're a full black." Spencer kisses Sarah on the top of her head, "I had all but given up on love until I met Sarah, but I lived in hate for years about being a slave and losing my family." He lifts his head and looks to Joshua "you need to get past it my friend, or it will destroy you, we all have a story, but not everyone lives to tell their tale." Spencer escorts his lover to the steps, but Sarah steps back and walks over to Joshua.

"I'm going to stay and make sure he's okay" Spencer, looking concerned, takes a step toward the two.

"All that silver may make him crazy, and I'm not sure the chains will hold him; you could be in some serious danger." Sarah looks to her man and shakes her head.

"I have nothing to fear from my son, he will never hurt me, but you should leave my love, he may hurt you if he gets confused," Spencer nods and begins walking up the stairs but turns.

"We open at 4 pm for the after-work crowd and what few mortals I have that comes in, the walls are thick, and I've insulated the floor as best I can, but you may want to change and change back before 4 pm." He looks to Sarah "I love you" is all that's said before Spencer walks up the stairs and closes the door behind him. Sarah turns as her son begins removing his clothes. Joshua stops undressing, looking embarrassed, he turns away from his mother.

"I carried you, and have seen you naked as a baby, a boy, and as a man, so get undressed, so you can change and get healed up." Sarah, looking impatient at this point shrugs her shoulders "would it help if I took my clothes off?" Joshua removes his shirt and lays it on a limestone shelf.

"No mama that would be about a hundred times worse" he removes the rest of his clothing and looks at his mother. "You know, when I change back, I sometimes get, well, I get, you know, excited" Sarah crosses her arms and begins tapping her feet.

"Trust me son, it's not the first erection that I've seen in my life, so don't worry about me." Joshua closes his eyes and thinks about Anna, he smiles at first but soon remembers how her face looked before John killed her, and begins to clench his teeth. He opens his eyes to see his fingernails grow claws and his skin turn black as fur covers his body. He looks at his mother and notices her getting shorter, but soon starts to tremble as his nose begins to grow and protrude from his face. He growls, realizing that his teeth had sharpened and that he was fully changed. He reaches up, but can't as the floor is only a few inches above his head. The injured werewolf begins to panic as he soon realizes that he is chained to the floor and begins to scratch at the ceiling before looking down to see Anna looking at him.

"Are you okay honey?" Comes from Anna's mouth, but sounds like his mother. Joshua shakes his head as he looks again, and sees Anna beaten up with an arrow sticking out of her chest. He looks and roars at the woman, Sarah remains calm and looks up at her son, unafraid "it's okay sweetie, it looks like you are healing." He looks at the woman covered in blood, holding a dead baby, with John standing behind them laughing. He begins hitting the concrete and walks toward the woman but is stopped by the chains that are holding him. Joshua begins to go berserk as he cannot save his beloved. The woman walks over to him and hugs his midsection "It's okay, I'm here "he looks down to see his mother looking up at him and realizes that his Anna is gone. The healed werewolf looks down at the concrete and begins to shrink as he changes back to human form.

Joshua sits on the concrete floor, lost in his thoughts, and is startled when Sarah places his clothes beside him. Nothing is said for several minutes as she sits down beside him. He stands up to finish getting dressed, and looks to his mother, as he buttons his shirt.

"Do you think I would have been a good papa?" Sarah stands up and walks over to her son with pride in her eyes, swallowing hard before answering.

"You would have been a very good papa" Joshua looks down at his mother and smiles.

"I would have made you and papa proud of me" he speaks just above a whisper as his eyes drift to the floor.

His mother reaches over and adjusts his hair before responding.

"Your papa would have been proud of the man you've become, and I'm proud of you every day" Sarah said.

Sarah and Joshua walk up the stairs and enter the small room they slept in the previous night. Spencer walks in, wiping his hands with a towel, looking Joshua up and down.

"Looks like that did the trick, everything okay here?" Sarah nods her head as Joshua silently walks out to the kitchen. Spencer, sensing some tension, walks up and wraps his arms around the woman he loves. "Is he okay? He looks like he's got a lot on his mind" Sarah leans up and kisses him passionately.

"He went through a lot, for a moment he thought I was Anna, and it all came back to him." Sarah looks around Spencer, at her son staring at the large metal table in the other room. "I know we've been apart for a while, and I appreciate your understanding by allowing me stay down here last night, but until he gets past this, let's not share a bed for a while in the apartment upstairs" Spencer walks over to the door that leads to the kitchen.

"Whatever you need, I'm in this for life my love. This is your home, and he can stay as long as he wants" Spencer said.

Spencer walks to the large metal table and begins pounding the steaks with a wooden hammer. He looks at Joshua and points to a large sack of potatoes.

"I need you to start peeling and get em' in that large

pot to be boiled and mashed."

Joshua, without hesitation, begins peeling the potatoes as he looks to his new friend, "I thought you cater to our kind, do many werewolves eat potatoes?" Spencer smiles, laughing briefly as he turns and cuts on the large electric skillet behind him.

"We used to only get our kind in here, but after your mother started cooking in the kitchen, business picked up quick. She is one fine-looking woman that knows how to cook," he places the steaks in a pan and sits them aside while he grabs some hamburger meat and begins forming them into patties. "The early crowd is all mortals, and we get a good after-work crowd. When they find out that she's back, we're gonna get busy."

Sarah enters the room with her hair tied back "I checked the crocks, and the sauerkraut looks about right, we can place it in canning jars for later, or I can get some Sausage and make some dumplings if you want." Spencer turns and looks across the table.

"Sounds like tomorrow's special to me" he then turns to Joshua.

"You'll know when the wolves come, they'll know you're one of the stronger ones and may ask questions. As far as they know, me and Sarah are a couple, and no one gives a damn about skin color in this part of town." He turns to flip the burgers while he continues to speak "as far as anyone knows, you're dead, but John has eyes everywhere, so just stay back in the kitchen and go upstairs if you need to."

Sarah hears the bell that hangs on the front door,

alerting them that customers have arrived. She walks into the dining room, and after a few moments, you can hear her laugh. Joshua peeks out, as his mother is standing speaking to three large black gentlemen sitting at a table. "Two burgers each, and I assume we're starting with two beers each" Joshua walks back over to the large sack of potatoes.

"She's happy here, isn't she Spencer? Maybe I should leave so you two can have a life together." Spencer opens a large can of pickles, placing a spear on each of the plates holding the cheeseburgers and a pile of fries. He rings a bell as Sarah quickly enters the kitchen and grabs the plates of food.

"She cried every night over you, and leave for weeks every time she heard about John and his goons being somewhere, she would go check it out, come back, and cry some more." Spencer grabs another pile of potatoes, separates them into two piles and begins cutting one of the piles into fries. "I know you've got some things to take care of, but please stay" he stops briefly and in a somber tone. "I can't say that I would jump in front of a silver bullet for you Joshua, but I would for her, you make her smile and that makes me happy."

Weeks passed, and as predicted, business picked up, mortals and werewolves came in to taste the fine cuisine that Spencer's has to offer. Business got so good that more help needed to be hired. One morning, Sarah comes downstairs from the apartment she and Spencer shares, and greets Joshua, who is cleaning the kitchen. She enters the dining area and notices Spencer sitting down talking to an older black woman, who looked to be in her late fifties, it was obvious that she was a very attractive woman in her day. Sarah walks over to the table, places her hands on

Spencer's shoulders, and greets the older woman and young girl seated at the table. Spencer pulls out a chair and asks Sarah to sit down. "Sarah, this is Nell, and her granddaughter Jayde, they're going to be helping out around here for a while." Nell looks up at the blonde woman standing behind her man.

"Your biscuits melt in the mouth, and that gravy is the best I've had, I'm gonna be helping you in the kitchen, so I can find out those secrets of yours." Nell looks around Sarah and waves, "you must be Joshua, how are you doing baby" Sarah sits and looks at Spencer.

"I think we need to talk about this, I don't mind working long hours, but what about our illness? I wouldn't want her to catch anything" Nell looks and smiles,

"Nothing between Spencer and me anymore, he was my man for a while, but time caught me, and it's still chasing him." Nell motions for Joshua to come over before continuing, "but that's to be expected with him being a werewolf, I'm just glad he found someone." The older woman grabs Joshua's hand and begins rubbing her fingers across his palms before reaching up and turning his head from side to side. "You're a strong one, and your heart is good" she stands and hugs Joshua, "you may even be Loa, one of the protectors." Sarah looks at Spencer with a confused look, who laughs before leaning over and kissing her.

"Nell is a Mambo, a voodoo priestess, I found her years ago and asked if she could reverse the curse, but she can't" Sarah stands up and hugs her new coworker.

"I'm going to get some things to make chicken and dumplings tonight. Do you want to walk with me" Nell smiles and nods her head, indicating that she will not be tagging along.

"Why don't you take Jayde and Joshua? They'll be more helpful to you than me." Sarah smiles and exits out the back door. Spencer and Nell pass the time reminiscing about years past but are interrupted by a knock at the front door. The storekeeper mentions several times that they are closed, but the individual keeps knocking until Spencer finally walks over to the door, and freezes in his tracks at the individuals standing at the door. He opens the door and welcomes the two men inside.

"Hello John," he also nods at the large blonde man standing in the room. "Bull, we're closed, but I can get a few steaks browned up for you." John walks over to the black woman and gently grabs her hand kissing it gently.

"John Bennett, pleased to meet you" Nell looks up and smiles nervously, as John walks away. She looks down at the ground and whispers.

"Rougarou trash" John ignores Nell and turns to Spencer.

"I'm not here for a steak, but I am here to get my property" John walks behind the bar and pulls out a bottle of bourbon and a glass." You see, Anna is gone, and I need a replacement," he fills the shot glass and quickly takes a drink, slamming the empty glass on the worn wooden bar, before continuing. "And it's come to my attention that you have an employee here that's a fine piece of Amish ass that will be joining my pack." Spencer takes his stance, ready to fight for his lady, but is interrupted by another early customer.

"Hey, do you sell any moussaka here? If you do, I bet it's with beef and not lamb" the man walks up to the bar, looking around as he pulls up a bar stool. He rolls up the sleeves of his oversized sweater and then points to John, "and if you ask me if it's made with beef, it's not moussaka" John looks at the gruff, outspoken man and sighs.

"Get the hell out of here while you still can" John lowers his head and laughs for a moment before lifting his head, displaying his yellow eyes, anticipating that the Greek gentleman will take off running. Spencer approaches the stranger and encourages him to leave. Nell walks over, and pulls her former lover back before whispering to him.

"Trust me Spencer, that man isn't what he seems." The Greek gentleman looks to Nell and Spencer before removing his hat, and tilts his head before introducing himself.

"Pardon the intrusion, and please overlook my manners, my name is Lyle, are you sure you don't have any moussaka? Souvlaki? "He turns to John and points at the arrogant leader whose eyes are now yellow."Pretty eyes, Asshole!" John motions for Bram to come over.

"Take him out back and kill this clown," Lyle reaches behind the bar and grabs a glass, but turns to Spencer and points to the bottle of bourbon, before pouring a drink.

"Well it ain't ouzo, but those boys in Kentucky got it right as far as I'm concerned." He pulls out a silver Drachma and places it on the bar, "be careful with that, it could burn you Mr. Storekeeper." Lyle raises the glass but is interrupted by Bram, who attempts to drag him outside.

The mysterious stranger reaches up and grabs the large blonde man by his throat, slamming him to the bar, "there was a time when you would have been crucified for touching me, boy." Lyle throws Bram across the room and turns to face John with blood red eyes. He points to his eyes "mine's prettier asshole," John swallows and is obviously surprised at what he just witnessed. Lyle closes his eyes for a moment and opens them when they return to normal "I'm not going to kill you John, I should, but some things need to be learned, and our kind lives so long, this is gonna have to run its course." The Greek gentlemen pours himself another drink, and looks to Spencer, who is standing with his mouth open, "and trust me, assholes like this guy always gets it in the end." John walks over and helps Bull up and the two walk slowly to the door, John turns to the group, standing in the bar.

"I'll be back to get my property, if she runs, I'll find her, and when I do, my whole pack will take turns with her." John looks over at Lyle before leaving "this isn't over." Spencer gets ready to approach the senior wolf but is stopped by Nell.

"Lower your head when you approach an elder" she kisses her talisman and lowers her head. Lyle walks over to the pair and removes his hat before speaking.

"Look at me gorgeous, there's been no need for that for some time," he tosses his hat on an empty chair before sitting down at a table and instructing the others to join him. The elder werewolf remains silent, giving Nell and Spencer time to comprehend things. "If I kill John, someone will take his place, and this cycle continues, this will end, but not here and not for a few years." He places his hand on Spencer's shoulder "they can't stay here, and I understand how hard it will be hard for them, but this is how it needs to be for now," Lyle gets up and walks to the door "if it helps they play a much bigger role than you may realize, when our kind looks back at this they will be legends."

The restaurant remains open for the day per Lyle's instructions. Spencer and Nell pull up to an older home nestled in the woods outside the city limits, the house had a rusted tin roof, and the boards lined the house was weathered, but no one noticed as the sun had gone down and it was now dark outside. Spencer gets out of the old ford pickup, with Nell getting out of the passenger side. Sarah runs out of the house and embraces the man she's come to love. "What's going on? No one will tell me anything," he swallows hard and looks deep into her eyes.

"John found us, and he wants you baby" Spencer looks up at the porch to Joshua, "but I don't think he knows about you." Spencer's eyes begin to fill with tears as he turns back to Sarah, "I can't lose you again, I was pretty good at fighting when I was in the war." He grabs her hands hard before finishing "I have no problem running away with you, and I'll die fighting for you," Sarah reaches up and places her hand on his face.

"I know you would my love, but you have a life here, and our kind needs you." She pulls his head down to her and kisses him passionately, "but know that you have my heart now and forever." Nell pulls a car around from the back and motions for Joshua to come down from the porch where he has been standing.

"The car is clean, tags and title are all good, and I put a few steaks in the back on ice." Nell pulls everyone in a small circle and lowers her head, speaking just above a whisper, then raises her head to look at the three members in the circle. "Blessing to these three and let no harm come to them" Spencer hands Sarah a paper bag; she looks in the bag and shakes her head, refusing the bag.

"No, honey, I'm not taking it, it's too much" he reaches over and places the bag on the hood of the car.

"It's a couple of hundred dollars and a few gold coins, it's not much, but it should help." Spencer reaches out and shakes Joshua's hand "if anything happens to her, you'll answer to me." Joshua nods as he truly understands the love they share. He grabs the paper bag before addressing the others.

"John stays mainly on the east coast so we should get as far west as we can, but John has some mini packs, and they may pose a problem but one thing at a time." He then looks to Sarah, "mama, it's time," Jayde comes out of the house and hugs them before they leave. Sarah gets in the passenger side of the car and continues to stare at Spencer until he disappears into the night.

CHAPTER FIVE

John walks out of the small shack, tucking his shirt in his pants, and looks to the four men standing outside, before pointing to the door at a nude woman he just killed "Someone clean that mess up and get that useless bitch out of sight," Michael approaches John as the other three enter the room to dispose of the body.

"Boss, you can't keep doing this, if you kill enough mortals, eventually someone is going to show up. Jesus Christ John, this is the third one you've killed this month." John walks over to the hood of the car and turns the bottle of brown liquor upward, sitting the bottle down before responding.

"I wouldn't need to if you would've caught that little blonde thing I turned." He looks into the bottle, almost hypnotized, "she's as ungrateful as her useless son, must run in the family" Michael grabs the bottle, sharing a drink with the pack leader.

"If she's smart, she headed out west, but Spencer is staying put so I don't know how we'll find her." Michael leans up against the car facing John, "you don't think that Josh or Anna survived, we didn't cut the heads off" John leans into his second in command.

"They're both dead, I put enough silver in both of them to make sure of that, she died the useless whore she was, and he died waiting for God to avenge him, we will find her, and she'll wish she was dead before I get done with her." The other three pack members circle around John, acknowledging the dead woman has been moved, the

Alpha nods, before looking at his pack. "After we change, I want you to go to your respective packs and spread the word about that blonde bitch, I've contacted Bishop Reed, his church will be the contact point for everyone, call him with updates." John reaches out and grabs Michael by his throat lifting him off the ground "and instead of questioning me, I suggest you find her because if anyone loses her again, I will personally rip their heads off."

The sun comes up to find the five men getting dressed and Michael quickly gets in the car with John, as the other three get in the other car and drive off. "Boss, I contacted Hector and Carlos; they will check things out in the south, mainly Florida and Georgia. Bull and James are heading down south to speak with them and will double back to cover the Carolina's and southern Virginia. Henry will stay in Richmond and cover Spencer's place, but I don't look for her to come back for a while" John nods his head in approval.

"I'm going to Pennsylvania and coordinate with the Bishop, he sent out a story about her leaving her kids and being addicted to drugs, so we have most churches nationwide looking for her. I need you to start checking on the others to make sure they know who's in charge," Michael starts the car and begins driving down the road heading north after discussing details of the plan to get Sarah with his leader but a few questions remain.

"I'm assuming that Antonio and his bunch are covering the north but if she headed west, we're screwed boss, and this will be for nothing. Did you reach out to anyone else?" John looks out the window, admiring the scenery, but doesn't say anything for several awkward moments before turning to Michael.

"I reached out to the nightwalkers, the ones that have the blood disease, and they will not help us, I also asked the witches' counsel for some help, but they don't seem to like me." John begins tapping on his leg, visibly agitated, as he explains things. "So we are pretty much on our own, I don't want word to get out about this, but if needed, we can deal with the west coast freaks that are afraid of the sun and to hell with the witches." Michael keeps his eyes on the road but shakes his head as he voices his opinion.

"The nightwalkers can be pretty tough, I understand you can handle them, but the rest of us may not be able to win a fight against his entire nest, and I understand staying away from the witches, given your history." John slams the dashboard, cracking the plastic coating and placing a large dent in the red coating of the cars interior.

"I'm so happy that I have your fucking approval Michael, but last time I checked, I don't need it, we will handle this in our own way as we always do." Realizing his mistake, Michael hesitates to speak but takes a deep breath as he isn't sure what will happen.

"I had no problem killing Joshua or that prissy bitch Anna, but if word gets out that she was carrying a pureblood, we're gonna have bigger problems than night walkers, witches, or other packs. If anyone finds out, we're screwed" John crosses his arms and looks to his driver with a tired look.

"Well, last time I checked, the only ones that know about Anna is my pack. We told everyone that Joshua killed her because she wouldn't screw him, and we killed Joshua, no one knows about the bastard child growing inside of her, pureblood or not." Nothing more is said on the trip, but after several hours, the car pulls up to a pristine church in Philadelphia. A large man, with graying hair, emerges from the large red doors of the brick church, and rushes down the concrete steps, to greet the two werewolves parked in the asphalt-covered parking lot. John opens the door but looks at Michael before exiting.

"If Antonio and his pack give us any trouble, tell them that I will personally come up there and find someone that will follow my instructions after I erase him and his strays from existence." John exits the car extending his hand as the Bishop rushes up and grabs the hand that has been presented and shakes it vigorously.

"This is indeed an honor, I'm hoping this will show my commitment to you, and be granted the pleasure of being part of your pack." John, looking uninterested in the ramblings of his familiar, removes his hand from the Bishop's grasp.

"All in good time, have you set up accommodations?" John looks up at the large stained glass at the front of the church before turning to the Bishop, handing him a list." I will also need a few items, including several young pretty things that don't mind me doing things they will not like and probably not live through." The Bishop nervously accepts the list and nods his head after reading the instructions.

"I will see what I can do, but if many girls come up missing, it could get complicated." The Bishop escorts John to his room, asking if he needs anything, and waits for a response. John walks over and sits on the leather chair at the large wooden desk, and looks at the nervous religious leader.

"If I need you, I'll call you" John looks out the window at the departing car. "now go get the things on that list, including someone for me to screw."

Michael pulls up to a small trailer sitting in an open lot in New York City, and gets out of the dusty car, before looking around at the construction workers that are performing the various duties on the building being completed. A tall man in a tee shirt and jeans approaches the car and removes his hard hat, exposing his black hair and stubble that covers his face. "What the hell are you doing here, Mike? I'm not real big on arrogant John clones coming on my lot," Michael walks up to the tall man looking up at him as he notices the sun going down behind him.

"John needs you to keep an eye out for a blond woman that ran away from him after he changed her." The second in command stands defiantly, not waiting for a response. "Antonio, he's even more brutal than when you ran with the main pack, I would not piss him off, not about this." Antonio looks up at the wooden steps at the large overweight man standing outside the door.

"Bobby, close up for me, I've got things to check out, tell the others to keep an eye out for a blonde woman like us." He places his arm around Michael shaking him and laughing "we need beers, shots, and broads my friend, time to catch up." The two men soon enter a dimly lit bar, Michael smiles, admiring the smoke-filled air and the smell of beer and urine. The two men walk up and take a seat at the bar, Antonio holds up two fingers. "Joey, two drafts and two shots of bourbon" the men start a very long night of drinking and reminiscing about days long past. Antonio returns from the restroom, and grabs the beer sitting at his stool. "I heard about Anna, but I also know John, and there's more to this Mike, this is a lot of trouble for one blonde woman, and given what he does to them, I'm pretty sure he can find that anywhere." Michael smiles and slams a shot glass on the bar after finishing its contents.

"I just do what the boss says, but he's obsessed with this woman Tony" Michael raises his hand, acknowledging the shot glass being refilled. "Anna could keep him in check, and keep him from getting too crazy or stupid, but now that she's gone, he's went completely nuts." Antonio looks into the amber fluid in his glass before responding.

"I hear things, I heard that this Josh dude and Anna was getting it on, John got pissed and killed both of them." Antonio replaces the shot glass with a beer mug "now that story I believe, but I don't want to get on his bad side so we'll check things out for you guys."

The next morning Michael wakes up to a red-headed woman and looks down at her as he gets dressed, admiring her contours as she lays in bed asleep. Michael exits the room and enters the kitchen, grabbing a cup of coffee and taking a seat at the small table. Antonio soon enters the kitchen and pours a cup of coffee, taking a seat with his guest, in the tiny kitchen. "You can say what you want, but there's always a bigger wolf somewhere, and I think John's time is about up. I'll keep my place in his pack, but this isn't going to end well my friend" Antonio said, Michael takes a final drink of his coffee.

"Whatever happens is meant to be Tony, I protect the boss and the pack, so if I die fighting, I'm okay with that." Michael grabs his jacket, leaves the apartment, and begins the drive back to Philadelphia.

Meanwhile, Bull and James pull up to a large wooden warehouse in Georgia, near the Florida state line. James gets out and looks around, admiring the fields of peanuts that surround the warehouse. A short, balding Hispanic man exits the warehouse and walks to greet the two men, but stops at the large flatbed truck and gives the driver his paperwork, before reaching the two men that are standing outside the car. "Hello, it's been a long time, my friends, Hector is in the warehouse, handling the shipments, but he'll be out soon enough." James smiles at the Hispanic man and wipes his forehead.

"Damn Carlos, how do you take this heat, my friend?" James said, Carlos nods as he looks at Bull

"I've been down in these parts since the Mexican war ended but I see Bull is as happy as ever and still not smiling." The large Swedish man shoves the Mexican man back, and takes a defiant stance as the workers in the area surround them.

"I'm the new pack leader, anyone have…." Bull's statement is interrupted as a slender Hispanic man with a long mustache exits the warehouse with a shotgun in his hand. The crowd forms a path for the man as he raises the shotgun to his shoulder and pumps the gun, loading a shell.

"I told John we would help, but if you two think that you're gonna come down here and start pissing on trees; you should get in that car and go back to where you came from." The thinner pack leader stands confidently as he points the gun at the trespassers, "and don't worry, I have silver loads, so we're good on my end." James steps in between the two men holding his hands up.

"Hector, Carlos, we're just here to keep the southern

packs up to date my friends. We all ran together for a few years, and you know how Bull is," James lowers his hands, and a sly grin crosses his face. "Right now, I want some of that Mexican beer and a fine young senorita to drink with, who knows, we may even get Bull to smile before we leave." The slender Mexican starts laughing and lowers his gun, he yells, ending the day for the workers who graciously accept the short workday. Before long, the lot is empty, except for a few workers who stand behind the Hispanic pack leader. Hector turns and speaks in Spanish, instructing the others enter the warehouse before turning back to Bull and James.

"Come on in, we can talk in the back room, I sent Pablo to get women and more beer, but we have enough to get started." The four men enter a room at the back of the warehouse, and take a seat in one of the chairs at the round wooden kitchen table, in the center of the makeshift break room. Two of the men take stations at each corner of the dingy, almond-colored room as Carlos goes to the rusted refrigerator, and grabs four beers. He opens the beers and sits them down in the center of the table.

"The three that stayed back are part of our pack and will keep quiet about anything that they may hear." Carlos takes a seat beside his Alpha, who sits the beer down and leans back in his chair.

"We heard about Miss Anna and what that ungrateful *demonio* did to her, she will be missed." The two men lower their heads as they raise the beer bottles in their hands. " To Miss Anna," Bull leans in and smiles as he looks around at the men sitting at the table.

"It's about loyalty my friends, loyalty to the pack, and loyalty to each other." The men all nod in agreement, but James sighs as he sets his beer down.

"We've all ran with John for years, but he's different now and I would not want to get on his bad side these days." The group talks for a short while before they are interrupted by the scent of perfume. A young Hispanic man, with a narrow mustache and chin beard, enters the room with four women, who immediately begin rubbing the shoulders of the four men at the table. James looks to the man reloading the refrigerator with beer.

"Isn't he that kid that used to hang around the Mexican store and beg for change?" Hector nods his head.

"We changed him around 25 years ago, when we needed another pack member." Hector nods as two of the women sit on Bull and Henry's lap and begin kissing their necks. "We have a few rooms with some beds for the drivers through those doors, enjoy, my friends."

The next morning Bull wakes up to the smell of pork and quickly enters the break room, to find Carlos standing at the gas stove. Carlos points to the table, where Hector and James are sitting. "Its blood sausage, take a seat, it's about done and I have plenty." Bull sits down as Carlos sits a cup of coffee down in front of him, James looks at the large blonde man.

"Be careful with that Bull, its Mexican coffee and may knock even you on your ass." Bull shakes his head and looks to the others in the room as he takes a large drink of the coffee. His eyes open wide as he sits the coffee down and almost falls out of his chair.

"That's strong, reminds me of coffee back home" the four take a seat and begin devouring the large plate of sausage. After the food and coffee are gone, James stands up and stretches, before looking to the two gentlemen.

"We're just a few hours away, but let us know if you find anything, John's gonna give this a few years before he moves on." The four men walk outside, James and Bull turn to the two men.

"We'll keep in touch, but we won't come around for a while. Michael may be around to check on things but call this number if you hear anything." James said, then gives Hector a piece of paper with a phone number written on it. The Hispanic man places the paper in his shirt pocket and nods.

"If we hear anything, we'll let you know" Hector said.

Henry sits in a car parked near Spencer's bar and grill, almost mesmerized at the building that he has been staring at for so long. He is snapped out of his trance when he notices a young black girl approaching his car. The young girl walks up to the car as Henry rolls the window down.

"Spencer and Mama Nell would like for you to come inside and have some breakfast," Henry laughs and soon enters the front door to see Spencer waiting for him. The storekeeper presents a large plate of steak, eggs, and bacon. Henry sits down at the table across from Spencer and begins eating his breakfast.

"Thank you" is all that is said for a few tense moments. Nell comes and places a pot of coffee in front of Henry and takes a seat at the table.

Spencer pours a cup of coffee for his guest and

refreshes his own cup before speaking. "She's not here and will not be back for some time" Henry nods as he takes his first bite of food.

"I run in the back of the pack, and I chose to not have a pack of my own, so I'm here to stay out of John's way, no one expects her to show up." Nell pours a bit of cream in her coffee and turns to Henry.

"You're a good man, but John Bennett's the devil and you need to get away from him" Nell said. Spencer turns his attention to the window behind him, and looks to the outside for a moment, while Henry reaches for his cup of coffee.

"The bad thing about running in the back of the pack is you don't know where you're going until it's too late, my friend." Spencer turns back to face his two breakfast companions, "were you there when they were killed?"

Henry slams his fork down and takes a deep breath before speaking, "What do either one of you know about running with a pack? Not all of us are as fortunate as you, Spencer." He picks up his fork as he rubs his forehead with his other hand, "I was there when they were…removed from the pack, and I pray for both of them every day, it brought back some unpleasant memories from the past, I don't approve of what John does, but I stay for my brother." Spencer smiles and asks Nell for more bacon and sausage, then turns to Henry as Nell gets up and walks to the kitchen.

"I was attacked when I was in the union army, I woke up like this and have been this way ever since, but I would never follow someone like John, that much I do know my friend." Spencer moves his cup as Nell lays a plate of food in front of him before continuing, "I also heard about her being pregnant with the pureblood." Henry's facial expression changes slightly displaying a concerned look, but years of running with John has trained him to show little emotion when needed and to think before speaking.

"The only people at that cabin were the pack, and I can assure you no one said anything, fearing John's wrath, and since Anna is dead, that just leaves my other dead friend Jo…" Henry looks up and stares into Spencer's eyes, nothing is said for a few seconds, that seem like an eternity for the two men. Henry sits back in his chair and places his hands on the table, "she's not traveling alone, is she?" The pack member thinks about how his former student was tortured and how the last time he saw him, he was near death, before turning back to Spencer. "Did Joshua survive?" Nell rushes out of the kitchen to the two werewolves.

"You leave em' alone, dammit, they've been through enough" Spencer, with his eyes still locked with Henry's, raises his hand. Nell steps back after placing more food on the table but remains close to the table where the two men sit.

"Don't worry Nell, he's not gonna say anything, but if Anna was carrying the pureblood and John killed her, he's finished." Spencer takes a moment to gather his thoughts before continuing, "He killed the white wolf Henry, the one to lead us all, the one to make us all one pack." Spencer nervously begins tapping his fist on the table and takes a deep breath, "It may be in Joshua's nature to forgive, but not mine, I know what they did to Sarah, and now this." Spencer finally slams his fist on the table and leans into his friend "I know you to be a good man, but if you stand with John and the rest of those bastards, you'll lose your head too my friend." Henry lowers his eyes as he takes the last bite of food. He remains quiet for a while as he stares at the empty plate in front of him.

"I will say nothing as I do not know if it's true, John spreading us out among the sub packs is just a show of strength and nothing more, he may eventually stop searching for the woman, but if he finds out that Joshua is alive, he will never stop looking." Henry takes his last swallow of coffee "he will continue with this for a few years and then move on, the blood diseased ones on the west coast will not tolerate him, so if they remain on the west coast, they should be fine unless the vampiri have an issue with them." The spying pack member looks out the window before turning to his host "the witches have a lot of records on John, and none of it is good, the grand coven was quick to tell him to get lost."

Henry gets up and walks to the door but is stopped by Spencer "you're not going to find anything here, so use the cot in the back." The pack member smiles and soon returns with a small bag of items. Henry graciously enters the small room in the back, and immediately notices the bloodstains on the cot, despite all attempts to remove it, and smiles to himself, realizing his friend is alive. Spencer exits the small room to find Nell waiting for him.

"This is a bad idea" Spencer walks across the kitchen to the black woman.

"He's a good man, and we have nothing to worry about" Nell shakes her head and then looks up into Spencer's eye's

"Okay, we'll do it your way, but I'm here if you need me" the older, attractive black woman reaches out and strokes the bulge in her former lover's pants. "She could be gone a long time baby, but if things get too hard for you," Spencer removes Nell's hand and nods.

"I love her and will wait for as long as it takes" Spencer kisses her hand gently. "I can't do that to her," Nell jerks her hand away from Spencer and refuses to look at him.

"I guess I was just something to fuck and nothing more," Nell turns to go back to the kitchen "go to hell, Spencer." The former lover's words hang in the air long after she leaves the room.

CHAPTER SIX

Joshua and Sarah pull up to the small diner located in upstate California, they have been driving for several weeks, picking up small jobs on their journey to the west coast. The two enter the restaurant, and quietly sit at one of the red vinyl-coated booths lining the glass front. The business was booming, and this was the only booth available. An overweight brown-haired waitress waves her hand at the new arrivals that are waiting patiently at the booth, still dirty from the previous occupants.

"I'll get to you when I have some time but menus are on the table, just give me a minute." Joshua looks around as Sarah gets up from her chair and starts clearing the table. She gathers the items from the table and carries them to the end of the long counter in front of the fountain area. Sarah returns to the table with a damp cloth, and begins wiping off the table. Joshua looks to his mother and shrugs.

"You're doing this here too? Mama, you don't work here, or any of the other places you have a need to clean." Sarah taps Joshua on his denim-covered forearm, instructing him to raise his arms.

"They're busy and it never hurts to help out, and by the way, elbows off the table, you know better" Joshua sighs and removes his arms from the table. The two have been traveling for a while, and the stress of looking over their shoulders, finding places to transform, and driving was beginning to take its toll. The large blue apron-clad woman eventually makes it to the table with her pen and paper in hand.

"Thank you sweetie, it's been a day, what can I get for you two?" The mother and son don't order anything fancy. Just burgers, grilled rare, and some lemonade. After writing down the order, the middle-aged woman soon returns with the food to Sarah and Joshua, she looks down at the quiet pair. "Are you sure you don't want me to get Luis to put these burgers on the grill a little longer? They're almost raw." Joshua looks up and smiles as he notices the woman's name attached to the front of her apron.

"No, this is fine Brenda, but no lemonade?" Joshua said. The waitress shakes her head.

"No, sorry honey, the best I can do is some iced tea with a lot of lemon wedges in it," both parties agree, and the waitress soon returns with the tea in hand. The dinner rush was over, and the crowd had left, with the exception of Sarah and Joshua. She takes a seat across from them, lights up a cigarette, and begins speaking to her two remaining patrons. "You two just passing through?" Joshua takes a bite of his burger and swallows, making sure that he doesn't growl or draw attention to himself before answering.

"I'm looking for work and we were told that a sawmill around here may need help." The waitress extinguishes her cigarette and looks to Sarah.

"You looking for work too?" Sarah nods. "Tom Johnson owns the sawmill, this diner, and most of the mountain, but Luis and I take care of things here. I can call him with your info and probably get you started tomorrow." She turns her attention to Sarah, "and I can use some help here if you're interested" Sarah smiles nervously and looks to Joshua, who remains quiet.

"We don't have any information but we are good

workers" the waitress walks over to the door and turns the sign to closed. She locks the door and returns, taking a seat beside Joshua at the booth.

"Tom's a good guy and doesn't ask many questions, I got messed up with a truck driver in Nevada years ago, that son of a bitch beat me all the time before I ran away, after he almost killed me one night. I know someone on the run when I see em' but I also know good people." She instructs the two to remain in their seats as she walks behind the counter and picks up the phone. After a few moments, she looks over at the only two remaining occupants. "He'll be here in a few minutes."

The Portuguese cook pours a glass of tea for himself and lights a cigarette while they wait. Luis comes over and smiles as he refills the glasses with tea and simply says, "Good people, we need to help them out," as he walks past Brenda. Before long, headlights fill the front of the diner, Brenda opens the door, and a man wearing jeans and a tan coat, enters the diner. He removes a cigar from his jacket before removing his coat. He looks to Luis and asks for some matches before sitting down at the booth removing his cap, exposing his graying red hair and weathered face.

"You two looking for work?" The man lights his cigar with his newly acquired matches as Brenda places a bottle of beer in front of him. Joshua looks to the red-haired man across the table.

"Yes, sir, and we'll work hard for you, but..." Tom takes a drink of his beer and places the cigar in the small tin ashtray.

"Brenda told me, but it's obvious that you both have

seen an honest day's work" the business owner grabs his cigar and places it to his lips, filling the area with smoke. He looks to Brenda and points to the beer, "one more, I'll cover what they had and get them a few sandwiches before they leave." Brenda and Luis go to the kitchen to honor Tom's request, the businessman looks to Sarah "I've hired convicts and a lot of other people down on their luck, we can pay you out of the register, and you can keep your tips." Brenda returns with a bag of sandwiches and another beer that she places it in front of Tom, who turns his attention to Joshua. "And I can pay you cash weekly, sound good?" Sarah and Joshua smile and nod in approval. Sarah looks to her new employer.

"Thank you, Mr. Johnson, and God bless you" Sarah said, Tom looks to the blonde woman sitting in his diner, shaking his head.

" Call me Red, everyone calls me Red" the man stands up and places his hat back on his head and walks to get his jacket but turns to say something before he leaves. "Where are you two staying?" He then looks to the dusty car sitting in the gravel parking lot "you two planning on sleeping in that car?" Joshua stands up and nods as he reaches out and shakes Red's hand.

"Just for now, but we'll be fine" Red strokes the graying stubble on his face, points to Sarah, and sighs.

"I can't have her stay at one of the shacks, not with that crew" Red puffs on his cigar while he thinks, and after a few moments, looks at his two new employees. "I have a place at the edge of my property just down the main road, it's a little hard to get to, but no one wants to live there anyway, it's near that weirdo cult, but it has running water and electricity. If you're interested, how does $25.00 a month for rent and $2.50 an hour?" Joshua nods and extends his hand; Red grabs Joshua's hand with a firm grip. "Son, if you're not afraid to work, you'll do just fine."

The road to get to the house was bumpy, as Red described, but it was a nice place, and the two werewolves were very grateful to have a place to stay. Joshua looks to his mother "I can sleep on the couch, and you can sleep on the bed" Sarah looks at the couch and smiles. She removes the cushions and pulls on the small handle at the sofa's center, exposing a mattress.

"It's one of those sofas that turn into a bed sweetie" Joshua looks at the bed proudly.

"It looks like our luck may be turning around for the better" Sarah enters the small kitchen. She notices the small Formica table in the center and begins opening the faded wooden cabinet doors as Joshua plugs in the refrigerator and stove. Sarah looks across the room to her son.

"God has blessed us and we just need to keep the faith" Sarah said.

The next morning, Joshua drops his mother off at the diner and continues down the dirt road beside the establishment to the job site. He enters the dark green painted office and walks up to Red, who is sitting at his desk speaking on the phone. Red abruptly hangs the phone up and then turns his attention to Joshua. "Looks like I hired you in time, my high climber just quit, how are you with heights?" Joshua looks down at his new employer with a determined look.

"I helped my papa tend to the barn roof, and that

was pretty high. I'll do whatever you need me to do, Mr. Johnson" Red looks to the man leaning up against the wall.

"Charlie, get him a rig and show him what to do" he looks to Joshua and smiles, "I think it may take a few times to remind you to call me Red, but if it works out with you, it's another fifty cents an hour." Joshua turns and smiles at the bearded gentleman behind him eager to get started. The man leans into him, placing his flannel-covered arm on his shoulder.

"I'm Charlie Murphy, and before you get too excited, you may want to see how tall the trees are, because son, they're a lot taller than a barn." Joshua smiles as the two gentlemen exit the office and get in the pickup truck sitting outside. Charlie looks to his new climber as he drives down the makeshift dirt road to the job site on the hill. "I'm the foreman, and I run the crews. The new guy usually works as a high climber and faller. If it works out, you can be a bucker one day or work at the sawmill, that is if a widow maker doesn't get yah." Joshua looks at the crew chief, not quite knowing what he just said. The truck stops, and the two men walk up to the tall trees that align the edge of the field below, where the sawmill and equipment are kept. Charlie throws Joshua a pair of leather chaps and a large leather belt with straps attached. "Put on the chaps and your rig, climb until the trunk starts to get small, then start cutting. We'll have you climb for a few weeks, and then you can work on dropping the trees."

While Joshua was getting used to his new job, Sarah was starting her job at the diner. She put on the blue apron and began walking around the diner, getting used to her surroundings. Brenda sits at the end of the diner, smoking a cigarette and drinking her coffee. "We feed the men lunch at the job site; Red pays for lunch but not breakfast or supper." She takes a drink of coffee and continues, "He pays a decent wage and lets the men stay in the bunkhouses for free, so they can afford to eat here if they want, Still, we get plenty of business from the main road." Brenda points to route 101 as Sarah walks over and pours herself a cup of coffee, before sitting with her coworker. At the same time, Luis places four large metal pans in the large oven, then walks to the dining area and pours himself a cup of coffee, after closing the oven doors. Sarah smiles at Luis then looks at Brenda with a puzzled look.

"Why did he let me and Joshua rent the house?" Luis looks across the counter as he leans on the fountain area behind the counter, while Brenda answers.

"No one wants to live up there, and you can't stay in the bunkhouse, those guys would never leave you alone, and some of those guys are dangerous." Luis speaks up, adding to his girlfriends' explanation. Sarah listens intently as she has some trouble understanding Luis due to his thick Portuguese accent.

"Brenda and me stayed up at that place for three days, it's not a bad place, but I walked outside to smoke, and a pale white guy approached me. He was either half-dead or wearing face paint so we moved to the cabin out back the next day. I quit working at the mill and started to work here as the cook," Brenda nods and then adds to the conversation.

"We've heard the crews find skeletons on the ridge, but Red doesn't say anything because the police would cause problems. He's a good man, but doesn't ask that many questions and some of his crew have some messed up backgrounds." Brenda gets up from her stool and begins cleaning the counter, stopping briefly to warn her new coworker. "You and your man aren't the only ones that come here to hide but trust me, there are things in those woods that you need to stay away from, and as far as I'm concerned, it feels evil." Sarah doesn't say much, or correct anyone that she's Joshua's mother. Luis stands up and stretches, before walking to the large steel doors that swing freely when entering or exiting the kitchen.

"I have the beans cooking, time to make the biscuits" Sarah follows Luis in the kitchen to offer her help.

"Can I help? We're not busy, and I know my way around a kitchen" Luis shrugs his shoulders, and allows Sarah to work in his kitchen. Sarah begins removing items from the large wooden shelves as Luis places a large bowl beside the mixer. Luis smiles at his new kitchen helper.

"You cook good, don't you?" Sarah begins mixing the ingredients and nods as she starts the mixer.

"I can make a pretty good biscuit Luis," nothing more is said as Sarah removes the dough from the bowl.

Joshua looks intensely at the large tree in front of him as he clips the steel cable to his belt and begins making his way up the tree. He pauses for a moment to admire the view from the treetop before starting the chainsaw that has been dangling from his belt. He notches the tree, and before long, the wood begins to splinter, and a large portion of the tree falls to the ground. Joshua stops the chainsaw and yells, "Coming Down!" Charlie is at the base of the tree, waiting for his new climber to reach the bottom. Joshua soon reaches the ground and begins removing his harness.

"Did that look about right, Charlie?" Joshua said, as

he removes his hardhat while Charlie laughs, slapping him on his shoulder.

"You're natural at this kid and you don't mind the rig or the heights, you may want to climb a little higher next time, but you did okay for your first time." Most of the morning is spent with Joshua topping trees. A whistle blows, signaling lunch, and the men climb in the back of the large flatbed truck that drives them to the chow hall. Joshua sits quietly as the men talk to one another; a young dark-haired man in a flannel shirt begins yelling at Joshua arrogantly.

"Hey farm boy, how the hell did you end up a high climber? I was told you don't sleep in the cougar den with the rest of us. What makes you so damned special?" Joshua doesn't say much as the others begin laughing. The truck soon pulls up to a large tent area with rows of wooden tables. Joshua waits in line quietly and presents his plate to Luis, who fills his plate with a large helping of beans. Joshua grabs two biscuits as the Portuguese gentleman leans in.

"Sarah is doing good, and she baked those biscuits" Joshua smiles as he finds a place to himself, sitting quietly as he eats. A grey-haired man sits across from Joshua and begins eating his lunch. The man wipes his face making sure to clean the hair around his mouth, including the mustache that is perfectly curled on both ends before speaking.

"They call me Lefue, pleased to meet you" Joshua shakes the man's hand but says very little. The grey-haired man shakes his head, "you're gonna have to toughen up boy, everyone knows that Dom's an asshole, but he'll walk all over you if you let him." Lefue takes another bite of his lunch and continues to instruct Joshua on how to deal with the crews. "The next time he mouths off, hit the son of a bitch, I mean, knock the shit out of him." Joshua remains respectful but quiet and nods to Lefue, acknowledging that he heard his advice. Lefue waits for a reply but after a few minutes shakes his head "you're not gonna do a dammed thing are you?" Joshua smiles as he knows the gray-haired man is only trying to help.

"It's not my way, but I thank you for your help" Joshua bites into the biscuit and smiles, recognizing his mother's cooking. Days turn into weeks, and Joshua does his best to endure Dom's taunts. He speaks with his mother about things, but she offers little help as it is becoming difficult to live with the English and still follow the old ways. Today is payday, and everyone goes into town on Fridays to celebrate, all but Joshua, who keeps to himself. The former Mennonite tries to find a way to fit in but always seems to come across as awkward, regardless of the circumstance. Today is harder than most days due to the full moon coming that night. Joshua simply climbs the trees and remains quiet, attempting to avoid people as much as possible, especially Dom, lunchtime comes, and Dom continues to taunt Joshua as he does most days. The truck drops the field crew off for lunch, and the men hurry to the office to get paid before eating, but Joshua holds back and waits patiently at the end of the line. The sawdust covered former Mennonite eventually finds himself standing in front of Red's desk, who glances up at Joshua and writes paid in the blank beside his name. The red-haired owner hesitates to give Joshua his wages before offering his advice.

"Son, I've been around a while, and I see things, you are a good worker, and I could see you running a crew one day, but no one is gonna pay any attention to you if you keep letting people walk all over you." Red hands him his money and then leans back in his chair, "you're not a convict or troublemaker like most that end up here, but trust me boy, If you want to make it up here, on this mountain, you better grow a set of balls." Joshua smiles, he has been told this by several coworkers, and offers the same response to Red that he does the others. Joshua puts the money in his pocket and walks out to the chow line. He grabs a plate and waits, but before he can get to his Portuguese friend, he feels someone shoving him forward. He turns only to find Dom standing behind him.

"How much did you get paid today? I know for a fact that high climbers make more than the ones that actually do the work on the ground, so how much is in your pocket? Looks like a bigger wad than I got." Joshua looks at Dom then turns around to move forward in line but the arrogant coworker keeps shoving and is more aggressive with each shove. "I guess I'd make more money if Red was giving it to my old lady, does he let you watch when he screws that bitch of yours?" Joshua turns to his tormentor.

"It's nothing like that, Dom, now please leave me alone so I can eat," Dom shoves Joshua again, leaning forward.

"I'm either gonna get half your money or screw your old lady, so what's it gonna be farm boy?" Joshua lowers his head, struggling to remain calm but has trouble fighting his instincts on the day of the full moon. He raises his head, regaining his composure, and simply responds with.

"Don't push me again," Dom laughs, looking around, making sure he has an audience. He has been waiting for Joshua to say something that would allow him to bully him some more. Dom hits the plate of food that Joshua has been holding and attempts to shove him again, but Joshua raises one hand and easily shoves Dom into the open area that surrounds the makeshift dining area. He takes a deep breath and turns to Luis to make sure he's okay, not realizing his green eyes had turned color and were now amber. Luis says nothing as Joshua's nose and jaw begins to extend from his face and a low growl escapes him, but after a few moments, the werewolf's face returns to normal, including his eyes. Dom rises up from the ground and re-enters the tent area.

"Hey, if that's how you want it, no problem," Dom throws dirt at Joshua's face in an unsuccessful attempt to blind him, then steps forward and swings at Joshua, who grabs his fist mid-air. A scream follows the sound of bones breaking as the attacker finds himself being thrown farther than before. Joshua walks toward the injured man but stops when Red and Charlie rush around the corner of the building to see what is going on. Both men look down at the injured man on the ground.

"Anyone wants to tell me what the hell is going on?" Charlie waits for a response but all remain quiet except for Luis.

"Mr. Charlie, that man's been an asshole to him for weeks, this guy just had enough and finally took up for himself." Luis looks to the former Mennonite and smiles as Red looks down at Dom.

"You're more trouble than your worth Dominick, when the truck takes the guys into town, don't come back." Red looks up at Joshua and grins, "didn't think you had it in you" he walks past his former employee to Joshua, who is unsure about his future employment. "I have a guy working on the ridge that wants to work in the mill, and since this piece of crap no longer works here, I'm moving him to the mill, and you start as a faller tomorrow."

Luis pulls up to the back of the diner and begins emptying the back of the truck with the dirty pans and plates. Brenda comes out to help but is soon concerned at the look on Luis's face, "You okay, Louie?" Luis leans into the truck and lights a cigarette before answering.

"I just saw a *demonio*" he then points to his eyes and explains what happened, including Joshua's face changing, and how he broke Dominick's hand. Sarah walks out back to assist but is stopped by Brenda.

"I think Josh may have gotten in a fight, he's okay, but the other guy may not have been so lucky." Brenda grabs the cigarette out of Luis's hand and takes a puff, while the Portuguese cook picks up another armload of dishes, "and Luis thinks he saw something weird, something about yellow eyes and growling." Sarah looks concerned and afraid that this may be the moment when their secret comes out. Brenda walks over to Sarah, looking up at the back door. "I'm sure it's nothing, just overgrown boys being boys" Luis exits the back door and stops at the bottom of the steps.

"Nothing, did you say nothing? You didn't see what I saw; it was like looking into the eyes of a demon" the cook looks at the two waitresses, nodding his head in disbelief. "I almost shit myself."

Joshua and Sarah say very little on the way to the house they have been living in the past several weeks, and they soon enter the small dwelling that Sarah has turned into a home for them. The walls that were once vacant now have paintings and various other hangings, purchased at the yard sales she frequents, the Mennonite woman has even started to knit again. Sarah lays her simple handbag on the small wooden table that sits at the entrance of the tiny house, before entering the kitchen.

"Did you mean to hurt him that bad?" Joshua sighs then looks to his mother. She removes the apron she wears at the diner, before taking a seat on the chair at the kitchen table across from Joshua. "You were supposed to turn the other cheek, not break the man's hand and get him fired" Joshua remains calm and emotionless as he ponders his Mother's statement. Both of them have been through a lot, but Joshua's time with John has changed his perception of things. The first few years, he held onto his faith, but eventually realized that he is no longer a practicing Mennonite. His mother realizes that she isn't the woman she was when she lived in Virginia, but still holds onto the hope that she will be able to return to Spencer, and her life in Richmond.

"It's easy to turn the other cheek when everyone else is doing the same thing, but when a man like Dom keeps trying to start something and never lets up, things happen." Sarah grabs her son's hand from across the table and pats it with her other hand.

"It was hard for me today too Joshua, with the full moon coming tonight, but it must have been almost too much to bear for you." Sarah removes some steaks and browns them lightly on both sides before they eat. She lays the steak in front of her son before taking a seat across from him, "but we need to be careful and avoid drawing too much attention to ourselves."

The two werewolves change as they do every month

with Joshua running in front, and Sarah following a little behind him. This isn't for rank, but it allows the black werewolf to protect his mother if needed. The pair runs through the woods bold and unafraid of running into anyone, as they have searched the mountain the past few weeks. This is what keeps Joshua and Sarah sane, both have endured a lot over the years, but none of that seems to matter at times like this, and all the troubles fade as they run through the forest, fully aware of their surroundings. The pair runs for miles making sure to not disturb the large open area at the top of the mountain, where the cult lives. They spend most of the night running free, not worrying about the pack that is chasing them or the past. Werewolves know their surroundings better than mortals, the black werewolf senses that they are being watched but cannot detect a heartbeat or see anyone near them. An experienced werewolf can also sense when the sun is about to rise. Joshua can change back or stay in his wolf form, but Sarah is tied to the moon's cycle. Morning comes as it always does, forcing the pair to return to their normal lives.

Later that morning, Joshua stands at the treeline beside the man who will be training him to drop trees. He has seen this done on the farm in Virginia, but it was far less efficient as chainsaws were not permitted in his past life, but before long Joshua is dropping trees like an experienced lumberjack, always watching his surroundings and where the tree will land, as this is what makes dropping trees so dangerous. Weeks pass by, and the clearing in front of the woods gets further away from the mill area. While dropping trees is still dangerous, it doesn't require as much attention to detail as when Joshua was assigned the position, but he still keeps an eye on things while performing his duties and steps in to assist anywhere needed. One day Charlie comes up to the ridge and waits patiently as Joshua helps the others trim the limbs off the tree that lays on the ground.

"Josh, me and red want to talk to you, get in the truck, It won't take long" Joshua sits his chainsaw away from the work area, then removes his gloves as he takes a seat in the truck. Charlie looks across the cab of the truck, shaking his head, "you're not winded at all, are you? You must be in good shape," the foreman continues, not waiting for a reply. "I never see you drink with the guys or light up a cigar, it shows on yah boy, but it looks to be a boring way to go through life," Joshua looks over to his foreman.

"It's how I was raised, and I have never seen anything about getting drunk or smoking that appeals to me." The werewolf smiles at being called boy, as he is technically in his sixties, and older than Charlie. Joshua looks out the window at the field of stumps, and finishes his conversation with "but to each his own." In a short time, the truck pulls in front of the green building, and the two enter the office to find Red sitting at his desk. The red-haired owner points at the chair in front of his desk, indicating that he wants Joshua to sit, before grabbing the cigar resting in the amber ashtray on his desk. The red-haired owner relights the cigar as he waits for his employees to sit down.

"Josh, you have done better than I could have hoped for; you never miss a day and work right up to quitting time." Red removes the cigar from his mouth, checking to see if it has been lit properly before continuing. "I look up at the ridge and see a group of men not doing a hell of a lot of anything, but you're always busy" Joshua smiles back, nodding his head in approval.

"I believe in giving an honest day's work" smoke

quickly fills the small office as the businessman puffs on his cigar, before looking at Charlie sitting at the other desk across from his own.

"Charlie and me have been talking, I'm gonna start checking out some other areas for wood rights, but he can't run the ridge crews and the mills without help. I want to bring you in the mill as a foreman, Charlie will run both areas, but you'll primarily be in charge on this end." Joshua smiles and accepts the position before reaching across the table with his hand extended.

"I'll do a good job for you, Red" Joshua said, the owner shakes the hand in front of him as he continues to puff on his cigar.

"It will be more money, good money, and a good career for you, but it also causes some issues" Red leans back in his chair. "Most men working for me have been in trouble more than they've been out of trouble, so I get why they want to get paid cash, it's just part of this business." Charlie, who has been silent up to this point, places his forearms on the metal desk and leans forward.

"If the police come looking for someone, it could be a problem with you being a foreman, and we don't have any info about you." Charlie looks to Red, wanting him to say something. The red-haired man extinguishes what's left of his cigar as he looks to Joshua.

"Anything you want to tell me about your past?" Red looks to Charlie briefly then turns to the nervous young man sitting across from him, " If you're straight with me, I can help you son." The red-haired owner turns his head and coughs before continuing, "I like you Joshua, but can you at least tell me why you don't have a social security number?" Joshua looks to the two men sitting across from him. Honesty has always been the best policy, but he cannot explain that he and his mother are werewolves or how they ended up on the west coast, so he answers the question as honestly as he can.

"Sarah and me are Mennonites and were told to leave our community in Virginia," The former Virginian shifts nervously in his seat as he continues to explain his situation. "We never received any social security cards, and as we do not go to hospitals, we have no birth certificate." Joshua looks to the floor, hoping not to get too many questions; Red looks across to the young man sitting across from him and laughs.

"I remember when ol'e FDR started social security, and here we are on the short side of the 1950s with someone that Uncle Sam doesn't know about," Red points to Joshua smiling. "You may have the right idea boy, but we can work around that." Charlie nods in approval as he stands up and puts his hat back on his head.

"You ready to get started?"

CHAPTER SEVEN

The 1960s came and went, Joshua settled in his role as the mill foreman, and Sarah continued to work in the diner. As promised, the police came looking for people from time to time, but Joshua was quick to get out of view while Charlie took care of things. Joshua and his mother have come to call this place home and were happy for the first time since they had arrived. Every month, they roam the countryside in their true form, with Joshua always careful not to draw attention to themselves. Joshua picks his mother up at the diner as he does every evening and begins the drive to the small house they share in the wooded area isolated from everyone. The pair gathers their things and exits the car; it was mid-fall and always dark when the day ends for the mother and son, even darker when the car door is shut, extinguishing what little light is available. The darkness does not bother them as they can see as clearly at night as they do in the day. They have also gotten used to hearing the creatures of the forest as they can hear and smell as good as any wolf can. Sarah enters the cabin, turns on the lights, and stands silently as she turns around to face Joshua.

"Someone's been in the house" Joshua looks around and smells before answering.

"I can't place the smell, but it smells like a mixture of a dead animal, and a dirty penny" Sarah looks around the small house, shaking her head.

"Well, they didn't take anything or make a mess" she removes the food from the brown paper bag and places it on the table. Joshua sits down and removes the foil that covers the plate in front of him, then reaches for a fork but is stopped by his mother, who is quick to smack his fingers. "We give thanks' first" the pair prays over the food before eating. Appearances are important when a werewolf eats in public but is not needed at home, so they quickly devour the food. Joshua goes outside and sits on the wooden chair leaning up against the house and his mother soon joins him after speaking to Spencer, as she frequently does after work. They sit outside looking around with only the light of the kitchen shining through the window above the sink. Joshua looks to his mother.

"What did Spencer have to say tonight?" Joshua said, Sarah smiles and shrugs her shoulders

"Henry is still hanging around the restaurant but isn't asking many questions these days, but everyone is okay, John is still in Pennsylvania, and Michael has joined him. Bram and James are heading back to Virginia" Joshua looks at his mother with a puzzled look.

"How does Spencer know about John's pack? You haven't told him where we are, have you?" Joshua said.

Sarah nods as she sits down beside her son. "He doesn't want to know where we are, but Henry has been telling him things. I think your friend isn't happy with his pack and suspects that you're alive."

Joshua looks out in the distance. "Henry's a good man, and he deserves better" Sarah begins to speak but stops as Joshua lowers his head, and stares at an area in the darkness, a small growl escapes him as he rises from his chair and leaps into the wooded area that surrounds the small house, that has become a home for them, and easily overpowers the pale white female that has been staring at them in the darkness. "She's the one that has been spying on us, she has no heartbeat, but we should have smelled her." His growls soon grow louder as he tightens his grip around the throat of his stalker. The small pale female hisses and attempts to claw at him, but fear takes over, and the creature begins to whimper and beg.

"JOSHUA, STOP IT! Can't you see she's afraid of us?" He looks to his mother with yellow eyes as she shoves him away from the pale creature that lay trembling on the ground. "It's okay, sweetie, he's not gonna hurt you" Sarah helps the girl off the ground and begins wiping the dirt off her clothes. The young girl opens her mouth, displaying her fangs, and then runs into the darkness.

Weeks pass, and nothing is said about the girl, but Joshua is quick to notice others observing them when he sits outside at night. The two werewolves are cautious not to ask many questions about the pale white female or the cult that lives a few miles from them. Sarah also notices the creatures observing them from a distance, but neither werewolf does anything to antagonize or harm the onlookers. The senior werewolf has gotten the curious creature's scent and can easily track them at this point, but does nothing as his mother continues to chastise him for tightening his grip on the young girl's throat, and continues to lecture him on turning the other cheek. One night Joshua and his mother pull up to the cabin they call home to find a tall thin man sitting on one of the wooden chairs waiting for them. The tall man isn't as pale as the others but is unique in appearance with his elongated arms, and towers over the pair when he stands up.

"Hello, my name is Bernard, and I have been sent to

get you by my master, he would like to speak with you both." The stranger extends his arm, exposing his shriveled hand, and points to the woods. The two werewolves are cautious as they follow the tall, well-dressed gentleman through the woods. They realize they have been watched for the past weeks after grabbing the young girl and are unsure what awaits them, but they soon find themselves standing in front of a very large simple wooden structure. The building is much larger than it may appear, as it is painted black and has no windows. The tall man opens one of the two large black doors and instructs them to enter and wait until someone comes for them. Joshua and Sarah enter the well lit structure, and are in awe of carvings that are embedded in the wooden archway, at the entrance, and the green ceiling adorned with winged dragons facing each other. The walls are adorned with paintings of an ancient oriental village with mountains fading in the background, and the two werewolves are enamored at the detail of the painting that covers the walls of the foyer. Bernard soon returns, and escorts the pair to a large chamber, aligned with chairs and a long table on both sides of the green, felt-covered room. They also notice a pale white oriental man, with long graying hair and a goatee that extends to the base of his neck, sitting in front of them, with two guards standing on opposite sides of the large chair, where the man is seated. The Chinese leader rises from his chair, and adjusts the long silk red robe that hangs mid-thigh and the black sash, that matches his loose-fitting black pants. Bernard escorts the pair to some chairs on the right of the oriental gentleman's chair. Joshua and Sarah sit down and remain quiet, as they are still unsure of the situation, but continue to admire the bright colors of the walls, and the carvings on the large wooden chairs at the tables. The oriental man steps down from his chair, which sits in the center of the wall between the long tables, exposing a carving of a dragon's head on the back of his chair. Sarah points to the oversized chair and leans into her son, telling him how beautiful everything is, as the two werewolves have never seen anything like this. They are also startled at how quickly their host reaches them. The oriental man leans forward and bows to the pair. He stands upright and adjusts the long ponytail that hangs loosely behind him. The host motions for his guests to rise. After the two werewolves stand up, he looks them over and smiles.

"It is customary for you to also bow" the nervous guests bow, unsure if they are in trouble or not. "I am Chang Wei, Swordsman and foot soldier for King Zao" he points to the foyer. "The paintings you have been admiring are of my homeland" the host goes on to explain his role in the many battles he fought for his king. One of the guards leaves but returns with two servants; one of the servants brings a platter of steaks, while the other brings two large glasses of lemonade. Joshua soon notices that one of the servants is the young woman that he met weeks ago. Sarah leans in and smiles as she places her hand on the servant's robe.

"Are you okay? I was worried about you" the servant girl nods, acknowledging that she is okay. Chang waves his hand, instructing everyone to leave the chamber as he returns to his chair, which sits at the head of the tables.

The leader rests his hands on the thick dark wood slats that serve as his armrests, as he leans to his two guests. "She's still learning to hide her fangs, and most of my kind does not learn to speak for several years after being changed, the blood burns the throat for a few years." The pair begins eating the steaks that were presented to them, while Chang continues to speak in a soft yet direct tone. "Why did you spare one of my children? It's not in your nature, especially for one as strong as you," Chang points to Joshua then locks his fingers in front of him, waiting for a response.

Sarah places her hands on her son's shoulder. "He got a little ahead of himself but we don't want to hurt anyone" Sarah said, Joshua nods as he swallows a bite of his steak.

"We don't want any trouble, and now that I know what is going on, you won't have any trouble from us." Joshua said, Chang sighs a bit and rubs the hair on his chin that surrounds his mouth.

"You share the same blood, but neither of you has the smell of death on you, I believe that you want to live in peace, so you are welcome to remain on the mountain." The Chinese leader lowers his head, exposing the ponytail that hangs down his back. "Where is your pack?"

"John Bennett turned us, he killed my Anna and left me for dead, we have no pack, but we are good people." Joshua lowers his head, trying to keep his composure as his mother speaks up.

"He's looking for me, but he doesn't know that Joshua is alive, we've been on the run but we're settled in, and John seems to have forgotten about us." Chang smiles softly at his guests' innocence.

"John has certainly not forgotten about you, and he has asked if any of his kind has made their way to the west coast. He is an abomination and will be dealt with if he comes here," Chang motions for the servants to gather the dishes, and clean the area before speaking. "I would like to speak with you often, we are not that different, it is in our nature to be distrusting, but for now, you are welcome in my home."

The next morning Joshua sits at the diner drinking his coffee before heading to the mill to start his day. Brenda approaches him offering to refill his cup, and Joshua is quick to take her up on the offer. Joshua grabs the sugar and begins pouring until the coffee reaches the top of the cup.

"It must be a lumberjack thing to need that much sugar in a cup of coffee," Brenda places the pot back on the burner and turns back to Joshua. "Personally, I like my coffee like my men, sweet and light brown" Joshua laughs, but doesn't respond as Luis comes out from the kitchen to get a cup of coffee. He turns to Joshua after filling his cup.

"You hear about that asshole you beat up in the chow line?" Luis said, Joshua nods his head with a look of concern, Luis is still not sure what happened that day at the mill, and knows the young man is hiding something, but he also knows good people, and as far as he's concerned, these two are some of the best. "They found him and two others washed up on the beach, not a drop of blood in any of them."

"Do they have any suspects?" Joshua finishes his coffee and gets up from his chair after asking his question. He waves to his mother before exiting but is left with some advice from Luis.

"I still say it's that bunch up behind you guys, I realize the beach is a bit of a drive from here, and I know you can handle yourself, but just be careful, amigo." Joshua shakes his head and smiles as he exits the diner.

Joshua enters the office, as he does every morning, and grabs the clipboard off Charlie's desk. "We need to get some of the hardwood cut and drying" Charlie said, as he looks up at Joshua. "I have some of the ridge crew coming down to help, so that means you just run the floor and not try to do everything."

The new foreman enters the mill and surveys the area and is quick to assign the crew to their designated work stations. Lefue approaches Joshua before starting his shift, "you hear about Dom?" Joshua nods but is quick to remove himself from the conversation. Later that afternoon, a police car pulls up in front of the office, and two officers exit the car. Charlie comes out to meet them and the officers present a photo of the dead ex-employee.

"Do you know this man?" Charlie nods his head at the officer's question.

"Um yeah, his name was Dominick, and he came here looking for work with a guy named Paul, we get all kinds up here but most of these guys don't give us a last name." Charlie remains quiet, and is careful not to give the officer more than is needed, the other officer writes down some items on a notepad, while the other officer continues with his questioning.

"How long did he work here? And what was the reason he left?" The officer shows no emotion as he waits for a response.

"He was here around two years and left because he was an asshole that couldn't get along with anyone." Charlie hands the photo back to the officer, who looks down at the photo before asking one last question.

"Was there any specific individual that he didn't get along with?" Charlie looks around at the crowd that has formed around the officers and nods.

"No, not really, he was an asshole to everyone" the officer turns, holds the photo up to the crowd, and asks if anyone has any information. The crowd all nods and responds with a resounding no before returning to work. The men go back to the mill where Joshua is going over paperwork, and attempting to calculate how much wood can be processed that day. The crew returns to work, but one of the recent hires stops at Joshua's platform.

"Did you do it? I heard you knocked him around pretty good" Joshua attempts to answer the question presented to him, but is interrupted by several other employees expressing anger at the question. Lefue emerges from the others and looks to the new hire.

"Listen, Dom was nothing but a boomer, and everybody knew it, but Joshua is good people." The others nod in approval as the new hire backs away as Lefue continues, "the boss is okay in our book, so shut the hell up or move on."

Charlie enters the area and waves for Joshua to join him in the office, to make sure Joshua is okay, before letting him get back to work. The day finally ends, and Joshua returns to the diner to pick up Sarah. Nothing is said about Dominick as they both know who drained him of his blood. A few weeks go by, and before long, it is time for the next cycle of the moon. Joshua and Sarah have monthly visits with Chang a few days before changing. The mother and son walk through the woods, but Sarah turns to her son before they approach the door. "Are you going to mention that man to Chang?" Joshua turns and answers, but both are a careful and only whisper.

"And say what mama? We have nothing in that" the pair looks up to see Bernard waiting, and enter the door as they do every month, since meeting the vampire leader. The couple enters the main hall to find Chang waiting, and take a seat before being served steak. The young woman they previously met smiles and lifts her upper lip. Her hair has turned back to its red color, and her eyes have a hint of blue. The young girl's skin is still pale, but she smiles with a look of innocence, despite having to drink blood to survive.

"I've learned how to recess my fangs" Sarah smiles as she rises to hug the new vampire.

And you can speak now, that's wonderful" the red-haired young lady looks up to Chang, and bows before leaving. She is careful not to turn her back to her leader, but she looks at the two werewolves before she leaves.

"By the way, my name is Meadow."

Chang waves his arm, signaling the room to be emptied; he has come to enjoy his meetings with the werewolves and considers them his friends. The vampire leader steps down from his chair and takes a chair beside Joshua and Sarah."I would like to ask for a favor" Chang leans back in his chair, collecting his thoughts for a moment before speaking. "There are many other creatures like us, which you may not know about, and you would think that we would all get along, but over the years most of the werewolves remains on the east coast, and my kind remain here on the west coast. Granted, our kind is worldwide, and Europe has more fights than you may realize, but everyone attempts to get along."

"You have been a good friend to us Chang, and if we can repay you, we will help in any way possible" Joshua said. Sarah adjusts her chair, before placing her hand on Chang's shoulder and smiles.

"All you need to do is ask" Sarah said, Chang places his hand over Sarah's and nods.

"Your kind has two recognized leaders, but neither has stepped up to lead. I speak with King Lycaon from time to time, but I haven't heard from the other elder overseas." Chang pats Sarah's hand before he continues "John is a concern, as he wants to force his way as the leader of your kind, he does not realize it is not his place, but if he assumes a large enough pack, he will need to be dealt with." Joshua turns to his mother and then back to Chang.

"I can't speak for my mother, but if you want me to help fight John and that bunch, just say the word." The stronger black werewolf looks down at the table as he tries to contain himself. "He took my Anna, my child, and most of my family" Sarah returns to her chair beside her son, and swallows before speaking.

"I have turned my back on most of our ways and have accepted that we follow the English way, I watch television, use electricity, the phone, and ride in a car, but I refuse to turn my back on a peaceful existence. I will remain close to God and keep my faith," Chang waves his hands, shaking his head back and forth.

"I was a warrior in my past life, and I will always be a warrior. I teach my children the ways of combat to help them focus, but Sarah, I admire anyone that stays true to themselves. My kind takes life to remain alive, it is what we do, but I would never ask either of you to do anything against your beliefs" Joshua looks to his mother.

"I'm sorry mama," he turns his attention to Chang," John is always careful to move around to hide how many people he kills, but he's an evil man." Chang looks to his friend tapping his fingers on the wooden table where his arm lays.

"John dines on flesh, he is a man-eater, and doing these things changes your kind, he dines on humans as a choice, not as a necessity. I also suspect he isn't the only one in his pack to do this," Chang ponders briefly before speaking. "This makes him untrustworthy to my kind, as he chooses to be evil, and it also raises concerns about those that follow him." Joshua looks with his mouth open struggling to speak.

"I never saw him eat anyone, but I was curious why he never ate the deer, bears, or anything else we found. He barely ate any hamburgers, but I thought it was because he was a full black." Chang nods and leans forward in his chair.

"You are one of the strongest of your kind, and you do not dine on man, in fact, you are the only senior wolf to refrain from such things. This is what I want to speak with you both about," Joshua and Sarah look concerned as they fear what Chang is about to ask them to do. Chang laughs briefly before continuing, "Do not worry my friends, I am not asking you to do such things; If you did I would have ended you both when you first appeared." The Chinese vampire looks to the two werewolves from his seat on the chair, and pauses before continuing. "I have a council showing up in a few weeks, it is a vast undertaking getting these people here, some are from other countries, some local, but I would like you to attend as a symbol of a new beginning for our kind." Joshua and Sarah both agree to attend, but remind him that they are not diplomats, and are simple people that just happen to be werewolves. Chang does not attempt to hide his excitement, but looks to Sarah before the two werewolves leave. "When you watch television, do you watch Marshall Dillon, he is an honorable man and always takes the path of honor," Sarah smiles.

"We watch the show every Saturday night and we also like the Andy Griffith show, it reminds us of home."

The next morning Joshua shows up at the mill and enters the office. Red returned, and sits at his desk smoking his cigar, reviewing the paperwork covering his desk. He removes his glasses and looks up at Joshua, "I've been looking over things, and I have a question for you." The red-haired owner extinguishes his cigar as he offers his mill chief a seat. "How in the hell did you get all that hardwood processed so fast?" He looks over to Charlie, who is waving his hand back and forth.

"I gotta tell you Red, I didn't miss those damn cigars one bit, but we're ahead of schedule, the boards will be dried, and we'll be able to make shipment a few weeks, ahead of schedule, thanks to that man." Charlie points to Joshua as he continues to voice his approval.

Charlie walks with Joshua to the mill area, where he sees one of the men from the field crew. "Kevin is coming down to the mill full time, we'll have him unload the truck, and then he can work the saws at some point." Joshua looks to Charlie while he reviews his clipboard.

"Are you reducing the field crew?" Joshua said.

"We are not downsizing and we just hired a guy, I think his name is Eric," Charlie walks to the large open steel doors and waves his hand. A black-haired man enters the mill area and offers his hand to Joshua.

"Hello, pleased to meet you, my name's Eric" Joshua takes a moment to notice the clean-shaven individual standing in front of him. He shakes the new guy's hand and immediately notices his hands are not calloused, and does not look like most of the guys that show up. Joshua says very little, but after the mill gets started, he enters the office to speak with Red.

"Eric doesn't look like someone that has dropped many trees" Red looks up and nods.

"Yes, I noticed that his hands didn't look like it has seen a hard day's work, but things may change around here, and I need some guys to help me run things." Joshua looks down at his boss, obviously concerned.

"Everything okay?" Red takes a moment and leans back in his chair but doesn't say anything for several minutes.

"I didn't go check out new sites son, I've been to the hospital" Red picks up his cigar and puffs deeply before continuing. "It appears that these damned things have killed me, I've got cancer, they can't operate, and the drugs may or may not help" Joshua sits down and says nothing as he can't find the words. Red grins at his employee, "I have a daughter somewhere, but I couldn't tell you how to find her, Charlie will run things, including the diner, and I'll figure something out between now and when I die."

Joshua has trouble most of the day staying focused but remains silent about Red's condition to everyone at the mill. The day ends, and Joshua remains seated at the small table, while Sarah calls Spencer. She hangs up and joins her son at the kitchen table, in their small home. "Are you okay?" Joshua looks across the table at his mother.

"Red has cancer" Sarah looks across to her son; she has come to understand her son's behavior over the years and realizes why he has been so distant most of the evening.

"What have you been thinking about?" Sarah said, while Joshua fidgets at the table.

"Changing Red into one of us" Joshua said, Sarah sighs and chooses her words carefully.

"So you have decided who lives and who dies? I understand that Red has been good to us, but it's not our place to decide these things." Joshua lowers his head and stares at the table, almost in a trance.

"We don't have a pack, and he may be someone to have on our side" Joshua said. Sarah continues to speak softly to her son.

"And do what? Fight John? Be the Beta in our newly formed pack?" Sarah doesn't wait for a response as she continues, "we may not kill, but changing Red is still taking a life, and we don't know if he will heal, or remain in pain for years" Joshua nods and swallows hard.

"He dies like everyone else around me" Sarah gets up from her chair and hugs her son.

"You didn't give him cancer" Sarah said.

After discussing the moral concerns about turning Red, the two werewolves change that night, as they do every month on the night of the full moon. Joshua has come to enjoy the times he changes, and forgets about Red and his other problems. His mother runs by his side, as the two roam the woods on their hands and feet under the full moon, both have come to accept the wolf is now part of them but wonder at times what side of their nature confuses them, as the times they are in wolf form, nothing seems to bother them. The next morning comes, and with it, a large breakfast for the two wolves, as they are always extremely hungry after they change. Before long, the car pulls up in front of the diner, it's a bit early, but Sarah is normally the first to arrive despite Brenda and Luis living just behind the diner. Sarah looks to her son before opening the car door. "Are you okay with what we talked about last night? About Red?" Joshua turns to his mother.

"I worry how we're more like the English than we care to admit, but it's who we are now." The concerned man smiles at his mother and nods his head, "but it's also not our place to decide such things. All I plan on doing is praying for Red and nothing more," Sarah opens the car door but looks to her son with pride.

"I knew you would do the right thing, and I am also proud of the man you've become" Joshua laughs and looks to his mother with a sly grin.

"You know, I am in my 60's, so that would make you around...." Sarah abruptly interrupts her son.

"Don't say it," and she laughs as she exits the car.

Sarah enters the diner and turns the sign to open, she starts making coffee and getting things ready for the mild rush that will be coming in a few hours. She enters the kitchen and greets Luis and Brenda, who begin getting things ready for the day. Sarah exits the kitchen with a plate of donuts that she displays on the counter, and looks up to see Red coming in as he does a few times a week. He takes a seat at the counter and quickly removes two glazed donuts. Sarah places a coffee cup and begins filling it. "So how are things today?" she looks with a soft smile as she waits for a response.

"I'll be damned, that man of yours told you, didn't he?" Red bites into his donut and soon takes a drink of his coffee. Brenda soon joins the conversation and lights up a cigarette, before long, smoke fills the air. Sarah looks to the man sitting across from her not knowing what to say. Red smiles and winks "it really doesn't matter at this point, sweetheart," he gets up but struggles to get out of his chair, walking slower than normal to reach the door. Brenda picks up her cup, which Sarah has just filled.

"What doesn't matter? Did I miss something?" Sarah walks over and places the coffee pot on the burner.

"It's nothing about you or me, Red wasn't clear on what it was" is all that is said.

Red enters the office and takes his chair as he does every morning; he lights up his cigar but soon starts coughing. He notices blood on the hand that was covering his mouth. Charlie enters the office.

"Josh has things covered at the mill, and the ridge crews have already started but we're gonna hit the property line in a few months, so we may need to start thinking about either relocating or just run the mill and buying logs." Charlie notices Red wiping the blood off his hand, "why don't you get out of here and do something you want to do?" The mill owner places the stained handkerchief in his pocket.

"And do what? Charlie, they gave me about a year with treatment and a few months without it." Charlie looks down at his desk but doesn't say anything as Red takes another puff of his cigar. "I'll keep going until I can't work anymore, then you can take over. Have you given any more thought about Joshua taking your spot?"

While Charlie and Red discuss the future of the mill, Joshua is busy with the day to day operations. He assigned Eric to pull the logs onto the conveyor to get him started in this business. Eric does a good job, but appears to be struggling with the physical duties of the position. Charlie soon takes a tour of the mill area and stops to speak with Joshua before leaving. "I see you have Eric running a bull chain; how's he doing?" Joshua looks to the struggling mill worker.

"He's not doing very good so far, he's just not cut out for this," he turns to Charlie. "I'll keep him busy, but there's something about him that I can't put my finger on." Charlie nods as he takes his leave. Before long, the whistle blows, and the crew finds themselves in line for lunch. Joshua waits to eat last, as he always does, then takes a seat at one of the open areas. He takes a bite of food and notices Eric walking toward him, who takes a seat across from him.

"So where are you from" Joshua takes another bite of the food and hesitates before answering.

"Virginia" is all that is said as the new mill worker continues, "and your wife works at the diner. She's that blonde that works there, isn't she?" Joshua looks a bit puzzled, but before he can answer, one of the workers at the end of the table speaks up.

"She's that good-looking thing with the nice ass that works there; Josh is a very lucky man." Eric nods while Joshua continues eating, but is still concerned about the question that was presented to him. The weeks pass, and the new mill worker is soon competent at his duties. Joshua shrugs off his concerns as nothing, despite the continued questioning. He and Sarah continue their day-to-day routine and eventually Eric stops inquiring about them, and Red's health is diminishing quickly. Most are aware of his condition at this point, but say very little about things. Joshua has stopped struggling with any decision on changing him at this point, and before long, the vampire council has gathered, and the two werewolves are getting ready to join the meeting. Joshua enters the living area of the house after putting on a shirt and pants, his mother nods in approval as she hangs up the phone. "Those clothes we found at the yard sale look good on you" Sarah stands up from the chair and adjusts her simple peach-colored dress.

"You don't look too bad yourself mama, what did Spencer have to say? Is Henry doing okay?" Sarah crosses her arms with a concerned look.

"John called everyone to Pennsylvania, including Henry, but before he left, Henry mentioned that John has gone crazy and his pack has grown to about nine members." Joshua looks to his mother shaking his head.

"That's a lot of people not to notice, and how do they move around?" Sarah walks over and begins adjusting her son's shirt.

"Well, it's not our problem; John remained in

Pennsylvania and stays at some church. Spencer said some of the other packs that come in the restaurant mentioned something about the police showing up to the church a few times because of all the killing." Joshua doesn't say much as the two begin walking to Chang's compound. Before long, they find themselves at the front door, but Bernard is not there to greet them, two guards with long swords stand on each side of the large door that is opened quickly at their arrival, one of the guards looks to the werewolf guests.

"Welcome, we're so glad you could come" the other guard nods with his approval and invites them inside.

The pair enters the room and is surprised to not see many people attending, but notice the various nationalities walking around, and is hesitant to approach anyone. Joshua soon feels someone hug his arm, he looks down, but before he can answer, his attacker speaks.

"Hello handsome, hello Miss Braun" Sarah looks to the young woman standing beside her son in her blue silk attire.

"Hello Meadow, what are you wearing?" The new vampire steps back, displaying her uniform.

"Master Chang told me to make you comfortable and to wear this; it's the color that the servants are wearing tonight." Meadow begins pulling on Joshua's arm "come with me, I have your chairs picked out, and I'll get the steaks for you two." As promised, Meadow presents a large portion of steaks in front of her assigned guests, and then takes her place behind the two werewolves, as previously instructed. Sarah looks to the young girl and points to an empty chair. Meadow nods her head and whispers, "I'm not allowed, but there about ready to start" before long, most of the chairs are filled. A Hispanic gentleman takes his seat beside Joshua and looks at the steak in front of the guests before turning to Meadow, instructing her to come closer.

"I prefer not to sit with the dogs" Meadow looks around, not knowing what to do, she leans into the vampire leader.

"I think all the seats are filled, but they are good people once you get to...." Meadow is unable to finish her sentence as the man leaps from his chair and grabs her throat, slamming her down on the table. The red-haired young girl begins to whimper and beg the Hispanic gentleman to release her.

"I am one of the oldest among us, I was an Aztec tribal leader, and I expect to have my instructions followed, so FIND ME ANOTHER SE..." The Aztec leader turns to find a pair of yellow eyes staring back at him. Joshua snarls, bearing his teeth, and before long, a loud roar fills the chamber as the black werewolf rises from his chair, displaying his claws, as he continues to snarl at the arrogant leader. Sarah grabs her son's arm as she looks to the worried leader.

"You need to let her go, I said let her go" Chang rises from his chair and motions for the Aztec leader to release the young girl, then points to his guests.

"A wolf shifter protecting one of us, this is our future, and it starts here with our new friends." Meadow rises up from the table and places her hands on Joshua's shoulder, who continues to stare at the man with the look of an attacking animal.

"It's okay big guy, I'm okay, just calm down"

Joshua's heart begins to slow down, and before long, his eyes return to normal, and his fangs recede. The Aztec leader smiles and nods graciously.

"You are welcome in my house anytime, you are honorable, and I do not smell death on you." He turns his attention to Chang, "how does he shift without the moon to guide him?" Chang surveys the chamber that is now filled with vampire leaders anxiously waiting for an answer.

"Because he is a full black and we can all agree from his scent, a master wolf shifter in time." Chang walks over to the werewolves, who are unclear at what has just happened. "He has not reached his potential, but no doubt he will be one of the strongest of his kind." The Asian leader looks at Joshua with pride, "well done, you bared your teeth to protect one of my children, I will not forget this."

The rest of the evening is spent mingling with the various leaders and making new friends. Sarah was as well received as Joshua, and the former Mennonites' simple mannerisms and way of life were endearing to everyone they met. Meadow never left their side as instructed and did a good job making introductions. Most werewolves have trouble being inside for long, and soon, the compound's interior feels like a cage. Joshua and Sarah walk outside accompanied by their eager young escort. They soon notice a few mortals gathered in the courtyard. Meadow looks to her friends.

"They're familiars; they want to be changed but need to prove themselves." She looks to the ground and, with a somber tone, finishes with "I was an accident." Joshua looks down at Meadow, still protective of her.

"A happy accident if you ask me" Sarah nods in approval. Joshua hears his name called and surveys the area to see Eric in the courtyard.

"Hey Joshua, I serve one of the senior nightwalkers, I'm hoping to get changed at some point." Sarah looks puzzled at the man addressing her son.

"Why would you want that?" Sarah said, as Eric shrugs his shoulders.

"I'm a night person anyway, so why not, and you live forever, the blood thing will be something to get used to" he then looks at Sarah."I mean, she's hot and will stay that way for a long time, actually being a werewolf may be better." Joshua looks to the dark-haired man standing in front of him.

"Be happy you're mortal" Joshua said, Eric looks at the two werewolves in disgust.

"Damned easy to say when you're changed and I'm still waiting. You know, I was a pastor at one time, and I'm supposed to believe in a better life waiting on the other side, but I like drugs and fucking too much in this life to take that chance." Joshua says very little as Eric arrogantly continues "but no worries, we're leaving tomorrow and I have a long drive ahead of me."

The next day, as promised, Eric is nowhere to be found, but people come and go at the mill, so it's not really noticed. Joshua starts his day as he always does, and Sarah tends to the restaurant. Red has lost weight and can barely make it to his chair at this point. Joshua enters the office with the clipboard in hand.

"We have a lot of the hardwoods drying, and the

pine boards are ready to be shipped out. We even have some cedar about ready that hasn't warped yet." Red looks up, smiles, and with a weak raspy voice, acknowledges what a good job Joshua has done. He looks over to Charlie and motions for him to exit. Charlie leaves as instructed, locking the door behind him. Red looks to Joshua with lifeless eyes.

"Something's been eating at you for a while, I thought that it was the cancer, but I don't think that's it." Red pulls a bottle and two glasses from his desk drawer, Joshua pours his boss a glass, but is instructed to fill both glasses. Red raises his glass, and Joshua grabs the glass and takes a drink with his boss; this isn't the first time he has taken a drink and being a werewolf makes it very hard for him to get drunk. "So, what is it?" Joshua sits for a moment and looks at his friend.

"I have some people chasing me, and I'm always worried that my mother and me will be found," Joshua ponders for a moment then continues. "But I'm worried that our luck is going to run out soon" Red looks with a puzzled look.

"Sarah's your mother? I didn't see that" Red struggles to take another drink, but points to the desk drawer on the opposite side of his desk. "I've got the solution to your problem in that drawer, a Smith and Wesson 45 caliber that hold eight permanent solutions, but given you don't believe in things like that, I don't know what to tell you son." Joshua looks to the drawer and realizes that his boss will soon be gone, and after a long pause, looks to Red.

"I also may be able to save you" Red looks at Joshua, nodding his head.

"I don't see how, unless you have a cure for cancer" Red looks to his employee, realizing this is what he has been struggling with. "It's just my time son, nothing more" he points to the floor and instructs Joshua to close the blinds on the windows in front of the office. Joshua does as he is instructed and pulls up a board on the floor, revealing a canvas bag. He removes the bag from the floor and hands it to his boss. Red pulls the bag open and looks to Joshua "found my kid, she's a schoolteacher in Nevada, she visited and assured me that her and my son in law are going to keep the place open, but I gave Charlie an equal share just to be sure." Joshua nods, but before he can say anything, Red pulls out a stack of money wrapped in a rubber band and soon afterward pulls out another stack of money. "I think that should be around three thousand dollars."

Joshua nods his head, "I can't take that."

Red looks to the werewolf sitting across from him "We made a lot of money on that lumber you dried out, so consider it a bonus," the dying mill owner pushes the money away from him, then leans back in his chair. "I'm pretty sure you're not telling me everything, and you can stay as long as you want, but if you need to go, this will get you started somewhere else." Red opens the drawer on the other side of his desk and presents the handgun to Joshua, "and this should solve the rest of your problems." Joshua takes the money after protesting but before he can leave, Red throws a set of keys on a key ring. "You're not gonna get far driving that rusted up antique either, take the truck." Joshua walks over to the desk, picking up the keys, but is unsure what to say, as he looks down at the weak man in front of him. He has heard both John and Master Chang mention the smell of death, but did not realize what that meant until now, as an unfamiliar scent fills the room. The werewolf remains respectful and quiet while his employer struggles to speak. "I've tried to be a good man for the last couple of years, but I was an asshole for a long time, you can't be both successful and nice son," Red begins coughing, spewing more blood. Joshua begins walking around the desk but stops as his boss holds his hand up shaking his head, "I don't have much time kid, but something tells me that helping you is important." Red wipes the blood off his mouth before continuing "and you're a good person, I'll have the truck signed over to you and if anyone asks, Charlie can cover." Joshua looks up to his friend and smiles but says nothing, as thank you didn't seem to be enough. The former mill foreman walks out of the office to find Charlie waiting at the blue Ford truck.

"He cares a lot about you Josh, and he knew you were in some sort of trouble months ago." The new mill owner places his hands in his pockets as he walks slowly to Joshua. "He insisted on helping you before he dies and is sure you're a good man," Joshua remains silent as Charlie stops before walking past his employee, "so don't disappoint him kid, the truck is yours, and you can stay as long as you want." The bald-headed leader looks down at the canvas bag and smiles," and I don't need to know about anything else," the former Mennonite pulls out of the driveway and heads to the diner to pick up his mother. Sarah gets in the truck after shutting the diner down for the night, and then looks to her son with a puzzled look.

"He just gave you this truck and a bag of money?" Joshua nods "but you had to take the gun to get the money and the truck?" Joshua and Sarah return to the place they have called home and sit outside as they do every night. The next morning the phone rings, Sarah hangs up the receiver, and after a brief pause, she looks at her son with a soft smile.

"Red died last night," Joshua nods; he knew that the conversation that he had yesterday would probably be his last, as he could smell cancer and death on his boss. "They closed the mill and diner down today, but he didn't want a funeral," Joshua looks to the floor, he was in a somber mood, but as he has seen so much death in his life, tears escaped him.

"He was a good man" was all that was said. Most of the day was spent doing very little. Sarah went to the store to get some supplies to bake in an effort to have something to take their mind off things. That night as they sit outside, Bernard emerges from the woods.

"Master Chang wants to speak with you tomorrow morning about an hour before the sun rises." Bernard does not reveal many details and quickly leaves after delivering his message. Sarah and Joshua get up early the next morning and arrive at the compound. They enter the door and are greeted by Bernard, who escorts them to the main hall, where Chang is waiting.

"Please sit down" the look on the vampire's face worries the werewolves. Chang pauses for a moment then looks to his friends, "when you get to be my age, money or status fades, and all you're left with is loyalty." Joshua and Sarah assure Chang that they have been loyal and have kept his secrets. The elder Vampire looks at the two werewolves and smiles "I always knew your journey did not end here, and I have come to consider both of you friends" he strokes the hairs that extend below his chin, "and please know you are always welcome in my house." Master Chang directs them to a door at the opposite side of his chair that they were not allowed to enter in the past. They are led down to a lower level, and enter a large room lined with beds in the center and on both walls. Sarah and Joshua don't say much as they walk down the makeshift aisle of the simple off-white room. Joshua stops abruptly and looks at the large wooden door in front of them.

"Someone like us is in the other room" Chang nods, but says nothing as he opens the door and instructs the pair to enter. They enter to find an attractive blonde woman chained to a wall. Joshua pauses for a moment as the smell of her flesh burning from the silver straps overwhelms him. Chang is aware of the black werewolf's past and helps him out of the room, but stops and nods to the vampire guarding the tortured wolf. The guard unsheathes her sword and places it against the pleading woman's throat as the door is shut.

"Are you okay?" Joshua clears his throat, but continues to rub the scars on his neck as he looks to answer his mother's question.

"I will never forget that smell mama," Joshua looks to his vampire friend. "John?"

"She is part of his pack and was sent here by John," Master Chang looks to the door they had just exited. "We will send him a message about this, but she's not the one who told him about you two." The pair is led back to the main hall and to the front door. Chang walks outside with his friends, and the three soon find themselves in the large clearing beside the building, where Chang's warrior's practice. Joshua and Sarah look at the far side of the dirt area, past the splintered wooden posts, to see Eric tied to a tree. The senior vampire continues to walk to the man whose hands are tied securely behind him to the large oak tree. Eric immediately begins begging for his life as they approach. Chang reaches out and grabs the young man's throat, unfazed at his pleads, "He thought he could find what he was looking for with your kind, and told John about you both." The elder vampire releases his grip and turns to the two werewolves, "but I was kind enough to fulfill his wish," Chang looks to the horizon as the sky begins to lighten "I will speak to you after the sun rises." The vampire warrior walks to a door at the side of the large structure before turning to the former pastor. "You were never worthy of my house...so enjoy your prize," the two werewolves say nothing as they watch the door shut, but soon turn their attention to the man in front of them, who continues to beg.

"We can still fix this; all you need to do is untie me and walk away, they changed me, do you get it now?" Sarah grabs Joshua's arm before he can start walking to a pleading Eric.

"If you help him, we'll end up in the basement" Joshua looks to his mother and nods in agreement, as Sarah attempts to offer the new vampire some comfort. "It isn't about the quantity but the quality of life that matter's" Eric up at the two nodding his head.

"He knows you're here, so fuck both of you, and I'll see you two in hell." The vampire's words are cut short as the sun rises, and shine's down on him. Nothing is said as Eric's screams soon stop as his flesh smolders and burns, until nothing is left but some ash, which is scattered by the wind. The two werewolves both lower their heads and say a brief prayer before walking to the front of the building. They pause at the front door and look at each other, unsure what to do, but soon enter and sit down at the chairs at the side of Chang's chair where they often sit. The elder

Vampire is aware of the Mennonite's beliefs, but this isn't the world that he lives in, and he offers no apologies for his actions.

"While I respect your commitment to peace, this house will not tolerate such behavior," Chang has come to care deeply for the two werewolves. "I consider you both worthy of my respect, and will defend you if needed." The vampire leader pauses a bit as the pair considers his offer, "werewolves and vampires have fought in the past from time to time." Chang strokes his beard while his friends remain silent. "But it always causes a lot of death among not only our kind, but also mortals." The ancient leader ponders for several minutes, lost in his thoughts, "we have been able to hide these battles with plagues and wars in the past, but times have changed." The two werewolves listen as they are told about the last war lasted a year and how the flu epidemic was used to hide the dead. Joshua looks to his mother, and holds her hand before speaking.

"We do not want harm to come to anyone over us" Sarah looks around with a look of despair.

"But we don't know where to go from here," Chang walks over to Joshua and Sarah with a piece of paper, and lays it down in front of them. Sarah picks up the paper "Chicago?" The vampire leader nods his head.

"This is the address for the record keeper of the grand coven, perhaps he can help." Sarah gets up and hugs the man she has come to call friend, and after a brief embrace, Chang extends his hand to Joshua. "I will miss you both and hope to see you again, but know you are welcome in this house, and we will protect you if needed."

The two make their way to the door where Meadow

160

is standing, "I can't cry since I changed, but I'll miss you."
She reaches out and wraps her arms around Joshua,
"especially my big bad wolf." Sarah rushes out the door as
the two embrace but returns with something in her hand.
She approaches the vampire and places a necklace in her
hand. Meadow looks down and admires the cheap red
ruby, encased in tarnished gold plating.

"It's not much, I got it at a yard sale" she looks to
Meadow, but is unable to hold back tears, as she hugs the
little vampire." You may not be able to cry, but I can, don't
forget about us," the two embrace, but eventually release
each other. Meadow looks to Sarah, struggling to find
words.

"I never knew my dad, and my real mom was
almost dead from all the men and drugs before she was
drained by a vampire." The Mennonite woman, that has
come to be a surrogate mother to the red-haired young
woman, places the necklace around the young vampire's
neck, who pauses for a moment to admire her jewelry. "But
you're the mom I always wanted, and I'll never forget either
one of you," Meadow steps back to avoid the sunlight as
the displaced pair leave, before she rushes into the large
room where Chang is. She walks up to the senior vampire
and proudly presents her necklace, who looks at the simple
ruby necklace, and nods his head in approval. He goes on
to tell the young vampire the details of what had just
transpired then points to the doorway that leads to his
chambers. Meadow does as she has been told, and walks to
the olive green phone on the long narrow table, just inside
the opening, and dials the number lying on the table.
"Hello, I was told to call this number and give you an
update on Josh and Sarah," the young Vampire listens and
soon replies, " he never talks on the phone, but said to tell

you that he sent them to Chicago, as you instructed." Meadow hangs up the phone and turns to Chang who is standing in the doorway, "are they gonna be okay?" The senior Vampire walks past the young woman and stops before entering his chambers.

"I hope so, little one but I think there is much more to this than we know."

CHAPTER EIGHT

John sits at the large wooden desk, gazing at the large stained glass window at the church, lost in his thoughts. It has been years since the pack has been together as they have been searching for Sarah. He turns his chair back to his desk and looks to Michael, who has returned after hearing the news about Sarah's location, and Joshua being alive. "Are the others back yet?" Michael nods, but is hesitant to say much about the former pack member being alive.

"Not yet boss, but they should be here anytime" Michael takes a seat on the leather couch, located on the far wall of the large office. "The others are coming back, but no one has heard anything, including our newest member Robert, but considering he can't get out of his own way, that's not much of a surprise." John looks up to his second in command in disgust.

"Robert is a soldier, nothing more, so are Peg and the Bishop," Michael sighs as he shakes his head.

"Say what you want, but Anna had an eye for talent, and I don't see her changing any of them, their light grey's at best, and I don't see em' getting any darker." Michael leans in, obviously disgusted, and ends his rant with, "and I don't trust the Bishop at all, he's too needy and will tuck his tail between his legs and run in a real fight." John looks unfazed by what he had just heard.

"The Bishop has his place, he can hide the money within the church and when he finds a main location for us, we can end him." The Alpha turns his attention to his Beta before finishing his thought. "Then we stop hiding and take our place at the top of the food chain, Robert and Peg has a place in the pack, for now." Michael looks to his leader, shrugs and in a condescending tone and asks.

"And what about our eating habits? Anna wouldn't chow down on a mortal like me, you and Bull does, hell, James has even started, so his brother won't be far behind." The Beta of the pack sighs and shakes his head before voicing his concerns. "Look boss, all I'm saying is we can't eat the mortals anytime we want, fuck whoever we choose and stay at one place, I thought that was the whole point of moving around like we do." Michael gets up from the couch and starts moving toward the door, "It looks like the gang's all here." He opens the door to let James, Henry, Bull, and Robert enter. John looks to the crew that has gathered in the large office space.

"By now, you realize Joshua is still alive and with his mother, I got a phone call from a wanna be familiar." The pack leader scans the room, trying to hold his temper. "I don't trust familiars, they're too needy, so I decided to send Peg out to double-check." John slams his fist on the wooden table in front of him. "I want that traitor dead and his mother can lose her head after she gives me what I want." The Bishop enters the room where the others are gathered, carrying a box, John looks at him and, in a disgusted tone, asks.

"Why are you here? Did I ask your worthless ass to join in?" The Bishop places the box on the desk and looks at the other's and points to the box.

"It's addressed to John, and it's cold" James walks to the edge of the desk, and shoves the Bishop back, as he opens the box, only to find a steel green cooler inside, with a letter attached to the lid. James hands the folded letter to

Michael, who looks at the letter before unfolding it.

"Nice paper" he proceeds to open the browned thick paper and reads out loud for all to hear. "Any wolf shifters caught near my house will be dealt with" he turns to John, and, with a raised brow, continues. "I have a bad feeling about this boss" James proceeds to open the cooler to find Peg's head in ice then looks up to his pack leader.

"Found Peg," Robert begins pulling at his hair and frantically proclaims.

"That's a head! I mean that's a real head" Bishop Reed approaches the box and begins praying. John walks around his desk and slaps the Bishop when he gets in reach.

"Quit praying over that useless bitch, It's her own fault for getting caught, I thought she may have been able to screw her way out of trouble given how she made her money." Bishop Reed says nothing as he backs away from an enraged John, who grabs Robert and shoves his head down just above the cooler, where Peg's head lays. "And yes, IT'S A FUCKING HEAD! It will not be the last one you see, so get used to it."

Michael grabs Robert and shoves him, making an opening between him and John. "Chang and his kung fu vampires didn't kill Josh or his mother; we did get that much from Peg, but what now? They're either protected by Chang or gone, so what's our next move?" John walks back to his chair as silence fills the room for several minutes.

"Get that thing out of here, her head doesn't do any of us any good like that," then turns to the pack. "We will go back to Virginia at our new location," and defiantly proclaims, "where we will eat, torment, rape or screw whomever we choose as we are at the top of the food chain." Still angry at his situation, John looks to Henry, "and since you don't do any of that, you can go back to Richmond and see if that blonde bitch or her useless son shows up." Michael holds his hands up and says nothing as he backs away from his leader, while John continues his rant. "Robert can shadow Michael for a while" then, without concern for anyone in the room proclaims, "and if Robert or Henry doesn't soon grow a pair, they can be lunch one day." John begins making his way to the door but stops in front of the Bishop, "you won't be much help, so stay here and keep the money clean and coming, since that's all you're good for."

While John and his crew are packing up for the trip back to Virginia, Joshua and Sarah pull up in front of a bookstore on a quiet street in Chicago. They have been driving for days, but were able to find a quiet place to change under the full moon the previous night, in a field away from traffic.

The store sits on a corner lot near Lakeview and blends well into the row of local businesses that line the street. Joshua is careful to look at the glass front, with a few books in the window, and how unassuming everything appears to be. His mother looks at the crumpled paper in her hand.

"This is where Master Change said to go and see if they can help us." Joshua turns his attention to his mother, still unsure how to proceed.

"It doesn't look like anything weird, are you sure this is the place?" Sarah nods as she opens the door.

"We're not going to get any answers in this truck"

Sarah slams the door behind her and strolls to the driver's door, stopping to look at her son through the glass. "Well, come on" Joshua gets out of the truck, and the two werewolves enter the front door, ringing a bell that alerts the owner of their arrival. A voice welcomes them to the store and they soon notice a bald man standing up from behind the counter. The hair around his mouth contorts to accommodate his smile as he stretches his neck to see who has entered his store.

"Can I help you find something? We have a very good selection of books," Joshua looks to his mother but nothing is said for a few uncomfortable moments, until Sarah speaks up.

"Please excuse us but we've been driving for days and was told you could help us," the tall bald man nods.

"I see, did Master Chang send you?" Joshua takes a deep breath and smiles.

"Yes he did" the storekeeper walks around from behind the desk and past his two patrons to turn the sign from open to closed, and lock the front door. The two werewolves remain guarded as the bald man approaches them and extends his hand. Joshua shakes the man's hand, but is quick to place himself between the stranger and his mother.

"I'm Frank, and I've been expecting you" the two werewolves are led to a door behind the counter, where additional books are kept, and look around at the various jars of herbs, and some items unfamiliar to them. Sarah approaches one of the jars and looks intently at its contents.

"It looks like peppermint" she turns to Joshua and

smiles, "I used to make peppermint tea for you and Liam to settle your stomachs." Sarah returns to the jar and smiles as her eyes begin to tear "my little Liam." Frank stands patiently at another door while Sarah reminisces, and after a few minutes, opens the door, revealing steps that lead to the basement.

"Whenever you're ready," The store owner and his guests soon find themselves standing in a room with a simple round wooden table. Frank points to two of the chairs that surround the table "Please take a seat." He then sits a candle in the center of the table, but the candle holder is nothing Sarah or Joshua had seen before; the brass handle of the holder forms a half-circle, which is suspended above the candle. He opens a box and begins placing some herbs in the small brass container dangling just above the melted white candle, then lights the wick while explaining its contents. "This is some lilac pedals, some mint and a pinch of wolfs bane" before long, a pleasant scent fills the air when the water in the container heats up. Frank walks to the small hotplate and begins digging in one of the cabinets that line the wall while he waits for the water in the teapot to get hot. "I'll use that one, oh yes, this one will work" he fills two copper tea balls with tea from a small wooden box. Before long, the teapot begins to whistle, Sarah and Joshua, are presented with a cup of hot water. Joshua looks as the water turns brown but soon turns his gaze to the storekeeper. Frank laughs as he assures his guests that they are safe, "I can't tell you what's in the tea; the first among equals drinks it when she visits, but I assure you it's safe." Sarah drinks her tea and nods graciously.

"It's very good, thank you" Joshua takes a sip as the store owner joins them at the table.

"So Master Chang told you about us?" Frank shakes his head as he lowers his cup.

"Master Chang Wei does not speak to many mortals, he contacted the first among equals, and she instructed me to assist you." The bald-headed priest looks to the two werewolves, "so how can I help?" Sarah and Joshua struggle to answer the question presented to them. The storekeeper clears his throat and begins explaining, "You two are lone wolves with no pack, John Bennett is chasing you, and you have lost your way. You are both Virginia Mennonites, and Joshua is one of only a few black Lycans." Joshua smiles as he and his mother are careful to never disclose their secret.

"We had a good life in Virginia and after a few bumps, found a good life in California, but John is obsessed with fornicating with mama, and he wants me dead because I got Anna pregnant." Sarah smiles and nods in approval as she strokes her son's arm. Frank is clearly stunned, and takes a moment to process what has been told to him.

"Anna Farlow got pregnant by you?" Frank looks to Joshua with his mouth slightly open "oh my, that changes things significantly." The store owner strokes his goatee as he shakes his head. "And she conceived after you were changed?" Joshua nods with a look of confusion, as Frank looks to Sarah. "That explains why he's so obsessed with you" Sarah leans in, intrigued, waiting for an explanation, as the Wiccan priest continues. "He wants to impregnate you with what he hopes is another pureblood, I assume he thinks it has something to do with the bloodline." Joshua leans back in his chair, trying to process what he has just heard.

"We mentioned losing our families to Chang, but

we never got into specifics, I just assumed he didn't care about our kind. He did say that Anna was an honorable person but that John smelled of death, we never asked many questions, he speaks in riddles but gets grouchy if you ask anything."

Frank gets up, refills the cups with water, and places the pot back on the burner, hesitating before speaking. "A Lycan pureblood is one of the strongest supernatural creatures on record, but I have only read about this, as far as I know the white wolf is only a legend." Sarah leans back in her chair after taking a sip of her tea.

"But doesn't the vampire have purebloods?" Frank returns to his chair, but turns to Joshua first "I am truly sorry for the loss of your mate and your child," he turns to Sarah "and for both of you, losing your family." The storekeeper takes another sip of tea and Joshua quickly notices his hands trembling as he explains things. "Vampires reproduce by infecting others, but they cannot reproduce naturally, granted, Master Chang and the other leaders are careful to limit this, and the dead that walks cannot reproduce, so as far as I know, the Lycans are the only ones that can, but most lose the ability to reproduce after being changed. The pureblood is supposed to be the emissary for all supernatural creatures and he or she would be the recognized pack leader," Joshua looks to his mother.

"That doesn't make sense, John is very protective of his pack," Joshua said, as Frank shakes his head, disagreeing with the black werewolf.

"Not just John's pack, all packs, and would be the ambassador between mortals and all supernatural creatures, If Chang or the other packs find out that he killed the emissary, it will start a war, divide the wolf packs and vampires, and it would cause casualties among mortals." Frank fidgets at the table collecting his thoughts "but if he can create another pureblood, it would solve his problem." Sarah reaches out and grabs her son's hand holding it tightly.

"We will find a way, God will protect us" Sarah said.

Frank gets up from his chair and walks to the far wall where three sets of double doors line the wall of the basement. He removes a key from his pocket and unlocks the doors, after a few moments, he returns to the table with an old tattered book, and begins scrolling down the pages. "We need to find a safe place for you two" he continues to scroll down the pages as he talks to himself, "neither of you is man-eaters, so that's good." Joshua looks to the record keeper, concerned about what he had just heard.

"You know about that? Chang told us just before we left," Frank lays the book in front of him, before addressing Joshua.

"In all the years we have recorded, I never heard about you or your mother eating flesh. I am assuming as Anna got impregnated that she never ate mortals, but John and his pack are well known for devouring flesh." Frank looks down at the book in front of him and proclaims, "Found it, John Bennett got a taste for flesh after he was first turned, in Montana, the Blackfoot Nation to be precise." Joshua looks to his mother stunned at what he had just heard.

"I never knew, but no one ever came looking for the bodies. John would leave me with Anna and venture out with the others, we'll all except Henry." Frank looks to his new friends and closes the book in front of him.

"Most of the nomadic packs are man-eaters, it's why they never stay at one place for very long and the grand coven only allows practicing in the light, the dark ways are forbidden, but we do watch and record what we see." Frank gets up from the table and returns the book to the shelf, he returns to his guests as he places the key in his pocket. "The Blackfoot Nation recognizes both good and bad lycans, the bad are evil, and the good are considered spirits of their lands." Sarah gets up and begins cleaning the table, Frank immediately stands up to assist, "you are a guest, I'll cleanup." He escorts the werewolves to the front door but offers a last piece of advice, "the Blackfoot Nation will protect you if they see you as good spirits." Frank waves as the blue Ford pickup pulls out and begins heading down the road. He turns the sign to open and returns to his desk, where he places a phone on the top of the desk in front of him, and dials a number, then begins speaking to someone on the other end. "I counseled them as you instructed, and recommended the Blackfoot Nation." Frank takes a moment to listen before speaking, "they mentioned the pureblood, if word gets out, it could be bad for everyone" after a brief discussion, the storekeeper hangs up the phone.

On the other end of the phone, a rather prim and proper lady sits at a chair; she hangs up the phone and takes a moment to enjoy the sun coming in from the window, at her house in Salem Massachusetts. She takes a moment to reflect on what she had just heard then turns to address the man who has just entered. "Hello your highness, I have news," the man sits down on a blue chair on the other side of the phone table, and attempts to make himself more presentable, despite his appearance.

"Maggie, no one has called me that for some time, call me what you want, but I go by Lyle these days." The former king raises his sweater-covered arm displaying a simple gold ring with his cress that is barely visible. "This is the only thing left from my kingdom, that I have," Margaret smiles sympathetically at her house guest.

"You are too hard on yourself, and no one has done more to atone for any wrongdoings." The middle-aged woman gets up from her chair and leaves the sitting area, returning with two large cups of coffee, that she sits on both sides of the phone table. "Cream and sugar as I recall your highness." Lyle laughs a bit and thanks Margaret for her hospitality, "Franklin has sent your associates to the Blackfoot Nation, and they are heading to Montana as we speak." Lyle takes a sip of his coffee and gets lost in his thoughts for a moment.

"This is gonna set things right Maggie, Cerberus will let me pass this time, and Hades will let me see my wife and kids." Lyle begins twisting the simple gold ring on his finger, lost in his thoughts. "If they want to see me" Margaret takes her seat beside Lyle, and listens while Lyle continues. "The Native Americans will take care of them, the chief is a good man, I never met the guy, but I did help his ancestors after that piece of crap John damned near wiped his tribe out." Margaret takes a moment to allow Lyle to finish before speaking.

"You spent one-lifetime doing questionable things my friend, but several lifetimes atoning, I sincerely hope they welcome you. Franklin mentioned something that is concerning, it is not my place to interfere if it does no harm, but he mentioned John killing a woman carrying the pureblood?" Margaret takes her seat beside her friend and leans into him. "If John killed the pureblood and it can be proven." Margaret places her hand above her brow, searching for something to say from her trembling lips. Lyle leans into his friend, who is obviously concerned.

"It would turn into a shit show in a hurry, but Maggie, I got it handled, but those kids need a break." Lyle pauses before looking to the Wiccan leader "and trust me, John and his bunch will get what they deserve," Margaret lowers her hand after adjusting the bun on the back of her head.

"Please call me Margaret, and I trust you will do the right thing as you always do, your highness, but if your European companions hear about this, they will come to see for themselves, and may not be as understanding as you have been over the centuries." Lyle gets up from his chair and gently holds Margaret's hand.

"I got this beautiful, and trust me, when the truth comes out, they'll come, and most of my kind will not be a problem." Margaret gets up from her chair and escorts her guest to the front door. Lyle turns and hugs Margaret before taking his leave, "I just hope the unbelievers don't cause any problems" Margaret nods.

"Nor do I, my friend" Margaret said.

Joshua and Sarah pull into a parking lot at a roadside motel, just inside the North Dakota state line. They walk into the small office located at the end of the row of doors, leading to the motel rooms. Joshua and his mother enter the small office, and an older woman approaches the desk area from the door leading to the back of the main office.

The woman looks the pair over and responds in a less than pleasant tone, "Need a room?" Joshua nods, indicating that he would like to stay for the night. "Queen bed okay?" Joshua turns to his mother briefly before answering.

"A room with two beds would be better" the woman removes a key from the wall behind her and lays it on the desk in front of Joshua.

"Room twelve at the very end, you need to pay in advance and be out of here by eleven tomorrow morning." Sarah approaches the desk and grabs the key off the desk. She looks up at the woman standing in front of her and Joshua.

"Is there somewhere close, where we can get something to eat?" The elderly woman scans the room for a moment before answering, and then sighs before responding.

"Flint's is just down the road, but you better get there before too long, it gets rough when the drinking starts." Sarah thanks the unfriendly manager and walks out the door, to the room. Joshua pulls the truck in front of the light brown cinder blocked wall that surrounds the dark brown door, and picks up two brown paper bags, before entering the door where his mother is.

"Not too bad, did you just want to go get something to eat before we settle in?" Joshua nods, and both of them soon find themselves pulling in a gravel parking lot with a large building at the end of the property, with Flint's displayed proudly at the top of the building. The two werewolves enter the front door, and laugh as their feet stick to the floor, making a sound with every step. They look around the darkened area and find a table against the wall of the bar area, and before long, a waitress comes over and greets them.

"Can I get you two a beer?" The waitress said.

Sarah looks to the woman dressed in a tight pair of jeans and a shirt that leaves little to the imagination. "No, just iced tea or a coke if that's easier" the woman leaves, and returns with two cans and two glasses of ice, "and please bring us six hamburgers, rare." The waitress soon returns, and to Joshua and Sarah's surprise, the hamburgers were better than some they have eaten. Joshua looks to his mother, as he finishes the last of the hamburgers.

"I still can't believe that Red just gave us his truck and all that money" Joshua said, Sarah looks to her son, and sighs, as she surveys the room noticing that a crowd is starting to gather at the bar.

"It's a nice truck" Sarah said.

"It's only a few years old" Joshua said, Sarah nods as she looks up at the unkempt scruffy man approaching their table. The man stumbles, as he is obviously intoxicated, but catches himself on the table where they are seated. Both lean backs as the smell of alcohol overwhelm them.

"You know, I've been looking at you for a while now, and I figure since you're the reason for this hard-on, you should be the one to take care of it." Joshua pulls his chair back, but before he can get up, two large overweight men walk up and grabs the drunken man.

"Okay Bill, time for you to go" Sarah looks at Joshua and laughs; they spend a little more time in the bar, but leave to get an early start. They leave and begin walking to the truck but are soon approached by the same man they met earlier.

"Hey Bitch, I'm still hard," the man staggers as he attempts to walk in a straight line "why is he the only one that gets to screw you?" Joshua steps in to meet the drunken man, who pulls a knife from his denim jacket and lunges at Joshua, who easily pushes the man back. Sarah steps in and stands in front of Joshua.

"Don't hurt him, he's just drunk, and I've heard worse" Joshua looks down, shaking his head. His mother turns around to face the drunken man, but soon falls back into her son, who catches her. Joshua looks down at his mother and notices the knife sticking out of her shoulder.

"Mama!" Joshua leans his mother against the truck and begins walking to the drunken man, who realized what he has done, and begins apologizing. Joshua's eyes begin to change, but he is interrupted.

"Get over here, we can't have the police involved" Joshua does as he is told, but looks down at the man and demands his jacket. The drunken man quickly takes off his jacket, and begins running down the gravel parking lot. Joshua lays the jacket over his mother's injured shoulder, and helps her into the truck. In no time, the two werewolves are back at the motel room. Joshua rushes to help her to the bathtub; he inspects the wound for a moment, and then gently presses his mother against the olive green tiled wall, before removing the knife from her shoulder. Sarah grunts a bit and clenches her teeth as she feels the knife being pulled from her shoulder.

"It's bad, but it could have been worse, mama"

Joshua continues to press a towel against his mother's shoulder.

"Just let me get undressed and take a look for myself, if we can wait a few weeks, it should heal when I turn." Joshua leaves and shuts the door to the bathroom, where his mother remains for several hours, with the shower running. Joshua turns the beds down and waits, his mother soon appears with a towel wrapped around her. The wound was cleaned and covered with a roll of toilet paper, which she continued to press against her shoulder. "The bleeding has stopped and hopefully it will stay that way until I change."

The next morning, Joshua takes his shower and cleans the motel room, surprisingly, not much blood was spilled. Joshua grabs the remaining clean towels and lays them on the back of the seat before assisting his mother in the truck. "I have all the bloodied clothes gathered up and put them in a paper bags to burn later, so don't worry." Werewolves are cautious with blood, they often fornicate, so semen doesn't seem to cause a change, and as far as anyone knows, a bite is the main way to change someone, but the bite normally involves the joining of blood, so caution is always used in this type of situation. He pulls the truck up to the main office and hands the older woman a twenty-dollar bill for the towels. She graciously accepts it and is silent, but also hands Joshua some additional towels suspecting there is more to his story.

Michael pulls up to the modest home surrounded by acres of land, this was Elkton. The large farmhouse is near the center of the 200-acre farmette. The Beta gets out and surveys the area, including the vast wooded area that divides the property, but soon notices dust coming from the dirt road as James pulls up with Bull. He turns to John, who has exited the car with Robert following behind him.

"Not bad boss, plenty of room to run, a decent barn that we can use for something but why here? Elkton, Virginia?"

John points to the car as he shoves Robert away from him. "Get the clothes and start taking things to the house, the main bedroom is mine, got it?" Robert nods his head but fails to remain quiet.

"This is an excellent choice, sir, Elkton is almost the center of the eastern United States, and it's very isolated, very good choice, sir." John reaches out and grabs Robert by his throat, lifting him off the ground.

"Nobody asked you or needs you're fucking approval" Michael looks downward as the snap of Roberts's neck is heard from the rest of the pack. John throws the body in the center of the cars, where his crew is standing. "Put him in the freezer until we get closer to the moon rising." Michael stares briefly at the corpse lying in front of him.

"Boss, he was new to the pack, you may want to give these guys a chance before killing them this quick. He's the third one you've changed and killed before they can learn anything." John walks over to Michael and places his hand on his Beta's shoulder, as he speaks to the others.

"Bishop Reed was a mistake, and as soon as he is no longer useful, he will be removed from this pack." He turns to James pointing his finger "and if your brother doesn't step up, he will be removed, I need fighters, not poets." Nothing more is said, as the other's quietly unload the car, all except Michael.

"Henry has his place John, but he may not be as easy to kill as this guy. I have concerns about him, but how are you gonna know when his time's up?" John looks to his second in command, and a sly grin comes across his face.

"Henry's not the only person watching Spencer, I know for a fact that he has spoken to that bunch, and is getting a little too close for comfort." John crosses his arms as he surveys his property. "I also have spread word that I want to know where that red-eyed prick is, and he will be dealt with, by me personally." Michael leans up against the car facing his leader.

"You know the rumors just like I do, he's the first of us, and to my knowledge, the only red-eye that anyone has heard about. We dodged a bullet with Anna and her baby, but dammit John, if you kill the first of our kind, we're dead, and these mountains ain't gonna save us." John turns his attention back to Michael, and in a very calm manner, addresses the concerns given to him.

"The only true way to lead all the packs without the emissary, is to kill the recognized leader, but if I can find Joshua's mother and get her pregnant, I can lead the packs and kill that arrogant son of a bitch, regardless if he's the first or not." Michael hesitates but asks John a final question.

"Then what? Let's say that you get what you want, what happens then?" John looks to the house, where his pack has finished unpacking

"We stop hiding and use these mortals for the sheep they are, and then take our place at the head of everything, with the emissary in my pack and a dead red-eye at our feet." He looks to the others and points to Robert, "and anyone that disagrees with me will end up dead, like that whimpering, useless son of a bitch."

At the same time John is settling in his new headquarters, an older black car pulls up in front of a large warehouse, near the Georgia Florida state line, a large muscular Hispanic man in a tight tank top approaches and taps the fender as he approaches the driver, who has yet to emerge. He begins speaking in Spanish to the passenger. Lyle emerges from the car and addresses the man in Spanish but ends his sentence in English.

"Could you please take me to Hector or Carlos?" the Spanish man turns to see the two gentlemen approaching, Carlos looks to the farm worker.

"It's okay Juan, we got this" Lyle removes his glasses and squints at the sun beating down on him. He looks to the two farm owners.

"They call these thing's sunglasses, best-damned invention to come along in a while if you ask me." The larger man begins to approach Lyle, who quickly addresses the large gentleman. "Look big guy, I'm a firm believer that we don't harm the decent members of our kind, but I've driven here from Massachusetts, and I need to talk to these guys." Hector looks to the bold older man standing in front of him and smiles, he begins to speak but stops as he notices the ring on Lyle's finger, he looks to Carlos.

"He's the one that helped me in Mexico shortly after I turned" after speaking with Carlos, he turns to Lyle.

"You're the one who shows up and takes care of things for our kind, aren't you?" The former king nods respectfully, Lyle is a legend, but most werewolves have only heard about the Alpha. "You're welcome here, sir, we heard that you're a king," Lyle smiles solemnly.

"Not for some time, but can we go inside, I'm okay with the moon, but this sun is brutal" Lyle said.

Hector and Carlos enter the large warehouse with Lyle, who surveys the area, including the various workers in the large metal structure. Hector opens the door that leads to the back, and takes a seat at the table with the two Hispanic leaders. Lyle graciously sits down and smiles at the two werewolves sitting across from him.

"I gave up on those New York goons some time ago, they're so far up John Bennett's ass, it's a waste of time, the same can be said of most of the east coast packs." Lyle sits back in his chair "but then there are you guys," Carlos smiles nervously and addresses Lyle for the first time.

"Can I get you something? I don't know what to say, you're a legend, but most of us have never seen you," Lyle scratches the stubble on his face.

"Water is fine, I've helped a lot of people, but I like to stay hidden, it makes my job easier," Hector sits a glass of water down in front of Lyle and returns to his chair. "My loyalty is to the good people that have normal lives and struggle with being different. People like you and your pack."

"I don't have much loyalty to John, especially these days, he's gone loco since that religious boy killed Miss

Anna," Lyle sighs a bit before correcting the two Hispanic leaders.

"Anna and Joshua found each other and wanted to go out on their own, settle down, and try living normally but then Joshua became a full black." Hector begins nodding his head and points to Carlos, shaking his finger.

"I knew something didn't feel right about this, John looked at Joshua as someone trying to take over his pack, so he killed him, but why Miss Anna?" Lyle leans into his host.

"Because he's a crazy son of a bitch, now this brings us to why I'm here" Carlos steps in and nervously speaks. Both know there's more to the story but say nothing out of respect and fear. Lyle's also known to be one of only two red-eyed blacks on record and can kill most packs with little difficulty.

"We heard that this Joshua is alive, John told us to look out for his mother, but then we were told to look out for both of them, do you want us to look the other way?" Lyle nods his head as he looks across the table.

"No, they're safe and don't worry, John and his crew are going to be dealt with. I just need you to stay put and not go when John calls," Hector collects his thoughts before addressing Lyle.

"No disrespect, but there's more to this, has the packs overseas mentioned anything?" Lyle shakes his head.

"Everything overseas is okay for now, I take care of things here and have no desire to return to my homeland, just know that everything will be dealt with in time." Carlos gets up and refills the glasses as Hector thinks for a moment before looking at Lyle.

"As far as I'm concerned, you're the pack leader of us all, if you tell us to stay put, then we'll stay put." The door opens, and Pablo enters the room, covered in sweat, he looks down at the guest sitting at the table, then turns to Hector.

"That's a powerful dude, isn't it" Hector looks to Lyle as Pablo goes to the refrigerator and pulls out a large jug of what appears to be iced tea.

"I am sorry, he's still a pup and not housebroken yet, I am sorry sir." Pablo sits the glass of tea back in the refrigerators and stares at the older man, sitting at the table.

"You're the one who shows up and fixes things "Pablo said, as Lyle nods.

"I help when I can" Carlos places his hand to his chin and ponders for a moment.

"Where have they been hiding?" Lyle grabs his glass and takes a drink of water before continuing.

"The nightwalkers protected him for a while, but after John found him, they left to avoid any trouble." The senior wolf runs his finger along the rim of the glass and pauses before speaking. "If John showed up on the west coast and started killing vampires, it would be bad for all of us, so they left to avoid a war." Hector shakes his head and looks to Pablo before turning to Lyle.

"Chang protected two werewolves? I would have never seen that coming, given what happened before. I wasn't around then, but I heard that's why Chang started requiring his guys to practice that Kung Fu crap." Lyle nods his head and raises his eyebrows.

"I was around then, and was the one to get the nightwalkers to calm down and end the fighting." Lyle scans the room briefly to see who is listening. "Joshua is a full black who gets along with the nightwalkers and the covens. He also has good morals and is not a man-eater." Pablo steps forward and finally addresses Lyle.

"So what does a human taste like?" Hector stands up, staring intently at his pack member.

"Don't worry about it Pablo, we don't eat humans. I can't speak for King Lyle, but Carlos and I ate mortals for a while. It can become an addiction." Lyle looks at the young werewolf.

"I ate mortals for years after I was turned, it can be an addiction, but trust me kid, it never ends well, and it changes you." Lyle stands up and approaches Pablo, stopping in front of the young man. "When you eat humans, you take a part of their soul, and it's never the good parts that stay with you." Lyle turns to his host and asks about staying for a few days as he doesn't get this far south. "My home is your home and stay as long as you want; it's an honor to have you here."

CHAPTER NINE

The drive to the reservation seemed longer than it actually was, as the smell of Sarah's blood was stronger than when they started, indicating that her shoulder was bleeding again. The bloodied towels also alerted Joshua to his mother's injury, as his senses is more acute. Over the years, the two werewolves have been careful to not be noticed, and blend in the background. One of these lessons is to not drive over the speed limit, Joshua understood this, and as hard as it was to see his mother suffer, it would be harder to explain his mother's injury. Maintaining a safe speed was important but this became less of a concern, the closer the two came to the reservation. Joshua has been on the reservation for several miles, but was told that the Glacier Mountains were his destination from Frank, so he did not stop, despite the looks from the Native Americans that he passed on the way to the mountain. The black werewolf looks to his mother and smiles, "We're almost there, mama," but his smile soon fades as his mother does not respond. Joshua can still hear his mother's heartbeat, but it is hard not to worry when she doesn't respond, and the smell of blood that fills the cab of the truck did not help things either.

The truck pulled up to a building where the road ends and a large crowd of people had gathered, and despite the fact that resources are limited here on the reservation, word of a strange truck had made its way up the mountain. Joshua exits the car and rushes to the other side and opens the door to pick up his mother, who has almost passed out from her injuries. No one approaches or says anything as he scans the half-built buildings that make up this community.

Joshua turns to the building in front of his truck and notices an older man well in his seventies, dressed in a denim jacket, with a younger man that appears to be in his forties, wearing a faded flannel shirt, standing beside him. Both men had their hair tied back, but the older man had a green hat with a John Deer emblem displayed proudly on the front of his hat. Joshua begins to back up against the truck holding his mother and looks to the crowd, who begins to back up as his eyes have turned yellow and a roar escapes him. The older man shakes his head and holds up his hand as he addresses the crowd, "Saa...Wakaan," instructing the crowd that he is injured and to stop. Joshua takes no comfort in this, and he continues to show his teeth that have started to sharpen. The flannel-wearing man approaches Joshua, who roars again and begins to bulk up. The younger man turns to his elder.

"Kayissta, Makoyi kayissta?" asking if this is a supernatural wolf spirit. The old man nods his head. Joshua continues to hold his mother tightly as the injured woman looks to the man standing near them, glassy-eyed and barely able to speak.

"Please don't hurt us, we mean no harm" The flannel-wearing man, still holding up his hands, smiles.

"My name is Twin Bears, and the older man is my father, he is Ninaa, the Chief, no one will hurt you." The smell of silver fills the air as a young man approach proudly, displaying a silver arrow that is notched in a bow. Joshua recognizes the arrow and begins to change. Twin Bears grabs the arrow and throws it away from the crowd. He turns to the half-changed wolf and points to the injured woman. "We only want to help, wolf spirit" the younger man, gritting his teeth, looks to the chief and says nothing as he points to himself and points his fingers down to his throat. The old chief shakes his head as his son shoves the eager young man away from the two werewolves.

"He is not a wendigo, they attack at night, eat people, and I'm pretty sure they don't pull up to the front door and announce themselves." Twin Bears then waves his hand and points down the road. "The doctor is here today, go get her and tell her to bring her bag and get here as soon as she can." The young man does as he is told, under the watchful eye of the chief. In a few minutes, an attractive dark-haired woman approaches Joshua. She sits her black bag down, as she points to the tailgate that Twin Bears instinctively lowers. Joshua sits his injured mother down but remains protective. The doctor begins removing the bloodied towels and places her stethoscope on Sarah's chest. She looks up to the large supernatural creature standing beside her.

"Her lungs seem to be healthy, so I'm pretty sure they aren't punctured, but I'll need to clean the wound before I stitch her up." After checking for any other injuries, she looks to the chief. "I'm going to have to remove her shirt, and the bed is cold. Could you please have someone get me a blanket and have everyone leave? Except him. He's not going to leave her, and I'm afraid of what will happen if we try." The chief waves his hand as Twin Bears runs into the building, and returns with two blankets. Twin Bears and the mute boy, that's his son, return to the truck while the crowd leaves as instructed. "I'm going to use some peroxide. Is she like you?" Joshua nods as he begins to shift back to human form, and is able to speak after a few moments.

"Is mama going to be okay?" Joshua said, as the

doctor nods and smiles.

"Most of her fatigue is due to blood loss, normally I would have her transported to the hospital and have her put on an IV, but this isn't a normal situation, is it?" The werewolf looks down, realizing that his shirt is ripped and covered in blood. He attempts to compose himself as the doctor finishes closing the wound on Sarah's shoulder. She wraps Sarah's shoulder with gauze and tape and places the other blanket over the injured woman. The attractive young doctor looks up at the porch where the chief and the other elders are located. "Grandfather," the chief is slow but joins the others, "She needs juice and red meat. The moon will not rise for a few weeks, so she also needs a comfortable place to rest." Twin Bears looks to his father, who points to the dirt path that leads farther up the mountain.

"Are you sure about this?" the old man turns to the other two elders on the porch, who nods in agreement. The doctor looks to Twin Bears with her mouth opened.

"Up there? Really?" she turns to Joshua, still keeping one hand on her patient, then looks to Sarah, who has regained consciousness, and is more alert than when she arrived. "Hello, I stitched you up, we're going to take you to a cabin up that path for you to rest, but we don't have electricity or indoor plumbing, so it will not be the best living conditions." Sarah laughs in her weakened state as she looks to her son.

"I think we'll manage" she looks to the two men standing beside her son. "Thank you for your help, my name is Sarah, this is my son Joshua, and you already know what we are." Twin bears, places his hand on the old man.

"This is my father, Chief Gray Wolf, my name is

Twin Bears, and this is my daughter Waubun." The flannel-clad Native American then looks to the teenage boy standing beside the chief. "And the boy is my son, Kajika," Joshua looks to Twin Bears.

"Sorry about earlier, I was just worried, it won't happen again" Joshua said. The old chief steps toward the blood-covered werewolf, wearing rags at this point.

"To go against your nature would have been an insult. I would never tell an eagle to not fly or a wolf not to bear his teeth, you are welcome here, wolf spirits" Chief Gray Wolf said.

Joshua carries his mother to a rundown cabin, just out of sight from the main hall, a few yards before the tree line. Twin Bears looks to his new guests. "This is where my family and I stay but my daughter stays in the white man's world in town, but me, my wife, and son stays here." The Native American then looks to Joshua, who is easily carrying his mother. "The other cabin is past the tree line in the open field, can we help carry your things?" Joshua looks up at the clearing just a few yards behind the small rundown cabin.

"Yes, I would appreciate any help you can give us, if it's not too much trouble." Twin Bears nods, and soon, the four individuals approach a small shack that sits alone in the middle of a large clearing. The cabin has no windows or a door and is open to the elements, it wasn't winter, but the ground still has some snow scattered in patches due to the elevation. A metal stove pipe stands the length of the exterior wall held in place by brackets. Joshua enters the dwelling entrance and immediately notices a large axe sitting in the corner of the room. The werewolf doesn't say anything, but keeps a close eye on his host as Twin Bears grabs the axe.

"This is only used in a ceremony but I'll get rid of it for you." The middle-aged host grabs the axe but notices the look in the young man's eyes. Twin Bears backs up slowly as he soon realizes this is the look of a predator, and it's a look that cannot be taught. The Native American host exits the small shack and can be seen walking toward the tree line.

Joshua sits his mother down on one of the army cots, and then turns to his other host, "if you could get me a blanket for mama, that would be great." Waubun leaned over her patient and checked to make sure it had not opened while she was being carried. She stands up and nods to Joshua.

"She will be just fine, but she needs to rest, I'll bring some juice and check on her tomorrow." Joshua looks and smiles at the attractive doctor.

"Thank you, Doctor Wachun," the young woman laughs, shaking her head.

"You're close, but it's Wabun with a B" the doctor smiles as she walks to the new houseguest. "Just call me Dawn, that's the name I use at the hospital," the young woman begins adjusting Joshua's shirt as she continues to speak. "Daddy will bring you some meat and some blankets. I'll also ask him to bring some wood for a door" she leans in and whispers, "but it may get done quicker if you ask." Joshua smiles not quite sure what to say. He looked to his mother, who had fallen asleep, before walking outside.

"Thank you" is all that is said as the beautiful doctor

walks down the road.

Twin Bears returns with a woman dressed in a weathered handmade leather jacket and faded blue jeans. She was attractive, and it was obvious she's Dawn's mother. She enters the small shack and places one of the blankets over Sarah, adjusts the small pillow, then places the other blanket on the cot facing the opposite wall. Before going outside to speak with Joshua, she wraps her arms around his large frame, and looks up at the Mennonite man. "I'm Twin Bears wife, you can call me Snow Bird" Joshua nods as she turns to her husband. "Wolf spirits or not, they need a door and some firewood for that little stove" Twin Bears looks to his wife and shrugs.

"We have no money or resources, my love, but I will try to find something for the wolf spirits" Joshua looks to his new friends.

"I can purchase some supplies and build a door" Twin Bears looks to his wife with a stressed look on his face.

"Me going into town is a bad idea" the Indian woman looks to the two men, ignoring what her husband had just said.

"I'll stay with her so you two can go into town" Joshua rushes down to the truck and returns to the small cabin with a tape measure. He measures the door entrance and returns to his truck with Twin Bears, after changing his shirt, who looks at the truck.

"How did you get a truck in this kind of shape?" Joshua looks to his Native American friend.

"A friend gave it to me before he died "nothing else

is said about the truck as the two drives off the reservation, and to the main road that leads to town. Joshua pulls into the front of the store, but Twin Bears soon points to the side of the building.

"You should park over there" Joshua doesn't question and moves the truck to the side of the building, before looking to his friend, who simply says, "I'll wait here." Joshua enters the building and walks to the wood section, where he begins reviewing the wooden boards that line the back wall. One of the hardware clerks approaches Joshua with a smile.

"Can I help you with anything?" Joshua nods.

"I'm gonna need about six oak two by fours, eight pine one by sixes, a pound of eight penny nails, and a pound of 3 penny nails." The attendant soon gathers the items up for Joshua and places them in the front of the store. Joshua gets to the cash register, where he places a saw, hammer, and some other items to purchase. A man walks up behind him, waiting to make a purchase.

"You look like you're gonna be busy today, my boy." Joshua looks and smiles.

"Yes sir," the former Mennonite politely responds, and looks outside at the rusted-up truck and its contents. "How much do you want for those windows?" The bearded man looks outside and laughs.

"You can have anything on the back of that truck you want, I just got done finishing a job, and I'm just hauling that stuff to the dump" Joshua smiles and turns to the clerk.

"I'm gonna need four pine two by fours, two tubes

of caulk, and a caulk gun." The clerk smiled broadly at what was going to be a very large purchase. Joshua pays for the items with Red's money; he and his mother had not spent much of the money he was given, and helping the Indians felt like the right thing to do. Joshua places the items on the back of the bed, then drives around to the front of the building, and begins searching through the bearded man's pickup truck. He picks up a window frame that still has the glass intact and carefully places the window on the back of his truck along with four more windows. He also found a door and various items that he thought may come in handy. The bearded man exits the store and begins to speak but notices Twin Bears sitting in the truck.

"What's that tree monkey doing sitting in your truck?" Joshua looks stunned at the man's outburst as he continues to taunt his Indian friend. "Planning another uprising? I read all about your bunch pissing and moaning in Washington." Twin Bears leans out the window and looks to Joshua.

"I told you this was a bad idea" Joshua looks and nods to his friend. He begins to take his leave but is stopped again by the bearded man, who refuses to stop.

"You know it looks like we're going to end up in Vietnam, my boy got drafted last week, just out of high school." The man, who is red-faced by this time, shoves Joshua, "but I'll bet a healthy young buck like you don't know a fucking thing about that, you're one of those hippy objectors sitting up on that mountain, with the rest of those fucking tree monkeys." Before Joshua can say something, a police car pulls up beside his truck. A police officer gets out of the car and approaches the two men standing at the front door and looks at the bearded man.

"Everything all right, Gary?" the bearded man shakes his head, still upset.

"No Bob, I just caught this hippie stealing off my truck, throw his ass in jail, better yet, draft him in the army." The officer grabs Joshua and begins pulling him to the car but stops abruptly when the store clerk yells at the police officer.

"Hold on Bob! That's not what happened" the store clerk limps over to the three men standing in front of his store. Joshua immediately notices the clerk walking with a limp, "Gary told him to take what he wanted but got pissed when he saw that Indian." The bearded man starts to rant again.

"It's just not right Randy, I'm telling you, this is a bunch of shit, now I want to press charges and have those two draft dodgers arrested." Randy looks to the irate man, finally fed up with him.

"Gary, I got shot in the leg fighting Germans in world war two, and while I was in Fort Benning training with the fourth ranger battalion, your daddy and both of your uncles were sitting at home. I enlisted with a wife and a daughter, with a son on the way, but your bunch has never served one day in the military." The veteran continues to scold his friend, "so be proud of your son, since he's the only one with enough balls in your family to serve." The irate man gets in his car and leaves without saying another word.

The ride back to the reservation is quiet for a few moments until Twin Bears looks to his driver. "You get used to it, but things have gotten worse since they had that sit in at Alcatraz," the Native American looks out the window, admiring the scenery before continuing. "The government talks about helping, but we're still living with cardboard walls and bark covering the tops of our homes." Joshua ponders for a moment before speaking as he has become guarded over the years.

"I was raised in Virginia, in a small community, but we never had much contact with the English, and when we did, it was never good." Twin Bears laughs as he continues to admire the scenery.

"Wolf Spirit, every time the government shows up, it never ends well for my people either" Twin Bears said.

The truck pulls up in front of the great hall, and Joshua notices the rundown structure. He turns to look at the community and finds the other homes in the same condition, before looking at the back of his pickup truck, and being ashamed. Chief Grey Wolf motions for Joshua to join him at the front of the great hall, and turns to look at the other elderly individuals that are sitting with him. Twin Bears leans into his friend.

"Father assembled the tribal council to meet you while we were gone." Joshua begins adjusting his clothes and straightening his hair. Twin Bears admires his respect, but puts his mind at ease as they walk to the front of the building. The Chief looks up and introduces him to the other three tribal members sitting with him. Joshua is obviously nervous as he addresses the council.

"I got some lumber and some items to put a door and window on the cabin, but we can use it for something else." Joshua then pulls out what's left of the money that Red had given him. "It should be a little over two thousand dollars, and it should be enough to fix some things around here." The only woman of the council struggles to stand up, but rises slowly and hobbles to the werewolf with the use of a long stick.

"I am called Kay, please fix your dwelling as you like, and keep your money" she places her hands on the large man's arms and smiles. "You are the wolf spirit, the one who protects the sacred land. The great spirit told us of your coming in a vision many years ago after the wendigo came and attacked our people." The elderly woman looks at Twin Bears, who is standing behind his friend. "Tell him our story; you are the caretaker of the sacred valley."

Joshua speaks with the elders for a while and tells them about growing up in Virginia. He felt comfortable speaking and told the council about living in California, the vampires, and John Bennett. The elderly Indians immediately embrace the werewolf and respond with their own stories, this is an important part of the Indian culture, and the elderly are treasured. In truth, Joshua was about the same age as the four council members. Hours pass, and at the end of the conversation, the werewolf finally finds a place in this world where he and his mother fit in. He smiles and waves as he walks to the cabin to find Snow Bird roasting some meat over an open fire, away from the cabin. Dawn had left to go back to town. Twin Bears lays some boards on the ground but returns to the truck to get the remaining items. Joshua enters the opening to find his mother sitting upright on the cot.

"Are you okay? You look better," Sarah nods and reaches out with her good arm for her son to help her up. Joshua helps her up, and the two exits the building and go to the fire where Snow Bird is cooking.

"Taste this" the Indian woman cuts a piece of the

meat off and holds it up to Joshua's face, who eagerly eats what was presented to him. Twin Bears soon returns and walks up to his wife, who removed the meat from the wooden spit and hands it to Joshua." Your mother has been fed, so this is yours. I don't like hungry wolves this close to home" Snow Bird laughs, and her husband smiles at her lovingly.

"Why don't you take Ms. Braun down to our place while Joshua and I make a door," he then looks to his guests. "The chief wants a Pow Wow in honor of your coming, and he wants to have it in a few days so we can get some meat roasted up, and give everyone time to make something." He looks to his wife and sighs "the other tribal chiefs are coming, so he wants me to tell Joshua the story, why don't you tell Ms. Braun about what happened while she waits at our place."

Joshua walks over, picks up a board from the pile, and begins measuring it while the two women walk slowly down the mountain. He lays some other lumber out and begins sawing the board with the newly purchased hand saw and before long has several boars cut, and a door made. He attaches the door to the opening, using the old hinges from the scrap pieces he found in town, but looks around after the door has been closed, noticing the darkened interior.

"Now you know why we keep the doors off," Joshua laughs as he walks to the back of the cabin, and looks to the roof where the roof attaches to the stacked wood walls.

"I think if we nail boards to the interior wall and saw an entire section, we can make a good frame to hold the wall together and be able to get a window in. We can use some of the wood to insulate the opening afterward, that seems okay to you Mr. Bears?" Twin Bears laughs and shakes his head.

· "I don't know anything about construction, so I can't do much but hold a board, but you seem to know what you're doing, and it's Twin Bears, my friend." Joshua places a board up against the wall, after measuring, and begins cutting into the wall. Within a few hours, the window is in place, and the interior of the cabin brightened up. Joshua looks at the scraps of wood.

"I'm gonna make mama a stool to sit on, you wanna help?" Twin Bears looks and admires the window that had just been installed.

"You do good work, Makoyi" Joshua begins laying out the scraps that will make the top of the stool, while his Indian host shakes the newly installed door, and continues to admire the werewolf's craftsmanship.

"My papa showed me, and I've gotten pretty handy over the years. I also learned a lot at the sawmill," Joshua stretches as the two sit on the dirt floor. Twin Bears leans back against the wall and begins fidgeting.

"I have some things to tell you, Joshua" the former Mennonite puts down his hammer and gives his full attention to his host, as the tone of his voice changed. "Many years ago, an evil spirit showed up, a wendigo, he only came out at night, fed on my people, and sometimes just killed us as is his nature." The middle-aged Indian pulls out a wooden pipe and lights it, he takes a puff and hands it to Joshua, who, at first, refuses. Twin Bears smiles and insists he takes the pipe. "We're in council now, my friend, so we have to pass the pipe, its tradition." Joshua reluctantly grabs the pipe, and soon smoke fills the air as he puffs. He hands the pipe back to his host, who thanks him but hesitates briefly before continuing, while Joshua coughs, as this is the first time he smoked. "The chief asked the Great Spirit for help save his people, the Great Spirit cried after hearing the Chief, and his tears fell into the river, the chief gathered up the tears and used them to defend our people against the wendigo." The Native American takes a puff on the pipe and smiles as he hands it back to his friend. "The land we sit on is sacred, and it is the land where most of my tribe died, it's also home to the tears of the river." Joshua looks down and sighs as he places his hand on his forehead hiding his shame.

"So this is sacred ground, and I'm a wendigo? You let us come up here because you're afraid of mama and me?" The soft-spoken Indian taps the pipe on his denim-covered knee, emptying its contents.

"You are a wolf who walks, a guardian of this land, and one of the noblest of protectors. We bring tribute to this land when the seasons change and look to the Great Spirit to send you, and he has." Twin Bears disperses the ashes into the surrounding dirt before finishing "only the chief and the elders know what's next, we never ask as it is disrespectful, but the evil spirits will return, and the protectors will lead us into battle." Joshua looks to his host and ponders for a moment.

"It was John Bennett who came and attacked your people?" the werewolf looks nervously to his new friend. "His pack has grown, and I don't know if me, and mama is enough," Twin Bears stands up and places the pipe back in his pocket.

"I trust the council, and I also trust the Great Spirit,

you are strong Joshua, and a good man." The Indian host begins walking to the small path that leads to his house, but turns to his guest, "the Great Spirit will protect you and save my people."

CHAPTER TEN

Spencer sits and stares blankly out the window of his diner, business is good, and Mama Nell is doing a good job. Jayde left for college, and more help was needed for the restaurant to keep up, so Spencer hired another lone wolf to make sure his secret didn't get out. Rodney isn't as old as some of the werewolves that come to the diner and has only been a wolf since world war two, when he was changed in Germany. Rodney's injuries were enough to be medically discharged, but he didn't know about his curse until he returned home to southern Virginia near the Tennessee border. Mama Nell approaches the table, her age is starting to show, but she continues to come to work every day and she also holds ceremonies weekly in her duties as a voodoo priestess.

"I'm sure she's all right, Have you heard anything from her?" Mama Nell said.

Spencer shakes his head as he continues to stare aimlessly out the window. He looks to Nell and picks up his coffee. "It's been months, I should have gone with her and protected her like a man is supposed to do" he continues to look out the window as he leans back in the chair, holding his coffee with both hands before continuing. "And Henry's back" Mama Nell looks out the window before taking a seat facing Spencer.

"She needs hope and know she has a home to come back to, but getting killed doesn't make you any more of a man than giving that woman hope." A sound is heard from the back door opening, "Rodney's here, it's your business, but I still don't trust Henry and I damned sure don't trust Rodney." Spencer shrugs but doesn't respond, Rodney exits the kitchen and walks to his coworkers at the window. It doesn't take long to reach the window given his height, he is also thin with a thick mustache that runs down both sides of his mouth to his chin, and doesn't fit in with the Richmond height crowd. Sarah is also white, but everyone loves her as she lights up a room, but Rodney has a way of bringing out the worst in people. That's why Spencer keeps him in the kitchen.

"Hey Spence, I cleaned the grill last night, so I can mop in here before we open." Rodney said, Spencer turns and looks up at the tall man standing behind him.

"I already mopped, but I haven't filled the coolers yet" Spencer said, Rodney nods and goes behind the bar to see what is needed. Henry enters the room and joins Spencer at his table, waving at Rodney before sitting down. Mama Nell gets up and walks to the kitchen.

"I'll get him some coffee and refill your cup" Spencer turns to Henry, as Nell motions for Rodney to leave the main area with her, leaving the two men to talk.

"Have you heard anything about Sarah?" Henry nods, answering the question as Nell sits a cup in front of him and fills both cups.

"No, John knows about Joshua but lost track of them, he sent a pack member and a familiar to check on things. Chang sent her head back in a box, so I'm pretty sure the other one is dead too." Spencer looks emotionless at his guest and fellow werewolf.

"They had a good thing in California and I was hoping things would calm down. Why does he want those two anyway?" Henry takes a drink of coffee before answering.

"He wants Joshua for messing with Anna and going against the pack. I think he wants Sarah to replace his female Alpha." Henry sits his cup down, "I told Joshua when he first turned to walk away from Anna, but he didn't listen." Rodney exits the kitchen and places a plate of donuts between the two men.

"Nell said to bring these out to you" he looks to Henry. "You run with the Bennett pack? I hear they're badass." Henry grabs a donut and looks up at the tall white man, standing in front of him.

"Don't believe everything you hear," Rodney, unaware that he is overstaying his welcome, nods.

"I also heard he's a mean son of a bitch and an arrogant asshole, by the way, my name is Rodney" Henry looks to his host and smiles.

"Well, that sounds a bit more accurate" the door opens, and Lyle walks in, grabbing a chair at Spencer's table. He looks at the tall man standing.

"Why don't you get me a cup of coffee and take him with you, the adults need to talk for a few minutes." Rodney looks at the gentleman sitting with his button-toed hat and large sweater, in awe of the ancient Lycan.

"You're him aren't you? I mean, you're the one that everyone talks about?" Henry gets up and grabs Rodney by the arm, dragging him away from the table. Lyle looks to Spencer and grabs a donut from the plate, as Nell returns with a cup and a full pot of coffee that she sits down at the center of the table. Lyle looks at the woman and smiles.

"Thank you gorgeous, I have always said the only way to eat a donut is if you have a cup of coffee in your other hand." The elder werewolf takes a bite of his donut then leans back in his chair, after taking a drink of coffee, "they're okay Spencer but don't expect to hear from them for a while, and I mean a long while my furry friend." Spencer leans in placing his forearms on the table.

"I'll wait as long as it takes, she's worth it, but I should be out there protecting her, not sitting on the sidelines. I fought in the civil war, helped with the Underground Railroad, but here I sit like a scared rabbit." Lyle takes another bite of his donut before drinking his coffee but doesn't say anything for several minutes.

"Spencer, some things are bigger than your ego, you will be able to be with your woman after this is over, but you need to trust me." Lyle rubs his hands together as he reaches for the last donut on the plate. "I can never make things right with my family, and I get it, men are supposed to pick up a sword and fight to the death defending what's theirs." He then looks to the kitchen door, "you can come out now, I'm leaving" the others soon enter, and Nell begins cleaning up the table. "Hang in there kid, but don't trust anyone for now."

Lyle leaves, after offering his last words of advice to Spencer. Nell looks out the window as the rusted-up station wagon drives past the window. "What was that about?" Spencer gets up from his chair and turns to speak with the others.

"He told me that Joshua and Sarah are alive, he also told me that it would be a long time before I hear from them," Rodney is the first to speak up.

"If he's so damned tough, why doesn't he just kill the others and call it a day?" Rodney walks behind the bar and grabs a can of soda, before finishing his thought, "I haven't been a werewolf as long as most, I was changed in World War Two in Germany. Those kraut bastards killed my whole platoon, except me, and if it wasn't for this guy that just showed up. I wouldn't have made it. He just came out of nowhere and bit me" Spencer nods as he helps Nell clean the table.

"Lyle will not kill any of his kind, and he is trying to atone for the loss of his family. He could easily end things with John, and would have no trouble gathering up enough people to kill John and that bunch, but that bastard has a lot of eyes looking around for him." Spencer stands upright and looks directly at Henry. "Isn't that right, Henry?" Henry looks downward, searching for words.

"John has gone crazy, he sent me away because he wants fighters, not poets, but I am still loyal to my pack." Henry raises his head and looks Spencer in the eye. "But he has more eyes than mine on this place, my friend."

Nell walks behind the bar and places the coffee pot back on the burner. She turns to Spencer, looking directly at him "You never had this drama with me, but then again, I wasn't the love of your life like she is." Nell shakes her head as she gathers up the dishes "but I guess that's the difference between the love of your life, and someone you just fuck until she gets too old." Nell's words hang in the air as she leaves the room.

Michael enters the house in Elkton, the interior is a bit nicer than he is accustomed to, and John has done a good job of finding food without drawing attention to them. He enters the living room to find John hanging up the phone.

"That red-eyed prick showed up at Spencer's, and he also spoke to Hector." Michael takes a seat on the couch and turns to John, who is sitting on a chair beside the phone table.

"The northern packs are with us, and we're good down to about Louisiana, but I never did trust Hector or his pack." John looks to his second in command and shrugs.

"I will deal with the Florida pack in time, but I want Lyle's head on a stick first. We will find that blond ungrateful bitch, and give her a front-row seat watching her little boy get his head cut off, while I screw her." John gets up, and looks out the window at the front of the house. "And after she gives me my pureblood, we can cut her head off, and Joshua, his mother, and any anyone else who gets in my way can join them." Michael doesn't say much at first, but eventually speaks to his leader.

"The guys are getting restless, after we change I think we should take a little trip away from here to let the guys unwind, drink a lot, and if they should happen to kill someone, have it done away from here," John nods in agreement and walks out to the front porch to look around, he notices James walking out of the barn.

"How's he doing these days?" Michael leans up against the yellow wall of the house as he updates his leader.

"He's eating humans now, and I suspect he will be a darker shade of grey this month. Henry and the Bishop are the only ones that are left to get on board," John keeps surveying the area, lost in his thoughts.

"We have established identities now; we're not stealing cars or roaming up and down the coast anymore. So the Bishop will need to be eliminated after this is over. We can find better soldiers than him." he then turns to Michael, "as far as Henry goes, he will be the one to kill Joshua and eat him, or he will also need to be eliminated.

Michael looks to John as he slowly places sunglasses on his face. "Henry is not going to kill Joshua boss, and he's sitting in a bar having coffee with our enemies. It looks bad, boss," John turns his attention to his second in command. "Then we'll have to make an example of what happens when you go against the pack. Who knows, it may get Hector's bunch in line."

The two leaders walk to the barn and join the others. John looks to the Bull and Henry. "We're going on a trip to Pennsylvania after we turn this month. The Bishop needs to go, and we'll be hungry by then." Bram stands up from the ground, where he has been sitting.

"It's about time; I'm going crazy just sitting around doing nothing" Bram said.

"I understand, but things will get busy soon, we're cleaning house boys and need strong, new members, I'm thinking about three more people, so keep your eyes open." James looks to his leader with a confused look.

"You normally have seven members max, so why are we shooting for eight this time?" John walks over to James, and places his hand on the fit black man's shoulder.

"Because Henry will also have to be dealt with, I question his loyalty, but he's not one of us anymore. Is that going to be a problem?" James looks to his leader, realizing that defying John at this point would mean that he would also be eliminated.

"No boss, I understand" is all that is said before John exits the barn.

The moon rises as it does every month, John and his bunch roam the hills of their location. The woods are vast, so John doesn't worry about property lines, or running through the woods, as no one will see them. As promised, James is a darker shade of grey and is more aggressive. The pack comes upon a bear and easily kills it. James leaps in and rips into the bear's throat, but the entire pack eats humans, so killing the animal has no purpose. Bull comes up to join in, but James is quick to defend his kill, and slices into the other werewolf. Bram roars at James and is quick to remind him of the pack order. He easily grabs James and throws him to the ground, ripping into his chest and biting his shoulder. He is stopped by John, who picks him up and throws him away from James. Michael walks over and stands over James to protect him.

The next morning, the four men walk into the barn and get dressed. John walks over to James and checks out his injuries. The wounds James received the night before were not as severe as they appeared to be, but sent a message to the weaker Lycan.

"It doesn't look that bad; Bull must have only wanted to make a point. There is nothing new about one of us trying to rise in rank after getting a little darker." James doesn't respond, but his face quickly shows how painful his injuries are. Bram approaches the injured pack member and shoves him. John turns to the large blonde man, and grabs him by the throat with yellow eyes.

"You have made your point Bull, he's still a member of the pack but any more of that, and I may need another Delta, GOT IT?" John said, as Michael helps James off the ground and into the house. Bull nods to his leader and apologizes. "Bull, Michael will soon be leading the east coast packs, and I'll need you to step up as my Beta. Eventually, you'll be leading one of my territories, but you need to lose that chip on your shoulder." John doesn't wait for a response after speaking to Bull, and leaves to check on James.

Joshua stands quietly, admiring the scenery that the sacred valley has to offer. He looks past the open clearing around the house, and past the tree line, to the river that is barely visible to the naked eye. His mother is healing quickly, and both are beginning to appreciate the peacefulness and the solitude. This was different than the sawmill, this feels like home. The locals are aware of their secret, making things even better for the two werewolves.

"Beautiful day, isn't it?" Joshua turns to see Twin Bears walking up the path, carrying a long leather pouch. Joshua stands up, and watches every move that his host makes as he approaches the shack. Years of looking over your shoulder has made the werewolf suspicious of everyone, and considering that the last time Joshua saw a pouch like this, he almost died, so using caution is a matter of survival. Twin Bears quickly recognizes this, as he walks up to the two werewolves, slowly, realizing that Joshua already knows what he is carrying. He looks to Joshua and smiles, leaning over to see Sarah, who her overprotective son is guarding. "Are you doing better? Waubun said that the wound has closed, but you're still a little stiff." Sarah looks up at her son and nods her head.

"Would you please step to one side, so I can see who I'm talking to?" Joshua does as instructed while his mother continues, "he's a little overprotective, but means well, I'm okay. Dawn has been great; you've got a lot to be proud of with that one." Joshua is obviously concerned, and keeps staring at the pouch. His mother looks to her host, "what's in the pouch?" Twin Bears lays the pouch on the ground and removes an arrow. Joshua jumps back as his lips begin to snarl, and a throaty growl escapes him. His mother struggles to reach him as his growl turns to a dull roar. "I pulled those things from him, and Anna was killed with one of those arrows, Mr. Twin Bears, we mean you no harm." The Indian host places the arrow back in its container and steps back with his hands raised.

"You are safe here, the tears of the river will never kill its protectors, and this land will protect you." Joshua calms down, and his eyes return to normal. He respects the Native American beliefs, but also remembers the day that Anna died, when John stabbed them with the same arrows. Twin Bears looks to his guest's "I meant no disrespect."

"I have some bad memories about those arrows," Joshua takes a step forward, realizing that Twin Bears will not hurt him. "Those things took Anna and almost killed me."

"I am here to finish the story of the tears of the river" Twin Bears steps away from the pouch, and takes a seat on the ground. "After the Great Spirit cried and gave us his tears, he also gave us a protector to watch over the sacred valley," Joshua takes a seat on the ground, listening intensely. "He gave us the wolf who walks, his *tala*, the sacred arrows can only harm evil spirits like the wendigo."

"Those arrows damned near killed me, but they killed Anna and my unborn baby," Joshua looks to the ground. "No one was sweeter than Anna, and I refuse to believe that she was evil." Twin Bears reaches out and places his hand on Joshua's shoulder.

"I don't want to offend, your Anna was also shot with a gun, and I'm not saying she was evil, all I'm saying is the sacred arrows will never kill a wolf spirit." Sarah grimaces as she sits up in her chair.

"It's a lovely story, Twin Bears" the Indian sits upright, and offers Joshua his hand, to help him up. Joshua stands up with his Native American friend's help, but is unable to remove his hand from Twin Bears grip.

"I believe in this, I have sworn to defend the sacred valley and those who watch over it, including the wolf spirits." Twin Bears releases Joshua's hand, then looks to Sarah, "are you going to be okay? I want to take Joshua for a walk and show him a few things. Snow Bird can help if you need anything while were gone." Sarah nods and assures the two men that she will be okay.

Joshua and Twin Bears eventually make it to the river's edge. They begin walking toward the large mountain that stands between the rows of trees, which sit on both sides of the river. "Be careful when you run at night in your spirit form, the tears cannot kill you, but they may hurt you, my friend." Joshua stops and is in awe of the beautiful scenery after listening to his friends' advice.

"This is beautiful" Twin Bears smiles, and stops for a moment to let his friend enjoy the view.

"We can walk the river's edge for the rest of the

way, the Great Spirit cried from the mountain, and his tears fell where the river meets the mountain." Joshua and Twin bears begin walking the river's edge, toward the mountain. The walk was long, and took several hours that involved walking over downed trees and rocks. Joshua was amazed at how healthy his guide was. Joshua's eyes and mouth begin to burn slightly as the two men approach a clearing, where the river ends and forms a lake at the mountain's base. Twin Bears looks to his friend, "be careful from here on Joshua, this is where the sacred tears are." Joshua nods as his eyes water, eventually he gets somewhat used to the area, and his senses calm down.

"This area must be nothing but silver; it even burns when I breathe" Twin Bears points to an opening at the side of the mountain. The water is shallow at the lake's edge, and the two men enter the cave without getting too wet. The water narrows in the cave, and offers a sandy patch of ground at the entrance. Twin Bears walks over to a wooden box and removes an oil lantern that he lights, illuminating the cave: the walls and water sparkle in the light of the lantern. Joshua stands, amazed at what he is witnessing. He leans over and touches the water with his finger, and jerks his hand back, as his finger burns at the touch of the water.

"Be careful Joshua, this is the tears of the Great Spirit" Twin Bears picks up a piece of silver from the water, and presents it to Joshua. "Only the Elders and guardians of the sacred valley know how to make the arrowheads," Twin Bears tosses the chunk of silver back in the water. "John Bennett must have stolen one of the pouches from a hunter that was chasing him," Twin Bears points to the opening, we have to leave the cave now, he extinguishes the lantern and places it back in the weathered wooden box.

The pair walks in the shallow water and starts the journey back. Joshua stops and looks to his guide, "Why are you showing me this?" Twin Bears looks down at the water and skips a rock across the lake.

"You and Sarah are the guardian of all this, I wanted to show you, so you know that this is your home and we are your people." Twin Bears picks up another rock and throws it across the top of the lake, "I got seven that time" He hands Joshua a rock and smiles "this land, and these people, will protect you wherever you go, remember that." Joshua nods, and throws a rock across the lake.

"Looks like eight to me," Twin Bears laughs, and the two spend most of the day sitting by the river's edge, telling stories and skipping rocks. The two eventually start walking home, and finally make it to the clearing that surrounds the cabin. Joshua looks up to see his mother standing beside Dawn. Joshua approaches the doctor, who is dressed in tight jeans tucked into her boots that are laced up just below her knees with a simple white top. The Native American doctor is stunning, and Joshua is unaware of his surroundings, until he hears his mother's voice.

"I'm walking down with Twin Bears to help Snow Bird set up for the party." Joshua looks with a confused look on his face, but is reminded about the festivities from Dawn.

"The pow wow, remember?" Dawn reaches out and pulls the large man close to her, "and I have been elected to be your guide to all things Native American."

Most pow wows are usually held in the lower valley, closer to the road, and are mainly used to get money from tourists, but this is different, it is being held in the evening and in the mountains. Joshua walks down to the lower valley, and immediately notices his mother sitting in front of the great hall talking to the elders, but is soon pulled by Dawn to a large table of food. She picks up a piece of bread and hands it to him, "This is fry bread, fold it like this" Joshua folds the bread as instructed. Dawn grabs his hand and fills the folded bread with a mixture of meat and berries into the folded bread. Joshua's eyes grow wide as he devours the food that has been given to him.

"What's in this? I taste some meat, but what else is in this?" Dawn places her hand on the werewolf's stomach as she leans into him.

"Its antelope, berries, and nuts" she points to a large fire at a clearing. Joshua and Dawn slowly walk down to the fire, the beating of the drums gets louder the closer they get to the fire, and the former Mennonite feels his wolf side trying to emerge. The two approaches another table, but this table is full of roasted meat. Dawn reaches out and grabs a large piece of the roasted deer and hands it to her guest. "You have to try this; nobody roasts meat better than my people." Joshua bites into the meat and begins to growl a bit, Dawn backs up, but nothing is said when his eyes turn yellow. He looks downward as his eyes return to normal, and then looks up at Dawn, embarrassed at what he had just done.

"Sorry, my eyes turn when I eat if I don't concentrate" Joshua said, Dawn leans in, and pulls the large man closer and kisses his cheek.

"You don't have to worry about that here" Dawn said, Joshua looks down and smiles at his guide.

"They scare people, sometimes even other

werewolves" Joshua said, the Indian doctor strokes the broad chest in front of her.

"I know you would never hurt me, never fight who you are," Dawn said, the two roam down the small village, that is lined with wooden shacks in various states of disrepair, including the half-built structure at the end of the dirt path. Dawn points to the weathered structure "that was supposed to be a school, we had college students that were going to come and take turns teaching, but the college insisted that we have a proper environment for the staff." Joshua looks to his date and smiles.

"Mama and Mrs. Yoder taught me; I know the basics but not much more." Dawn wraps her arm around the large man, and the two watches the sun disappear into the tree line.

"You're smarter than you give yourself credit" Dawn said, as the couple continues to walk farther away from the crowd as they continue talking.

"None of this worries or concerns you at all, does it?" Joshua said, as Dawn looks up, barely able to see his face at this point.

"Well, I've been an Indian longer than a doctor, and I realize that there are things that cannot be explained" the pair finds themselves at the opening of the run-down schoolhouse. Joshua can see clearly in these conditions, but realizes that mortals cannot. He notices the structure is still intact for the most part but will soon be lost to the elements if not repaired. The former Mennonite looks up to the sky peeking through the large hole in the roof but soon lowers his head to see Dawn. It was dark inside the run-down schoolhouse, but Joshua could see her clearly; he notices her hair, which flows down each side of her perfectly contoured face, and swallows nervously, before leaning down to kiss her. Dawn falls into his arms, and gives herself to him. The werewolf is careful not to be too aggressive with her, as he is making love to a mortal, and could hurt her if he isn't careful, but eventually surrenders to his desires, and the two become one. Joshua kisses his lover passionately before lowering her to the ground. After their intimate session, the couple gets dressed and takes a seat on the weathered stairs that leads to the schoolhouse door. Dawn wraps her arm around the large arm of the man sitting beside her, and strokes his back while she leans into him.

"How long has it been?" Joshua looks around the darkened area before kissing the gorgeous doctor on top of her head.

"I haven't been with anyone since Anna" Joshua turns his attention to the night sky, he notices that his mind is calm and, for the first time in years, isn't worried about anything. "So about ten years," Dawn continues to stroke the man realizing how lonely he is. He travels with his mother but needs a woman that allows him to be a man. Dawn is not promiscuous, but could see the pain and desire in his eyes the moment she saw him. Nothing is said for a few moments before she turns and kisses the side of Joshua's arm.

"That's too long" the pair begin walking slowly back to the party. Most have left, but the food was left for anyone that wanted it. The lovers eventually end up at Dawn's vehicle. Joshua leans up against the wood grain that fills the side of the Jeep Wagoneer, and looks to the woman he has just made love to.

"I enjoyed being with you tonight, but why?" Dawn adjusts herself behind the driver's seat before answering.

"When we first met, the first thing I noticed about you after you changed back was the pain in your face." Dawn reaches out and gently strokes Joshua's hair, "wolf spirit or not, you're still a man" Joshua smiles as he reaches in and kisses her.

"I've been to the sacred valley with your father." Dawn smiles softly

"I can only go with an elder, a guardian, or the caretaker, my dad has never taken me." Joshua steps back from the vehicle.

"Why don't we go? I can take you, can't I?" Joshua said.

"I have to be at the hospital most of the week, but how about this Tuesday?" Joshua eagerly agrees and steps back as he watches the taillights disappear into the night. The next day Joshua awakens to the smell of the meat from the party. His mother has some bread and a few large pieces on the small table in the cabin.

"I've already eaten, but I brought you something to eat" Joshua gets up from his cot, and eagerly devours the meat. His mother returns and sits on her cot, "did you and Dawn have a good time last night?" Joshua begins rambling to his mother about Dawn, not caring about how he eats, but fails to mention the schoolhouse. Nothing else is said, but Sarah smiles softly as she knows what happened the previous night.

"And we're going to the sacred valley in a few days, you should come with us," Sarah leans back in her cot and laughs.

"I should probably stay here and let you two enjoy the day with each other." The two werewolves are soon invited to a council meeting. Joshua stands up inside the great hall to address the council, while the elders, Twin Bears, and his mother remain seated at the simple wooden table. It is apparent that they are seen as part of the community and someone whose opinion matters.

"I know enough about fixing things and can repair the hall and school; I think we should work to rebuild what was started." The chief listens, but does not agree with the newcomer.

"We appreciate your offer, but we simply do not have the money to fix or build anything" Kay nods in agreement with the others.

"Joshua, what little money we have goes to feed our people" Joshua nods, understanding how the Indians have struggled. "But we appreciate your offer" the council gets up from the table and disperse. Joshua turns to the Chief and Twin Bears before they exit the building.

"Dawn and I are going to walk the river of the sacred valley." The Chief looks to Twin Bears.

"Is that okay?" Joshua said

"He knows the way and has seen the sacred valley as a wolf and as a man, he knows the way" Twin Bears said, the Chief nods, approving of the journey.

"The sacred valley is your home and you are its guardian," The Chief looks to Joshua and gives him a final piece of advice. "Just be careful and don't get hurt on your journey *Makoyi*" Joshua leaves the hall, unclear about what the Chief told him.

Tuesday doesn't come soon enough, Dawn knocks on the door as Joshua and his mother exit the cabin.

"Are you sure you don't want to come with us, mama?" Sarah looks at the young woman dressed in denim and flannel.

"Very sure Joshua, but please be careful," the pair walk through the woods and soon find themselves at the river. Dawn stops, and admires the mountain that sets in the center of the trees lined on both sides of the river. Joshua surveys the area while she admires the view, and notices a black wolf just outside the range of a mortal's vision. The wolf does nothing but simply turns and walks away, leaving the pair alone.

"It's more beautiful than I have been told, but I never imagined it would be like this." Dawn said, as the two begin walking the river's edge, with Joshua lifting Dawn over the downed trees and large rocks. They stop briefly at a small clearing about a mile from the opening at the mountain. Dawn reaches up and pulls the large man down to her level and kisses him passionately. This time was different, and the werewolf soon began pulling at the beautiful woman's jeans. Dawn pushes him back and removes her clothes before giving herself to him again. Joshua isn't as gentle this time, as she leans over and allows him to make love to her again. After their intimate session, the couple gets dressed and eventually makes it to the edge of the mountain. Joshua grabs Dawn's hand, and lights up the lantern as he was shown when he was here with Twin Bears, Dawn picks up a piece of silver from the stream and turns to Joshua. "You know, I'm holding a couple of hundred dollars in my hand." Joshua looks down at his lover, confused.

"The silver is sacred and can only be removed to protect the land" Dawn tosses the silver back into the water and stands up.

"My people starve while they sit on all this, it would seem to me protecting themselves from poverty is a damned good reason to sell some of it." Joshua places the lantern back to the wooden box and carries Dawn to dry land. He sits her down gently then steps back.

"It's the way that it's been done for many years; these people stay true to who they are." Joshua smiles softly and places his hands in his pockets. "I admire and respect them for being true to themselves," Dawn grits her teeth as her face turns red.

"By all means, tell me about my people, I may have forgotten some things while you were inside me," Dawn shakes her head. "Joshua, I care about you, but you need to decide what you are. I assure you that I don't spread my legs for just anyone" the young Indian doctor walks over to her guide. "But I need you as much as you need me right now," Joshua wraps his arms around Dawn.

"Being with you gives me hope about not being alone, and finding someone that cares about me," Dawn falls into his arms, not knowing what to say.

"I'm going through some things, but how about we make a deal that this is nothing serious, okay?" Joshua reluctantly agrees, but has been told his entire life that a man and a woman should be married if they plan to fornicate. Dawn leans in, kissing his chest, "I never want to see you hide who you are or what you need from me." She leaves Joshua with a final thought before heading back to the cabin, "we're the only ones around here Joshua, so just promise me one thing sweetie, that when you want to fuck me, that you fuck me and not try to be something you're not." Nothing is said on the way back, Joshua and Dawn stop at the road leading to the cabin. Sarah watches from the cabin as Joshua and Dawn approach holding hands, the couple embrace, and Dawn kisses his chest before heading down the path that leads down the mountain. Joshua walks to the cabin, lost in his thoughts, he looks up to see his mother sitting on the stool that he made for her just outside the door.

"It looks like you and Dawn are getting along; did you have a good time?" Joshua sits down on the ground and looks up to his mother.

"She's amazing mama, she's so easy to talk to, and we get along great." Joshua can hardly contain himself as he fidgets on the ground. "She's so pretty, and she's a doctor, so if she lives longer, she can help more people." Sarah looks at her son but says nothing until he quiets down.

"So you're going to turn Dawn, and both of you are going to live forever? Are you going to adopt and then turn the children into one of us? Or just watch them grow old?" Joshua looks up at his mother briefly before looking around at the scenery, avoiding eye contact.

"Why can't I be happy? I thought you would be happy for us." Sarah looks down at her son, and stops to remember the little boy that she has seen grow into the man sitting in front of her, realizing that for as many years that he has been alive, he is still that same little boy.

"The only thing I want is for you to be happy sweetheart, but I worry that you're still in love with Anna, and trying to replace her." Sarah chooses her words carefully as she speaks to her son. "I see more than anyone how lonely you are, what does Dawn have to say about this?"

"She said that she's going through something, and we need to keep things casual." Sarah sighs, as there are some conversations that a son should not have with his mother.

"I know you were in love with Anna, but I also know that Dawn is the only woman that you have been with since she died." Joshua turns to his mother giving her his full attention, "just be sure you are truly in love with this woman, and not blinded from fornicating with her. Please talk to her before you make too many plans," an uneasy silence fills the air for several minutes, until Twin Bears is seen at the edge of the tree line waving his arms.

"Can you come down to the great hall Joshua?" The two guests of the Blackfoot nation walk briskly down the dirt path to find the elders and Twin Bears looking at the corner of the roof, which is drooping at the corner. Joshua walks up and notices the broken beam lying on the ground.

"It looks like its weight-bearing, we need to replace the post and pour a footer this time," Joshua shakes the other posts in front of the hall. He turns to the Elders with his hands on his hips, "we need to replace the other posts and change out the header board to fix this." Joshua looks to his mother and pulls out what money is left, "let me go to town and see what I can come up with." Joshua and his mother head to the hardware store that sits at the edge of town. Sarah quickly exits the truck, but Joshua is hesitant as the last time he was here, things didn't go well. The store was empty and Randy was standing behind the counter but smiling as the two approached the counter.

"I see you came back; what do you need today?" Joshua pulls what was left of the money from his pocket and looks to the back wall.

"I need a price on some lumber and eight bags of concrete" Randy begins walking around, writing down prices on a notepad. He returns to the counter and begins totaling the cost of the items. Joshua smiles as he has enough to purchase the supplies, but all that was left was a few dollars, before the two can start gathering up supplies, Joshua notices a phone behind the counter. "Can my mother use the phone? It's long-distance, but I'll be happy to pay" the storekeeper smiles and nods.

"Go ahead and don't worry about the money," Randy said, Sarah smiles as she goes behind the counter, calling Virginia. Sarah stutters a bit at the sound of Spencer's voice.

"Hi honey, it's Sarah, I just wanted to call and let you know we're okay." Nothing is said for a few minutes before the voice on the other end says.

"I love you Sarah, and it's good to hear your voice but I'm still being watched." Sarah and Spencer don't talk long, but spend most of that time proclaiming the love they have for each other.

"We're on an Indian reservation in Montana, I think it's near Glacier Mountain" Sarah doesn't wait for a response. "They know what we are and don't care. I know what you have in Virginia, but we can easily start fresh in

Canada or stay here." Spencer looks around at his surroundings before responding.

"I would give it all up tomorrow but John would eventually find us, we'll be together one day." Spencer hangs up the phone and turns to see Henry and Rodney behind him. "Did you hear any of that?" Spencer wasn't sure how acute both men's senses are. He has been a werewolf about as long as Henry, but Rodney is a young wolf. A chill runs down the business owner's back as he can't be sure how safe Sarah and Joshua are at this point. He walks past both men to the kitchen to find Nell in the kitchen cleaning up from the lunch rush. He looks to the woman he has known for years, things have been tense between them, and Nell has been vocal about how she has been treated. Spencer says nothing, but stops as he notices the phone on the wall of the kitchen.

"Is everything okay? That was too long of a conversation for a takeout order." Mama Nell said, while Spencer nods as he leaves the kitchen.

"It was nothing" he hesitates to mention Sarah to anyone, especially Nell. They were a couple for years, but time runs slower for a Lycan. It was a fling that lasted a short time for Spencer, but it was a significant part of her shorter lifespan. She spent years blaming it on his religious beliefs, but in truth, Spencer isn't a religious man. He spent a lot of time singing religious hymns in the fields as a slave, but that was to alert listeners about the Underground Railroad. He did worry about being cursed as she was angry for years, but it's hard to curse someone when they grow fur and fangs monthly. They eventually quit speaking, but time heals, and Nell has been a good friend the past few years. Spencer gets lost in his thoughts as worry starts to take control of him; he finally shrugs things off. *Get a grip; no one heard anything* before getting back to work.

While Spencer is getting his thoughts together in Virginia, Joshua and Randy are loading the wood on the back of his truck. The truck sags from the excessive weight but appears to be drivable. Randy places his forearms on the pickup and turns to Joshua.

"Not everyone is an asshole like Gary, and it looks like you're running a little low in money. If you need some side work, I can set you up" Joshua nods and extends his hand to the storekeeper.

"Anything will help, I'll stop in a few times a week to check" Sarah eventually returns to the truck, and the two begin driving back to the reservation. She was quiet for several minutes, but the smile on her face made it apparent that she was happy. She turns to her son and smiles softly.

"Thank you Joshua," Sarah looks out the window after speaking and closes her eyes as the air blows across her, pushing her blonde hair behind her. Nothing else is said as the two continue to drive quietly down the road and back to the reservation.

Joshua smiles as he notices a crowd of men standing in front of the great hall. He gets out of the truck and immediately turns his attention to the sagging corner. He surveys the front of the large building before turning to the men of the tribe with a plan.

"We can put the new header board behind the older ones, and reset the posts so they support the new board. A few feet shouldn't make a difference and it should hold" Joshua looks, realizing that his friends had little experience in construction. Everyone is quick to step in and do as they are told. Before long, the holes are dug, and the posts are set. Joshua inspects the recently repaired structure and gets nostalgic thinking of how similar the Native Americans are to the Mennonites. Whenever barns needed to be built or repairs made, everyone in the community pitched in, and money, prestige, or greed was never an issue, just the community's well-being. He turns to see his mother smiling at him, as she helps escort one of the elders down the dirt path to the elderly gentleman's home. Joshua spends most of the day making some additional repairs to the building with some extra lumber that was bought earlier. After gathering the rotted wood and placing it on a pile, he turns to Twin Bears, who stayed and assisted the werewolf after the other tribe members left.

"Thank you, Joshua" Twin Bears kicks the ground and appears to be struggling to find the right words. "I know you are fond of my daughter, but please talk to her before giving her your heart, things is not what they seem, and I am as protective of you as I am her." Joshua doesn't say anything, he understood his mother's advice, but this was coming from Dawn's father, and that was concerning.

CHAPTER ELEVEN

Joshua walks into the hardware store early Monday morning to find a man standing at the counter with Randy. The man looked to be in his early thirties, and was obviously a hard worker, with his calloused hands and dirty appearance.

"He's the one I told you about, he comes in a few times a week looking for work" Joshua walks up and shakes the dirt-covered hand of the man standing with Randy, and after a brief conversation, finds himself working for the day. He notices the large pile of shrubs and dirt on the back of the flatbed truck that is held down with shovels and other various gardening tools.

"I go by Matt, my given name is Matthew, but no one calls me that except my mother." The Sandy-haired man shifts gears on the steering column of the truck before continuing. "We're working at the hospital for a few days; they want to replant the shrubs around the building. To be honest, the job is a little bigger than I can do alone." Joshua smiles as the man drives down the road.

"My name's Joshua and I appreciate the work; just tell me what you want me to do."

The truck backs into the far corner of a lot at the hospital, where more dirt and shrubs are located. "I'm gonna let someone know we're here, you can start digging up the bushes in front of the building, but be sure to get all the roots, most of them have root rot, that's why they want them replaced." Joshua nods while he waits for the man to disappear, before walking over and pulling up each shrub from the ground, without any issue. Being a full black werewolf has its benefits as he keeps all his senses and is extremely strong, regardless of the moon. Joshua sometimes questions what side of his nature he struggles with, the human or wolf side. The former Mennonite begins pulling the brown shrubs up, carefully inspecting any remnants of the dying bushes. Matt returns from speaking to the maintenance head of the hospital, and stares at the pile of rotted bushes with his mouth open.

"How did you do that? At this rate, we'll get this done in a day." Joshua looks to his boss and points to the corner of the building.

"I'm gonna dig up the others while you start planting the new shrubs," Matt agrees as he walks off, pleased at how his day has started. Joshua finishes pulling the shrubs at the front of the building, being careful not to draw attention to himself. Being in the city has its challenges, and he must concentrate to block out a lot of background noise. His senses are stronger than a mortal's, but he has gotten used to it at this point, and doesn't get overwhelmed like when he first changed. He begins gathering up the dead shrubs but stops when a familiar scent fills the air. He turns to see Dawn entering the hospital and begins walking to the entrance, but stops when she starts talking to another man. Joshua has done a good job of respecting people's privacy. John would often tell his pack stories of conversations he overheard, but Joshua never enjoyed hearing the stories as it always felt wrong, but this is different, he has feelings for this woman. Twin Bears and his mother's voice kept running through his head, so with this in mind, he turns his ear to the entrance and concentrates until he hears Dawn's voice.

"Yes Andrew, I still have feelings for you, but I told you I need time." Andrew's voice begins to shake, and the pounding of his heart is making it hard to hear what is being said.

"And I've given you space but we're still married, and I don't want to lose you," Andrew reaches out and gently grabs her shoulder. "I'm getting tired of sleeping on Phil's couch," Joshua looks as Dawn leans in and kisses Andrew.

"I've got to make rounds; I have a patient with severe lacerations. It almost looks like he was attacked by a mean dog." Dawn said, as she pulls Andrew in and kisses him again. "I want to make this work too, how about you pack your things and come back home tonight. I'll make some fry bread, and we can share a bed like a married couple." Joshua's heart sinks as he hears her final words to her husband, "I love you, Andy."

Matt approaches his new employee with a concerned look. "You okay? You've been standing at that same spot for a while." Joshua looks to the groundskeeper with tired eyes. "I know that look buddy, my wife sent me a Dear John letter when I was on my last tour in the Navy, we've all been there my friend." The heartbroken Lycan spends the next few hours gathering up the rotted bushes and loading them on the truck. He looks down at his dirt-covered shirt and remembers the white coat that Andrew was wearing. More hours pass, and the two landscapers finally make it to the last three shrubs at the main entrance to the hospital. Joshua stands up to see Andrew and Dawn walk out the door. She stands for a moment, not sure what to say, and turns to her husband, not expecting to see Joshua outside the hospital doors.

"This will only take a minute, I'll see you at home" Andrew stops and looks at the dirt-covered man standing in front of him, visibly concerned at the larger man's size. Joshua swallows hard and breathes deeply in an attempt to keep himself calm. Dawn nervously walks up to her former lover. "You already know, don't you?" Joshua looks down at the woman who broke his heart.

"So much for being true to myself and not hiding anything from you." Dawn's hand trembles as she reaches out and begins stroking the werewolf's large chest.

"You need to calm down, I was going to tell you, but I also said this was just a casual thing." Joshua closes his eyes as the sounds of the city begin to overwhelm him. He opens his eyes that are now yellow, and struggles to speak.

"I AM CALM!" his voice begins to crackle as his neck thickens, but he then calms down as he remembers where he is. Dawn backs away from Joshua, unable to look at him.

"I'm pregnant Joshua," she finally looks up struggling to look at the man she is starting to fall in love with. "And its Andrew's, I never meant to hurt you, but I want someone to grow old with, and I want to raise children, not puppies." Joshua turns to find Matt quietly standing behind him realizing that Anna was the only love of his life and that he is truly alone in this world. Matt reaches out and slaps his coworker on the shoulder.

"Why don't you gather up the shovels while I go get us some money." Joshua watches Dawn walk away, feeling the weight of his chest pressing in on him as he cleans the area, and places the shovels on top of the dead shrubs that fill the back of the truck. The two begin driving down the road, but Matt turns his truck into a parking lot. Joshua looks up at the large neon light that spells "The Corral" shining down on the parked cars. "This one's on me tonight; you need a drink, my friend" Joshua looks at his boss and smiles.

"I'm not much of a drinker," Matt laughs as Joshua gets out of the car, and the two begin walking into the bar. The distraught man looks around at the various items on the wall, including the large painting of a long-horned bull behind the lacquer-covered wooden bar.

"After what she did to you today my friend, you need to start but you'll feel better after a few beers." The two men approach the bar, and soon, two mugs of beer are in front of them. "I have a son in San Diego; I was stationed there in the Navy. My son and ex still live there with a welder" Joshua sets his mug down after taking a drink.

"Dawn is the first woman I've been with since Anna," Matt motions his hand for two more beers.

"It's never too late and maybe this Anna misses you as much as you miss her." Joshua looks at the mug, mesmerized at its contents.

"She died years ago carrying our child," Matt shakes his head and places his hand on Joshua's shoulder.

"Died in childbirth, that's a tough one, and that doctor pretty much ripped your heart out today, didn't she?" Joshua and Matt spent most of the evening drinking. Matt pays for the beers and the burgers that were eaten. Before long, the truck pulls up behind the hardware store. Matt pulls out a wad of money and hands it to Joshua "here's $100 dollars, that job was going to take me three days. I have a few small jobs, but I can use you next week." Joshua shakes the man's hand and starts driving back to the reservation, Matt seemed okay to drive and Joshua wasn't concerned about being drunk as it was near impossible for him to get intoxicated. He pulls up to the front of the great hall and notices the Chief sitting at the front of the building. He gets out of the truck and walks to the Chief, lost in his thoughts. The elderly leader looks up at the heartbroken man and smiles.

"My granddaughter stopped by and told us what happened today" Joshua leans over and helps the old man get up, as he struggles to get out of his chair. "We've been waiting for you" the Indian Chief begins walking up the hill to the shack that Joshua and his mother share, but turns and walks down to the river, stopping a few yards from the water's edge, at an opening in a large embankment. Joshua notices the smoke rising from the top of the mound and the flickering light coming from a small opening. The old man takes off his clothes and enters the small opening. Joshua also removes his clothes and enters the opening, struggling to get inside with the others. He looks up to see Twin Bears, Kajika, and an elder called White Eagle. The Chief takes a seat and points to an empty spot on the ground around a fire. Joshua sits down and begins sweating due to the heat coming from the fire and the alcohol he drank earlier. Chief Grey Wolf looks around at the men sitting around the fire.

"The time is almost upon us when the evil spirits will return," he turns and looks directly at Joshua. "The wolf spirit that guards the sacred land is troubled, and we cannot lose our way." White Eagle tosses a small bundle of leaves and herbs in the fire, and Joshua breathes in the smoke from the fire, coughing a bit while the other elder speaks.

"We call upon the Great Spirit to guide us" Twin Bears begins chanting, and before long, the others join in. Joshua focuses on the flames and soon becomes hypnotized. He closes his eyes and begins to sway at the chanting, but notices John sitting across from him with a sly grin after he opens his eyes. The chamber disappears, and Joshua finds himself in the sacred valley alone at night, following a man dressed in colonial garb, his pants are tucked into his boots that rest just below the knee, and the long brown coat that hangs mid-thigh swings feely as he walks. The man begins to grow hair and turn into a werewolf but is dark grey and not black. He then trips over something and looks at his feet, where he sees dozens of dead Native American bodies covered in blood. Joshua roars and runs to attack the man, but is unable to find him through the smoke that surrounds the area. The smoke clears, and Joshua finds John lying on the ground with Anna helping him. Joshua begins shouting.

"Anna I'm here, it's me, Joshua" he is unable to get her attention as John overpowers her and begins to rape the woman who had just tended to his wounds. John looks to Joshua and laughs as he leans over and bites Anna on her shoulder. He continues to try and reach the woman he loves curled up by a fire crying as John pulls her up by her hair, instructing the crying woman to start walking. The sun comes up, but John and Anna are nowhere to be seen. Joshua soon realizes that he is standing in the clearing of the sacred valley. He turns to see Dawn covered in blood, with the entire Blackfoot Nation lying dead on the ground around her, and begins running to her, but is unable to reach the injured woman from all the smoke. He is awoken from his trance by a familiar voice.

"Joshua, wake up" he feels a hand slap his face and sees Twin Bears sitting beside him. "We need to get you outside," Joshua doesn't say anything as Kajika, and Twin Bears help him leave the small room. The Chief and White Eagle soon join Joshua, who is being led to the river. Twin bears look to his son, "ease him into the river a little at a time." The men clean the sweat off them and stand by the water's edge, after getting dressed, and after a few minutes, the chief looks to the werewolf.

"Did you have a vision?" Joshua looks to the three men standing with him.

"John killed everyone, and changed Anna after he raped her." Joshua looks to the river and pauses for a moment, "and he's going to do it again" Twin Bears looks at his friend.

"You were in there a long time; it must have been a powerful vision." Joshua takes a deep breath, and turns to the four men that he shared this moment with.

"I don't know what I was thinking; John will kill everyone on this mountain, then find Dawn and her baby, and do the same thing to them." Joshua feels the cooler air fill his lungs, as he stares at the four warriors standing with him with yellow eyes. "Just like Anna," the werewolf gets lost in his thoughts for a moment, before looking to the other side of the river at the black wolf howling into the air. The wolf lowers his head, and the two wolves lock yellow eyes before the creature disappears into the woods. Chief Gray Wolf remains silent until Joshua turns to him.

"You are the wolf who walks, but you are also a man, I told you when you first came to us to be true to your nature. Men lie with squaws, so never apologize for such things." The chief hobbles over to Joshua, who stands unashamed of what he is, and for the first time realizes what is at stake if John wins. "The wolf howls to tell the others about the protector of the sacred valley," the old chief looks across the water, unable to see as clearly as Joshua can. "It knows the wolf who walks, the protector of the sacred valley, has arrived" The old man turns and looks up at Joshua "our Makoyi warrior has arrived."

Joshua sits by the river most of the night, the others returned to their homes, but Joshua spends most of the evening thinking about his vision. He also ponders if he is strong enough to take on the entire pack alone, and if he will be able to kill John when the time comes. All his life, he has been told that killing is a sin and to turn the other cheek. He turned once when his family was killed and his home burnt to the ground, he turned again when he was left for dead after watching the love of his life die, as she begged for the life of their unborn child. Maybe he doesn't have what it takes to take a life, but he will not turn the other cheek this time. Joshua walks slowly back to the house to find his mother sitting outside the shack; she looks up and shields her eyes from the newly-risen sun that is now beating down on Joshua's back.

"Where have you been?" Joshua sits down beside his mother and leans against her

"Dawn's married, she doesn't want to see me anymore, and she's pregnant with his baby." Sarah suspected something like this would happen, and that her son's happiness would end.

"I had a feeling about her, but I am sorry she hurt you." Joshua sits up and leans against the shack that he and his mother share.

"I also had a vision last night; I sat around a fire with the chief and some others" Joshua rests his forearms on his knees and continues, "We need to help these people mama, something tells me that John's coming, and will kill all these people if we don't do something."

"We're not strong enough to take on John's pack alone, I can call Spencer if you want, maybe he can help." Joshua places his head on his arms and stretches his neck.

"Lyle may be enough to help, but who knows where he is, I don't think Spencer will be enough," Joshua gets lost in his thoughts for a moment. "Maybe it's time to stop fighting, it would be nice to see Anna, papa, and Liam again." Sarah looks to her son, no one has suffered more than she has, both she and Joshua have lost loved ones, but through everything, she has managed to keep her faith. Her son is starting to question some things, and Sarah understands that he needed Dawn, but fears that her going back to her husband may be more than Joshua can take.

"All life is precious sweetheart, including yours, and it's not your decision to make; only God decides when we get our reward." Joshua lays his head down on his mother's lap as she strokes his hair, she has cried as much for her son that is alive than the other family members that are now dead. The young man struggles to speak as he fights sleep.

"If God loves me, why does he torment me so much? Why doesn't he punish the bad people, mama?" Sarah doesn't respond as her son drifts off to sleep as she strokes his hair. Sarah looks up from her sleeping son with tears streaming down her face as she questions if he is strong enough. In truth, she has questioned God's plan, but remains true to her faith. John will eventually find them, and when that time comes, she will fight but will not take a life. Sarah looks to upward, as the tears continue to flow down her face.

"Please help us, we need you now more than ever" She leans back on the wood wall behind her and continues to hold her son as he sleeps.

Spencer walks down from the apartment above the restaurant and puts on the coffee, before unlocking the front door as he does every morning. Henry soon emerges from the upstairs apartment that he has been sharing with Spencer for the past several weeks. The two werewolves sit at the table in the kitchen but say little to each other; the restaurant is a cold, emotionless place these days and with the threat of John hanging over everyone's head. The other supernatural creatures are avoiding this place as they also feel something in the air. Rodney enters the kitchen to start the day and soon joins the other two werewolves. The three men struggle to have a conversation, but Spencer continues to keep an eye on everyone after his conversation with Lyle. The phone rings, breaking the silence, the business owner picks up the receiver and looks across the table with a puzzled look. "Hello, yes, he's here" Spencer looks to his houseguest emotionless. "It's for you" Henry takes the phone from Spencer's hand to hear his brother on the other end.

"Hello Henry, John has decided that you are no longer part of the pack," James whispers so as not to wake the others. "I warned you that getting too close to those people would not end well" Henry isn't surprised or angry at the news, but asks his brother if he's okay. James assures his brother that everything is going well for him, but everyone that opposes John will be killed, including Henry. He also reveals that John knows where the others are and is heading to Montana to end it; including making sure all the Native Americans are dead this time.

"What do you mean this time?" Henry listens as James tells him of recent events, including how John knows that Joshua and Sarah are in Montana, and how he will move up in rank after John takes over as leader of all the packs. Henry pauses for a moment, "you sound different, are you eating humans now?" James quietly laughs as Henry waits for an answer.

"You never got it, I'm stronger and darker than you because I do as I'm told, including eating the human sheep that you're so worried about." Henry swallows hard; leaving the pack was a blessing but knowing his brother is evil and lost to him hurt more than anything. The elder brother looks downward as tears fill his eyes.

"I love you" James says nothing and hangs up the phone. Henry is silent for a few moments realizing those were the last words he will say to his brother. The ex-pack member returns to his seat and looks to Spencer, sitting on the opposite side of the table, worried at what he has overheard. "I'm out of the pack and will be made an example with the others" the two former slaves look at each other, as Henry tries to remain composed. Spencer has known this man long enough to know the tears weren't for John. "And I've lost my brother" Rodney walks over to the abandoned wolf and places his hand on his shoulder.

"Welcome to the lone wolf club" Henry doesn't look up and continues to stare at his coffee as he responds to Spencer.

"John doesn't have ex-pack members; he has dead ex-pack members."Spencer looks across at his houseguest, worried the news will be what he has feared for years.

"Like the others?" Spencer said, as Henry looks up to his friend with a solemn look.

"John knows, and they're headed out for Montana tomorrow to finish it, he called everyone to join him there." Rodney scans the room and asks why he's inviting everyone to Montana. Henry looks to the younger werewolf and sighs, "because he's not only gonna kill Joshua, he's gonna kill everyone on the reservation." He then looks to Spencer, who is beginning to panic. "And Sarah will wish she was dead after those bastards get done with her," Spencer walks to the other side of the table and grabs Rodney, tossing him on the table as he closes his grip around his throat.

"WHY? Why did you say something to John?" Henry attempts to pull him off Rodney, but Spencer remains focused on the younger Lycan. "They don't know what's coming and what made you want to help those bottom feeders?" A voice comes from the entrance to the dining area.

"They didn't call John, I did" Spencer looks up to see Mama Nell standing at the doorway, proud of what she has just disclosed. "I don't know what you see in that Christian bitch, but I'm pretty sure she never did what I was always willing to do for you." The angry woman walks defiantly over to her former lover, "but I bet she gets used to having something in her mouth after John turns her into a whore for the next hundred years." Mama Nell attempts to shove Spencer, who doesn't move, "then she'll know what it's like to be something for a werewolf to fuck, and then toss out like a piece of trash." Spencer grabs Nell by the throat, blind with rage, but calms down, realizing that he needs to save the love of his life. He looks up at Rodney, and points to Mama Nell.

"Tie that voodoo witch up, and if things go sideways, the bar's yours," he walks over and slaps Nell hard. "And be sure to kill her if I don't come back," with his hands shaking, he pulls out a number from his wallet and nervously dials the number, after a few moments a woman's answers

"Hello, is Lyle there?" The Elder werewolf's voice is soon heard.

"Hector just called me, his pack's staying out of it, but you need to start hauling ass, I'm in Massachusetts and heading out now. I'll meet you in Chicago at a small bookstore; I'll give you guys more details there." Lyle gives Spencer the address and walks into the kitchen where Margaret is sitting. He looks down at his friend. "It's time, and I need to get to Montana ASAP" Margaret smiles as she takes a sip of her tea.

"That rust bucket of yours is not going to make it to Montana in time, your highness." Margaret tosses the keys to her car on the wooden table in front of her, "take my Buick." Lyle picks up the keys and looks down at the Wiccan leader.

"What happened to not interfering?" Margaret looks up at the werewolf and smiles softly.

241

"Only if it does no harm my old friend, and I fear much harm is headed for Montana." Lyle grabs the keys but leans over and kisses his friend on the cheek.

"You're the best Maggie," Lyle heads out in a rush, his host walks to the opening and shouts as she closes the door.

"IT'S MARGARET, NOT MAGGIE," she pauses after shutting the door and whispers, "Please be careful Lyle." Margaret immediately goes to the phone and dials Frank in Chicago, who immediately answers. "A pack war is brewing in Montana with some very powerful wolves, I'll contact the grand coven, but I need you to tell our members near the reservation what's going on." Margaret waits as Frank writes down his instructions before continuing, "they are planning on meeting at the store but do not ask questions at this time, these are extremely powerful creatures my boy, they will be on edge and can be deadly when they feel agitated." The record keeper is silent for a moment before responding.

"This could be bad, couldn't it Margaret?" Frank lays his pen down and continues. "If they fail in Montana, the man-eaters could start a war and start treating mortals like cattle." The first among equals pauses for a moment to collect her thoughts, as she has the same concerns.

"King Lycaon is one of the oldest living military strategists in history; he has seen civilizations rise and fall and knows more about what's needed than anyone." She pauses before continuing, "I'm sure he has gone over every possible strategy and is our best hope." Margaret hangs up the phone, trying to believe what she has just told the Wiccan record keeper.

Lyle laughs at what his friend said just before he started driving to Chicago. He knows that she doesn't like to be called Maggie but does so anyway. She is only one of a few mortals where he can be himself; he doesn't spend much time around the werewolves he helps as they have jobs, families, and obligations. Lyle has been there to help when the werewolves outlive their adopted children or mortal spouses. Other than the grand coven, Lyle is the only one that realizes just how many werewolves and vampires exist, if they did, no one would ever go outside at night.

Spencer comes up from the basement of his restaurant with a large pouch and opens the pouch, removing a handgun."This gun has lead bullets" he pulls out two additional clips from the dark green sack and sits them down beside the 357 magnum pistol. Rodney picks up the gun and tucks it in the back of his jeans and nods as Spencer gives him some final instructions. " I need you here in case shit hits the fan and people come to clean up loose ends; the two clips have silver loads, just in case, and you can find another box of silver rounds in the basement," Rodney nods as he tucks the clips in his shirt pocket.

"We don't change for three more days, what's he gonna do when he gets there?" Rodney said. Henry, who has been silently leaning against the counter, speaks up.

"John can change at will, so he can damn near wipe out the reservation in one night, or wait for the others to change then wipe out everyone." Henry looks down at the sack full of guns before addressing the restaurant owner, "he'll have over thirty wolves there." Spencer picks up his sack and begins walking to the door.

"I died a long time ago, but I started living when

she came into my life." He looks to Nell, who is sitting motionless at the table staring into space, "that's what she does for me, and what you never understood." Henry walks over to Spencer at the opened door.

"Got room for one more?" Spencer turns to the ex-pack member.

"Are you sure? Killing you and Joshua are gonna be high on John's list." Henry turns to Spencer with a determined look.

"I did nothing but watch something beautiful die when he killed Anna, and tortured Joshua." Henry's look changes from determination to anger. "I will not stand quietly this time, and if it's my time to die, I will die with honorable people, not hiding from those savages."

Spencer and Henry get in the older pickup truck parked at the back of the restaurant. Spencer fires up the truck and turns to Henry. "Last chance to get out" Henry looks to his friend and smiles.

"I have made my choice, and we're wasting time," he leans back in the truck seat and gets comfortable for the long ride. "Let me know when you want me to take over driving," Henry takes a deep breath and turns his attention to the parking area behind the restaurant "this is why I don't fornicate with mortals; it never ends well my friend." The two men laugh as the truck pulls out of the parking lot and onto the street.

CHAPTER TWELVE

John stands on the front porch of his house in Elkton, Virginia at the roughly twelve werewolves of various strengths. "I found the traitors and have decided to show everyone what happens when you go against the pack." John places the sunglasses on his face and stops to feel the sun beating down on him. "The northern crews are going to meet us at the reservation, and after we take care of things there, we'll start treating the mortals like the sheep they are." The crowd cheers as John leaves them with a final thought before starting down the road, "and take our place at the top of the food chain where we belong." The pack members get in the car and start driving down the road, Michael looks in the rearview mirror at his leader.

"How fast do you want to get their boss?" John lowers his glasses and looks at his second in command in the rearview mirror.

"James did as he was told, so take your time; I wanna make sure the strays in Richmond get there before we do" Michael smiles as he leads the convoy to Montana.

Henry pulls up in front of the bookstore, it was late, but the lights are on. The record keeper looks up and notices the two men standing at the door. He gets up and stretches briefly, before unlocking the door.

"You must be Henry and Spencer, please come in, I have some coffee brewing." The record keeper pours himself a cup of coffee from the coffee pot that he brought up from the basement. Neither werewolf accepts a cup, but takes a chair at the small reading table beside the counter for his patrons to use. Nothing is said for a moment until

Spencer speaks up.

"Thank you but we will not be long, Lyle should be here shortly, do you know what's going on?" Frank nods as he is eager to talk to the elder werewolves.

"I have some information, Margaret told me about Montana, and I am to call her when you head out." The record keeper takes a sip of coffee and keeps rambling, this is Frank's second pot of coffee, and the caffeine, combined with the stress of what may happen in the hours to come is starting to show. "This is an honor; we estimate that you two were born sometime in the 1830's." The two black men smile at the kind words. Henry speaks up in an effort to calm the nervous storekeeper.

"Lyle is the one you want to talk to, we're old, but he's the oldest and the toughest of us all" Frank laughs and eagerly nods.

"I have him listed at over 2500 years old, and you're right, he's one of the oldest" Spencer speaks up as he joins the conversation.

"We're going to need him," He looks to Henry across the table as each man sits, facing Frank with one elbow on the table. "You said around thirty?" Frank interrupts as Henry turns, and nods.

"The Florida packs are sitting it out, but the rest of the east coast packs are coming, including some of his contacts in Canada and the Midwest, it will be close to forty wolves" Frank said, Henry looks to the Wiccan store owner.

"How do you know all this?" Frank looks to the two men sitting at the table. Werewolves are known for being temperamental the closer it gets to the full moon, and tensions are high, given what's coming. He pauses for a moment, choosing his words carefully.

"We keep good records, I mean no disrespect," the conversation is interrupted by the opening of the front door. Frank stands up, adjusts his shirt, and respectfully places his hands in front of him as Lyle approaches the counter.

"How are you, young man? I'm assuming you're Frank?" The young Wiccan stands silent for a moment and stammers to get the words out.

"Yes, I'm Frank, and you're King Lycaon of Arcadia" the store keeper swallows nervously. "A 2500-year-old werewolf is standing in my store," Lyle smiles at his host briefly before turning his attention to his fellow werewolves.

"Are you two ready? I just gassed up the Buick so we can take that car, but one of you can drive for a while." The two men get up and head for the door, Spencer volunteers to drive and gets behind the wheel as Henry gets in the back seat. Lyle pulls two coins from his pocket and places them on the counter. Frank looks at the roman writing on the coin in disbelief. "This will easily pay for the car, and for your trouble." The elder werewolf leaves the building and enters the car. Nothing is said as the car drives down the road and heads for Montana.

It was the next night, and the werewolves had only stopped for gas and were exhausted from the long trip. Time seems to stop, and nothing is said as the three men head for the reservation. The night turns to day, but the three wolves eventually turn into the dirt road that leads to the reservation as the sun disappears from the sky. The lights of the Buick shine through the trees as it drives up to the great hall. Lyle gets out of the car with his crew and approaches the elderly Indian sitting on the porch. The chief looks up at the approaching werewolves.

"Howdy," he then points to the path that leads to the sacred land. "The ones you're looking for are up that path" Lyle takes a chair beside the old man, while Spencer and Henry stand guard.

"A lot more like me are coming, so you may want to consider gathering your people up and leaving for a while." The old man lights up a pipe and begins puffing on it, he hands the pipe to Lyle, who graciously smokes. The old man exhales and looks at Lyle.

"Soldiers came and told us we had to move a long time ago, so we ended up here. Then the government started telling us what to do. After that, a man like you guys came here and fed on us, but we stayed" The old man reaches out and accepts the pipe from Spencer, who had just smoked. "Were not leaving this time" Lyle gets up from his chair and looks to the others.

"We can sleep in the car tonight, but they'll be here tomorrow. The moon will not be full, but they'll attack at night, and then wait until the moon rises to finish it." Lyle looks down at the old man as he taps the pipe on his chair, emptying the contents on the ground. "Then they'll kill everyone and everything they see," the elder werewolf helps the old Indian up from his chair. The chief thanks him for his help and then turns to the others.

"Let em come," then enters the grand hall for the night.

Henry wakes up to the smell of meat being roasted, and looks out of the window of the large black car that served as a bed for the night. He gets out and stretches, feeling his back loosen up, as far as sleeping conditions, this was one of the better places he had slept in his many years of roaming the countryside with John and his pack.

"Wake up sleepyhead "Lyle said, Henry looks up to find Lyle sitting at a weathered picnic table near the car, talking to the tribal elders. He sits down to a cup of various leaves and berries in a cup, Kay grabs the cup and gently pours some hot water from an old metal pot. Henry looks down and smells the steam coming from his cup, the smell was surprisingly pleasant. "Just drink it, it'll get you going better than any coffee" Henry nods at Lyle's instruction before taking a sip and is pleasantly surprised.

"What's in this?" Henry said, while Lyle smiles as he takes another sip.

"Kid, when these people give you something, drink it, eat it or smoke it, but I find it best not to ask what's in it." Lyle said, Henry smiles and nods as Spencer gets out of the car struggling to get awake, he looks around searching as if he has lost something. "She's walking the woods with Joshua but she'll be back before long." Spencer walks up and accepts up the steaming cup of tea given to him and drinks, before thanking the elders.

"This has sassafras and mint in it, doesn't it?" Spencer said, the Chief looks up and nods, but doesn't say anything, as he understands that he is sitting with a pack of wolves, and needs to be cautious this close to the full moon. Spencer takes another drink as he leans against the front of the large black car "and the berries just blend well with the leaves." Lyle looks to the Chief and finishes the conversation that was started with the leader before addressing the others.

"We're going to walk the sacred valley today," the other two werewolves look to Lyle with a confused look on their faces. "John's not going to do anything until it gets dark, and I'm not much for sitting around doing nothing" Henry looks to the pack leader.

"Is one of the elders going to take us there?" Henry's question goes unanswered as Joshua's voice is heard from the distance.

"It's great to see you guys" Joshua said, Sarah runs, falling into Spencer's arms and the two lovers kiss passionately. She looks at the crew sitting at the table.

"They're coming, aren't they?" Sarah said, Lyle stands up and motions for Henry to also get up.

"Yes they are beautiful, and there's not one damned thing we can do to stop it." He looks to the other four werewolves that are his pack. "We're gonna walk the river today" he turns to Joshua. "You okay with taking another walk?"

Joshua agrees, and the five werewolves begin walking up the path to the clearing where the cabin is located. They notice Twin Bears and several men digging a large hole and walk up to the large pile of dried brush sitting beside the large hole. Lyle looks down at the large hole, "In case you're wondering, this is a grave to bury the dead." The werewolves also notice an unfamiliar smell that fills the air, Lyle laughs. "It's grease from the animals they kill; they let it ferment, then use it to start fires," he turns to Twin Bears who have stopped digging, "The five of us"

Twin Bears smiles and points to Spencer and Sarah walking into the cabin holding hands, "make that the three of us are walking the river today."

Spencer and Sarah enter the shack and close the door behind them. The two lovers quickly get undressed and lay on the blankets spread across the dirt floor. Sarah looks up at the muscular black man on top of her. She was promised to her deceased husband as a teenager, so she never fell in love or was courted, it was similar to honoring a contract. She never had the same feelings for her husband like she has for Spencer. The two remain on the ground and continue to be intimate with each other until Spencer rolls over on his back. Sarah immediately presses herself against him and strokes his chest and stomach. Spencer holds her close as he enjoys feeling her nude body pressed against him.

"I love you, Sarah" is the only thing that is said as Sarah gets up and begins to get dressed. She walks over to the only window in the shack while she buttons her shirt. Spencer walks over to his lover and pulls her to him, wrapping his arms around her as she falls into him, stroking his forearm, which is now covering her chest.

"I love you too, Spencer" she turns and looks into his eyes. "We can't win, can we?" Spencer leans into his lover and kisses her gently. The black man thinks about his past, and how he struggled after his wife and child were killed as slaves, and how he was filled with so much hate. He calmed down but remained angry, until she walked into the restaurant. He has helped a lot of werewolves and other supernatural types, but something was different with this woman. In time he came to know what it was to love someone again, and his happiest moments were waking up beside her and starting every day making love to her.

"I would rather die with the woman I love than live without you" nothing more is said as the lovers look out the window, holding each other.

The other three werewolves walk until they reach the river's edge, Henry looks up and is in awe of the view.

"It's beautiful and very peaceful," Joshua begins leading the other two to the tears of the river. They walk for a while and stop at some large boulders. Lyle stops and sits down on one of the rocks before looking at the other two.

"This is far enough, I just wanted to talk to everyone before tonight" Joshua and Henry take a seat, facing Lyle on the remaining rocks. "I've been around a long time and most of my life was spent in the old country" the ancient Alpha crosses his arms while he continues. "I woke up this way, I was a lousy king, and to be honest, a terrible husband and father." Joshua looks up to his leader and tries to console him in some small way.

"You helped mama and me, if it wasn't for you, I would've died." Lyle leans back and grins at Joshua.

"I've helped a lot of people kid, but there was a time when me and another older werewolf terrorized the countryside. We didn't care who we changed or the consequences of our actions," Lyle looks out to the rolling water and continues, "we heard rumors that the new world had settled down, and one of us needed to come over here and take care of things. Europe was overrun with vampires, werewolves, and other not-so-friendly creatures." Henry looks to the elder werewolf but hesitates to say something as he is still worried that Lyle doesn't like him.

"Why are you the one that came over? Why didn't you send someone?" Lyle hesitates briefly before answering the question.

"It was my decision to make, I am one of only two red eyes, but I wanted to leave my homeland. Everywhere I looked, I saw my shame. I woke up on a cross and saw my family dead, but I had children from other women, most were hunted down and killed. I hope that some survived, but I haven't smelled anything that feels familiar yet." Both younger werewolves look to Lyle with a confused look on their faces. The elder werewolf looks and sighs," you two don't know a damned thing, do you? Red Eyes are the last in line, most black werewolves have yellow eyes, but red eyes are rare. As a matter of fact, the other red eye is older than me, but that's another story." The eldest wolf gathers his thoughts for a moment before continuing, "being a werewolf doesn't make you evil, but make no mistake, this is a fight between good and evil my friends, and if that arrogant piece of shit wins, there will be war. John will start killing mortals, the witches will step in, and when it reaches the west coast, Chang will declare war. Vampires and werewolves will be fighting, and using mortals as cattle to replace their ranks, but things are not lost, or what they may appear to be." Joshua nervously agrees before he turns his attention to Henry.

"So John kicked you out because of me and mama?" Henry nods as he looks at the two men.

"John realized that I had lost my loyalty to the pack. I stayed to watch over my brother, but I fear he is like the others now. I never ate humans as I feared what I would become, but James was different when he called." Henry turns his attention to Joshua, "he sounded evil, and I know in my heart he has eaten man, something that Anna or I would never do. She protected you more than you realize; we never hunted deer before you joined the pack, Anna would sneak off and find us something or get something when we stopped at a store." Joshua looks dumbfounded as Lyle speaks up.

"I've had my eye on John's pack for years, I took a vow not to kill my own kind, but this guy is a virus all over the country for our people. Most that he changed ended up dead, and I managed to get some of the good ones settled in." Lyle turns his attention to Joshua "there are a lot of people like us out there and they have families, marry mortals, adopt children and live their lives. I show up and get them through the bad times, but some hard decisions needed to be made," Joshua swallows and fears what he is about to be told. "You darkened up quick, as far as werewolves go, so I suspect you'll be red-eye at some point. The other guy and I stopped eating people years ago, but a young red-eye, with blood in his mouth from eating humans, could be dangerous for everyone, and would be a lot bigger problem than John Bennett." Henry reaches over and places his hand on Joshua's shoulder.

"It's nothing to worry about, everyone knows you're a good man," the ex-pack member looks to Lyle, "but if you were not going to kill him, who would have?" Lyle scratches his head and stretches a bit.

"The Indians and our old buddy Chang had your number; I may have asked them to take you out if needed." Joshua doesn't say anything for several minutes, trying to process things. Lyle leans into his pack member and laughs briefly. "Twin Bears is the designated protector of these lands my boy, and he didn't kill you, even when you were screwing his daughter, and Chang wouldn't keep inviting you to his house if he was gonna kill you, so I think you're good." Lyle stands up and adjusts himself, "our kind damned near killed all these people years ago, and they have been trying to get on their feet since." The elder werewolf begins walking back to the cabin, "so it's gonna be made right tonight" the others stand up but do not move. Lyle turns to the others, "Are you two coming or what?" Both werewolves remain silent until Joshua speaks up.

"How is it gonna be set right? You and me are the only two werewolves, other than John who can turn tonight." The former Mennonite looks down at the ground, trying to stay composed, "you vowed not to harm your own kind, but I'm pretty sure none of John's pack made that same vow." Lyle smiles at the two wolves, but is silent for a few moments, he understands the fear that these two men are feeling, he had those feelings often when he was mortal. Only a crazy or arrogant individual would run into battle, unafraid of dying, but fear makes a warrior dangerous, and the will to live keeps them sharp. The two men standing before the elder wolf has been through a lot, more than most could handle, and Lyle can't help but question if they want to live.

"Things have a way of working out" when you live for thousands of years, you get a feeling for people, and Lyle is a master of reading people. He looks to the men who are visibly afraid. "But you have to want to live, you have to want it worse than anything else, and be willing to do whatever it takes to win." The military leader looks to the inexperienced soldiers standing in front of him. "John has taken almost everything from both of you...except your honor" both men look at each other, realizing that this is it, there's nowhere to go, and no more places to hide. Lyle looks at the two warriors standing in front of him. "Are you gonna let that son of a bitch take that too?"

It was early, so no one rushed to get back to the cabin. The three werewolves stop frequently, and Lyle is happy to provide answers to any questions asked. He tells them about Europe and the other red-eye, the vampire wars, and running through fields while mortals were shooting at him as he fled. Henry was especially curious and continued to ask questions, that were immediately answered, and the three emerge from the field as brothers. They walk past the large hole that has been dug but do not see anyone. The smell left the area, and all that remained was the oil-soaked brush that surrounds the sacred land. They approach the cabin and are greeted by Spencer and Sarah. Henry looks around and smiles at Joshua, who is lagging behind "Why don't we sit outside? The cabin looks to be small" Lyle, who is standing beside Henry, laughs as he shouts down the valley, "Take your time; I think Spencer and your mother are finished." Sarah looks down at the ground, red-faced, as Spencer looks to the elder werewolf and grins as he continues to hold his lover. Joshua walks past the others and smiles.

"I'm gonna check on the Chief and the others" he walks to the great hall but does not find anyone. Joshua proceeds to walk down the row of shacks that make up the mountain village, until he reaches the rundown schoolhouse. He continues to survey the area, looking beyond the village to the woods that surround the community, but finds no one. No smells or sounds are present, not even a heartbeat rings in his ears. Joshua continues to look around as he walks back to the others. "It's a ghost town down there and I didn't see or hear anyone." Spencer looks to the dirt path that leads to the lower valley.

"So it's the five of us against forty?" Spencer said, Sarah tries to console her irritated lover but is unsuccessful. The black man releases Sarah from his arms and stands with his hands on his hips, then looks to Lyle as he tries to stay calm. "Are you gonna man up and take care of things? Most of them cannot change until tomorrow, so you can kill the others while Joshua takes on John and gets the satisfaction of killing that arrogant son of a bitch."

Lyle turns to the people around him with a stubborn look, "I will not harm my own kind." Joshua begins to bite his lower lip as the stress of everything begins to show on his face. He was hoping that Lyle would take care of things but was starting to realize that this may be the end of them. He takes a deep breath and composes himself before speaking.

"I have only taken one life and it was a very nice woman that I killed years ago, when I had just been turned. I have prayed for forgiveness about her passing, and take no joy in hurting anyone, including John." Henry looks to his friend with a solemn look.

"You didn't kill that woman, John did" Joshua looks to the man that helped him when they were members of John's pack for so many years, stunned at what he had just heard.

"Why didn't you say something? I've carried that with me for years. WHY?" Joshua stands defiantly as Henry struggles to find the words.

"Because no one goes against the pack leader, I am sorry my friend." Henry and Joshua begin to argue as

Joshua looks to his former mentor, more upset than angry.

"You could have said something, I spoke with you about that, and you just stood there." Henry remains calm as years of running in a pack have changed his perspective. Spencer joins the two men and attempts to explain things.

"When the senior ranking office tells you to keep quiet, you keep your mouth shut, it's no different than when I served in the union army." Sarah rushes to her son's defense, and before long, all four werewolves are arguing. The stress of what's coming is starting to show, but this isn't unusual, and Lyle remains silent, listening to everyone's concerns. Spencer finally throws up his hands and in a disgusted tone, voices his concerns.

"I don't know why we're here if no one is willing to get their hands dirty" Sarah looks to the man she loves with her arms crossed.

"It's not Joshua or my way to take life, and Lyle took a vow" the others continue to argue, and the fear in everyone's voices can be heard. Lyle steps back and places two fingers in his mouth, whistling loudly.

"SHUT UP!" everyone quiets down as the senior werewolf sighs. "I've been in battle more than anyone here, and most will fold up when the shit hits the fan. Spencer and I are the only ones that have been in combat, and that's just not enough. You're right, I can take 'em all out, including John, but I'll lose a hell of lot more that I'll gain." The others stand silent as their leader continues, "I'm, gonna see my wife again one day, so running wild isn't an option." The senior Lycan steps back and looks at the scared wolves that stand before him, "I'm asking for a little faith, and for all of you to trust me, I think I've earned that much."

The others are silent for the rest of the day, Lyle has helped all of them at some point, and they owe him a lot. Waiting is hard, but waiting with the uncertainty of what's coming, is almost unbearable. Sarah's time is spent between consoling her son and her beloved. Henry doesn't say much as he spends his final hours as he has spent most of his life, in silence, thinking about his life and wondering if this is the end. Lyle sits on the small stool leaning against the wooden shack, asleep. The sun begins its descent as it does at the end of each day. Henry looks up from the river, takes a final look at the mountain, and walks back to join the others. Lyle stands up, stretches, and looks around in an attempt to awaken. "I could use some of that tea about now" Lyle said, Spencer looks to his leader.

"They should be here before long" Lyle looks down the mountain with a determined look.

"They're already here; I can hear them down at the base of the mountain waiting to come up when it gets dark," Henry finally joins the others. The pack leader looks at the newcomer. "You okay? Is your head right?" Henry nods, then turns and walks to Joshua extending his hand.

"I lost my brother to John, but I took some comfort knowing that I have another brother. I will not lose him too," Joshua grips his friend's hand and stares him in the eye.

"You haven't" is all that is said as the two embraces waiting for the others to attack.

The five individuals that are now a family stand defiantly, as the group of fellow werewolves emerge from the woods. John walks arrogantly with the others following and stands at the large hole, he looks to Michael and laughs.

"I like it when they dig their own graves" laughter erupts from the pack of forty-two wolves. Lyle stands in front of the four individuals, who are standing at the side of the small shack, unfazed at the arrogance coming from the crowd in the clearing. The sun finally rests for the night, and with no moon, darkness falls over the valley. Everyone can see clearly as the full moon is coming the next day, and senses are high. John emerges from the large crowd with Michael, Bram, and James following. Antonio and a nervous Bishop also join John at the head of the large crowd. The pack leader looks up at the five individuals standing at the small cabin above him. "I'm not an unreasonable man, and I had high hopes for Joshua, but you ended up being more trouble than you're worth" he looks to the small group standing beside his former member. "You know he's the reason that Anna had to die," Joshua lunges forward but is caught by Henry.

"We would've left and never came back! You didn't have to kill her" John looks to his former pack member.

"She was my property, and you took her, I told you to do one thing, be loyal to the pack, but all you wanted to do is bend her over every rock you saw and fuck her." John grits his teeth and looks with a lowered brow. "She died like the whore she was, and it's ALL YOUR FAULT!" Spencer places his hand on Sarah pushing her behind him.

"Get behind me" John looks up and turns his attention to the couple.

"Now, don't be shy Sarah, I have big plans for you,

your son took my woman, so I figure your family owes me another one." The arrogant pack leader steps forward and is now in front of his pack. "So after I get done breaking you in, I'm gonna see if someone here can get a baby to grow in that belly of yours." John laughs and raises his arms, "I may just get a collar and make you my little pet." Lyle turns and looks as tears stream down Sarah's face. He steps forward with his hands in his pockets and calmly looks down at John.

"You are really in love with the sound of your own voice, aren't you?" The elder werewolf removes his hands from his pockets and crosses them. "But every time you open your mouth, all anyone hears is an asshole" the red eyed alpha sighs a bit as he continues," but not just an asshole, an extremely stupid asshole." The two-pack leaders lock eyes as John replies to Lyle's taunts.

"I've asked around about you, the oldest of us all, King Lycaon of Arcadia." He points to the elder werewolf as he turns to his pack, "that's what happens when you're not man enough to embrace your destiny; you just crawl off and become a nobody." Lyle stands emotionless, unconcerned about John's reply, infuriating the smug leader. "I've also heard about your vow not to hurt any other werewolves so you may possibly find a comfortable spot in hell." The arrogant leader laughs and shrugs his shoulders "good luck with that." John pauses for a moment to admire the fear on everyone's face, confident that he will be the leader of all the packs, after killing the five werewolves standing in front of him. "Look around people, who's gonna lead us, a pussy farm boy, or a useless washed-up old wolf with no teeth" Lyle looks down at the crowd in front of him, unafraid.

"That was supposed to be the emissary's job, but you decided to kill Anna and her unborn baby because your seed didn't seem to be enough to make a baby." John's face turns red, and an uncomfortable silence fills the air for several minutes until the well-dressed leader calms down.

"An example needed to be made, they didn't follow my orders, so something needed to be done." John looks directly at Henry, who has remained quiet. "If you need a reason why I did it, just look at that traitor." The mob of werewolves looks to the former member, but the only one Henry looks at, is his brother, who is standing proudly with his pack. John immediately points at James and laughs, "by all means, take a good look at a future pack leader and he's darker now, thanks to me." Henry steps forward and looks down at the men he protected for so many years.

"My soul is not worth a darker shade of fur, and I stand proudly with honorable people." Henry continues to look at the large pack of wolves, trying to stay composed. "I know my mama and papa is proud of me," Lyle turns to the distraught wolf with a look of pride, any concerns about the former pack member vanished, and at that moment, the disgraced wolf became family.

"You don't owe them anything, Henry" Lyle said, the eldest of all the werewolves steps forward, and removes his hat, allowing his long curly hair to fall to both sides of his face, before looking to the black sky above them. Everyone is waiting for Lyle to do something and steps back when he lowers his head, displaying his red eyes. "I did make a vow, and it's worked out so far, but I know some others that made a few vows of their own." The oldest of all the werewolves turns to the people behind him. "This isn't our fight guys, we're just spectators here," Lyle turns and steps away from his pack until he is standing alone. "Sometimes being a hero is being brave enough to step aside and let someone else set things right." The senior wolf places two fingers in his mouth and whistles loudly. Chief Gray Wolf and Twin Bears soon emerge from the woods with yellow and red paint covering their face and torso. John looks and laughs, turning around to make sure he is the center of attention.

"That's your backup?" The Chief attempts to raise his arrow, but is unsuccessful as the bow and arrow fall to the ground. John continues to laugh at the two Native Americans, "This is almost sad to watch." He looks to Lyle shaking his head, "it's not even silver" Michael looks around and looks to the arrogant leader, concerned.

"This doesn't feel right boss, we need to kill these people and get the hell out of here." Twin Bears pick up the bow and arrow, and waits, as his father pours some goo from a pouch on the arrow, and ignites it. The future chief raises the arrow, shooting it high in the air. John looks up, shaking his head, and ignoring a concerned Michael.

"We're gonna eat good tonight after we kill all these people, something I should have done the last time I was here." Lyle looks at the small group standing at the small shack.

"Years ago, the people of this land asked me not to interfere, and grant them the honor of facing their enemy in battle, to allow the spirits of their ancestors to soar" Lyle said.

The woods appear to move as yellow, and red faces emerge from the woods. Everyone look as the Native Americans surround the open area. The chief nods as torches are dropped in the small trench surrounding the area, igniting the grease and brush. Lyle looks to the stunned crew standing with him, mesmerized by the flickering light from the fire, which now surrounds the open area of the sacred valley.

"I've seen a lot of warriors worry about dying in battle, but honorable people should never fear death." The Greek king slowly turns his attention to the large pack standing in the open field and sighs, "Death should only concern the evil."

The elderly chief is assisted by his son, as he steps forward, and raises a staff, topped with feathers and covered in the same paint that adorns the attacking tribe's faces. The Native Americans raise their arrows and points at the large crowd of werewolves, gathered at the newly dug hole. The elderly chief stands in front of his son, and with lips trembling, speaks, "you are not welcome here." Chief Grey Wolf stands defiantly and lowers his staff, alerting his tribe to attack. John turns as members of his pack start falling to the ground, and the smell of burning flesh fills the air from the silver arrows plunging into the attacking wolves. Michael slumps down on top of his Alpha with several arrows protruding from him, attempting to save his leader. John looks into his dead Beta's eyes, before using his second in command as a shield as he runs from the sacred valley. The disgraced leader lifts his dead Beta into the air, and throws him into the Native Americans standing in front of the dirt path leading down the mountain, shoving them backward, as he runs down the path. Joshua looks and begins running toward the evil pack leader. Sarah starts to follow, but is stopped by Spencer, who looks at her shaking his head.

"Not this time baby, this is his fight" the Native Americans lower their arrows as Joshua runs past them, determined to reach his former leader. He soon reaches the disgraced Alpha but is startled when John grabs him and throws him through the small shack that Twin Bears calls home. The inexperienced werewolf staggers and looks up to see his enemy running toward him. Joshua attempts to defend himself, but finds himself being thrown through the brush, and into the Buick that is parked in front of the great hall. Joshua struggles to breathe as his sides begin to ache from his broken ribs. The younger werewolf looks up to see an outraged John leaping at him.

"Remember these?" Joshua screams in pain as a silver arrow is shoved into his shoulder. John picks up the struggling wolf and begins slamming him into the side of the large black car. The evil pack leader stands defiantly in front of his injured former pack member that is struggling to stand. "I should have cut your head off when I had the chance," John continues to pummel his former pack member, "but I'll take care of that this time." Joshua roars and shoves his attacker backward, but John is quick to grab the arrow and twist, causing the younger wolf to cry in pain. The two black wolves lock eyes.

"You didn't deserve her, you son of a bitch" John soon realizes that this is not the same man he knew years ago.

"Spare me choirboy, I'll come back stronger with a pack that does what I tell em' to do" Joshua begins to move forward as the two continue to wrestle.

"It's over John, they're all dead, just like papa, Liam, and Anna" John looks into Joshua's eyes with an insane look.

"Don't forget about the little baby Josh that was growing inside that bitch." The young werewolf feels his enemy's claws dig into him and begins to fall backward as John's teeth begin to sharpen and hair grows from his face. Joshua roars but soon finds himself on the ground with John on top of him, almost fully changed, and screams as John bites into the forearm that fails to protect a struggling Joshua. The young wolf soon feels the silver running through his veins, one of the first lessons that was learned was to never change with silver in you. A werewolf can live for a very long time, but Joshua didn't need a hundred years, he only needed an hour. John looks surprised as the man beneath him begins to grow and is tossed into the wooded area surrounding the sacred land. The former Mennonite stands up and grabs the arrow with his good hand, and pulls it from his throbbing shoulder, with tears in his eyes. Joshua looks up at the light flickering through the trees and roars as he begins to grow even larger. The evil pack leader looks down at the growing figure approaching him and growls. Both men have fully changed, but John backs up into the clearing where his pack has just been eliminated. Joshua leaps into the clearing and rips into John, who counters by slashing into the other black werewolf's midsection, tossing him closer to the fire. No one interferes as Joshua stands up and roars as he catches an overconfident John in midair and slams him to the ground. Images of the distraught young man's father and brother fill his mind but soon switch to a bloodied Anna holding a dead baby. All the rage that has been building inside him for so many years comes out, and Joshua begins slashing into John with no mercy. The other's look at the two werewolves fighting and, for the first time, are visibly fearful of the passive young man's rage. Joshua stands up and roars at the night sky, before looking down at John with eyes that have changed from amber to red, and a low growl emerges from the black wolf, to the beaten and bloodied former leader, who has changed back to human form. Joshua raises his arm, baring his claws and sharpened teeth at the arrogant leader.

"STOP IT" Joshua looks up from a defeated John, with tears in his eyes, to see his mother standing in front of him. "This is not our way, sweetie" Sarah steps forward at the head of the beaten man lying on the ground and places her hands on her son's bloodied, fur-covered stomach. "I know more than anyone what you've been through," the overgrown, bloodied wolf looks at his mother, unsure of what to do, the blonde-haired woman looks up at her son with tears in her eyes. "But it won't bring her back or give you peace, honey" Sarah's lips continue to tremble as she speaks to her son, "give it to God...and let it go." Joshua begins to change back and is soon struggling to stand due to his injuries. Henry runs to the beaten man that he calls brother, and helps him stand upward with the help of Spencer, who has grabbed his other arm. Sarah places her hand on both sides of his face and kisses him as she cries. "It's over son, it's over" Joshua looks into his mothers eyes.

"She was pretty, wasn't she?" Sarah places a blanket around her son's nude body while the young man struggles to speak. "I would've made a good papa, but no one gave me a chance." Lyle approaches his fellow red-eyed werewolf and looks him up and down with a look of concern.

"Be careful, but take him down to the great hall," the four surviving werewolves help Joshua to the structure, away from where the bodies are burning. Henry lowers his head and prays briefly for his brother, before assisting Joshua.

John struggles to get up, but is quickly kicked back to the ground. He turns to see his pack members being beheaded and thrown into the large hole, where the fire continues to burn. He looks upward to find Lyle, the chief, and Twin Bears standing over him. Kajika soon joins them with a large axe that was used to behead the other members of his pack.

"I'm better than all of you, and I run in front of the pack," the former pack leader looks as Kajika raises the axe. "Go to hell" is the last word that comes from John's mouth as the axe is lowered. A thud is heard, and John's head soon rolls down the embankment toward the fire. The Native Americans toss the evil wolf into the burning brush pile with the others. Everyone is quiet around the fire and no one cheers or proclaims victory. The Chief begins walking slowly to the others and points to the fire, instructing his son and grandson what to do next.

"We will wait until the fire is out before covering the bodies," the elderly leader turns to Lyle. "Their spirits must not soar and we will bury them to make sure of that," Lyle nods, and leaves the area to check on Joshua, who is now lying in front of the great hall, with his mother sitting on the ground beside him, while the others instinctively stand at various places around the wounded family member.

"I think he has some clothes behind the seat of the truck" Spencer rushes to the truck, and eventually finds the clothes that Sarah asked about. Henry leaves, but immediately returns with a bucket of water and a clean cloth. Sarah begins to wipe off the bloodied man that is sitting in front of her. She looks at the deep puncture wounds on her son's shoulder and forearm, as well as the large gashes across his stomach and begins to cry, "please God, don't take another son." Everyone looks at the injured wolf with concern; only silver or losing your head can kill them, but Joshua has been severely beaten and may have given up. Everyone's attention shifts from their injured family member to lights from a vehicle, shining brightly up the dirt road that leads to the small mountain community. A Jeep pulls beside the wrecked black Buick, shining its bright lights on the crew surrounding the injured man. Spencer and Henry stand in front of their wounded friend, ready to defend but relax a bit when they hear a familiar voice.

"Please get out of the light, I need it to see how severe his injuries are," the two men step aside as a pregnant Dawn rushes to help, with her husband lagging behind. She looks at her former lover and gently wipes water over the lacerations that cover his stomach. Blood continues to seep out of the cuts, and the gorgeous Native American looks up to her husband, who is now standing beside her. "Andrew, these are deep, and his shoulder doesn't look too good either." The sandy-haired doctor looks down at his wife, who continues to wipe down the wounded man's injuries.

"We should get him to the hospital, in a sterile environment. Someone should call an ambulance" Dawn stands up and looks to her husband and fellow doctor.

"There aren't any phones up here, and we can't take him to the hospital" everyone focuses on the two doctors. Andrew knows about the affair but could not comment on it as it was his indiscretion that caused them to break up. Dawn is an emergency room doctor, but Andrew is a general surgeon. All doctors take an oath to do no harm, but no one said anything about stitching up the man who screwed your wife on an Indian reservation. Dawn reaches out and holds her husband's hand, "I can't stitch him up by myself, honey." The bearded doctor turns and walks away, but soon returns with a large black bag.

"We should start by giving him a few locals in his midsection, forearm, and one in his shoulder. I'll start closing the deeper cuts and then stitch the lacerations." Dawn looks and smiles at the man that she has learned to love for a second time.

"I'll start with his shoulder while you start on his stomach" Dawn said.

Spencer looks to the doctors that have started to tend to their patient. "Who called you to come?" a voice comes from the darkness.

"I did, I told her to come a few hours after the sun goes down." Lyle said, as he walks up to the small crew of people standing in the light after answering Spencer's question. Dawn looks to the flickering light coming from the trees that surround the sacred valley, but says nothing about the fire or the smell of burning flesh that now fills the air. Andrew looks up and wipes the sweat from his forehead.

"Is this an Indian ritual that went wrong?" The talented surgeon sniffs a bit, "and what's that smell?"

The fire that surrounds the clearing had extinguished, but the fire burning the bodies was still roaring, and offered little light to the ones at the great hall. Dawn advised her husband to remain quiet, and work on the patient. Andrew looks around at the small crowd of people that surround Joshua, and continues stitching up his patient. Dawn looks up to the pack members standing guard.

"Get out of the light and see if the lights on that car still work" the attractive doctor returns to Joshua but gives a final order. "I have another bag in the Jeep; please get it and the bag of gauze lying beside it." She looks to Sarah and hands her a clean cloth, "I need you to wipe him down as much as possible and keep him calm." Spencer rushes to retrieve the supplies from the Jeep, while Sarah does as instructed, and begins wiping the sweat from her son as she speaks to him. Joshua looks up to his former lover, glassy-eyed and in shock from his injuries.

"I saved the baby Anna, you and the baby are safe" Dawn strokes the injured man and smiles softly before turning to her husband, who smiles back at her. Andrew looks down at the injured man and truly feels for him, he lost Dawn for a few weeks, but losing her and their unborn child would be unbearable. The talented doctor continues to stitch while speaking to his wife.

"Give him a shot for infection. I would also get something in him for the pain." Dawn does as instructed and immediately fills a syringe. She looks around at the crew, who continue to stand guard. Andrew is new to this world, but she is very much aware of the situation. She knows what's burning up on the hill, and she also knows what may happen if he should die. She has come to consider the people that are standing around her as friends but is also aware that she is standing with a pack of wolves, tending to an injured member of the pack.

"This will help with the pain and numb the area" Dawn injects the needle into the man who used to be her lover. Joshua growls a bit, bearing his teeth while his eyes turn red. Andrew falls back shaking, holding his hands up.

"What the hell was that?" Dawn looks up to her husband.

"Daddy and I will sit you down and tell you everything, but we're almost done, and I still need you to help him." Andrew leans forward and recommends strapping him down, he reaches for his arms, but is immediately stopped by Dawn. "Not his wrists or his neck, it will do more harm than good, and he'll kill you before he knows what's happening, just trust me." She leans in and kisses Joshua softly.

"I'm proud of you for saving me and the baby" tears fill her eyes as she continues to speak to Joshua in a soft, calming tone. "But I need you to be still while I take care of you," Joshua does as instructed, and lies silently as the doctors finally finish tending to his injuries, and cover his injuries with gauze. Lyle hands the doctor's a bag of salve and instructs them to rub some on his shoulder. Dawn immediately coats the wound on her patients shoulder while Andrew inspects Joshua's sides.

"I think he may have some cracked ribs, but who knows without any x rays." Andrew says.

Twin Bears walks up to the others, checking on the protectors of his land. "How's he doing?" his daughter finishes wrapping his midsection with gauze, then stands up and hugs her father.

"He's stable and the bleeding has stopped, we gave

him something for the pain but he has severe impact injuries and has lost a lot of blood" Dawn looks down at injured wolf and attempts to hide her concern. "A normal man would have died but we'll have to wait and see how he's doing tomorrow," Twin Bears looks at Andrew and nods slightly.

"Thank you for tending to one of our warriors" Twin Bears said, Dawn looks at the two most important men in her life.

"We have a lot to talk about, and Andrew needs to hear our story" "Twin Bears nods proudly, while his daughter instructs the werewolves surrounding her."We can't move him very far, his injuries are too severe," Twin Bears looks to the rest of the pack.

"If someone can get him dressed, I'll get something for him to lay on." Dawn reaches down and begins wiping the blood off his legs. She grabs a pair of dark green pants from the ground while her father leaves.

Twin bears soon returns with a cot from the shack that Joshua and his mother shared. Kajika also returns, carrying an armful of blankets. Joshua is laid down on the cot and covered with a blanket. The others gently raise him up as Dawn, and her mother pulls the loose-fitting trousers up and gets him dressed. The young doctor looks to the small group of werewolves as she continues to wipe the blood off her hands and forearms. "He needs to rest, but do not move him until the cuts on his stomach close."

Sarah immediately grabs a chair and sits it beside her son, who has passed out. "I'll sit with him" Spencer leans down until he is at eye level with his lover.

"We can take turns sitting with him, this isn't all on you" the others nod in agreement but all hover around the injured werewolf, refusing to leave. Lyle looks up the ridge to see that the fire had died down before looking at the others.

"I don't think any of us will be getting much sleep tonight anyway," The elder werewolf walks up to the two doctors. "You helped one of my children and I am indebted to you both, If either of you ever need anything, just ask." Lyle leans up against Joshua's blue truck as the two doctors leave, watching the lights of the jeep fade into the distance, before taking a chair beside the injured man. Spencer takes a seat on the ground beside Sarah as Henry grabs the last seat. Kajika approaches the pack, with a large flattened rock and sits it on the corner post of the great hall. He stops in front of the crew that is sitting around a wounded Joshua, and makes two simple hand gestures before pointing to the rock. All turn and notice a diamond with two circles inside the symbol painted on the sandstone rock. Sarah wraps her arm around the teenager; in his culture, anyone that has faced an enemy in battle is now a warrior and a man.

"Thank you, Kajika" Sarah rubs his bareback that still has remnants of yellow paint as she consoles him, "he'll be okay." The young man turns to the others and nods, leaving as quietly as he came. Nothing is said for several minutes as the pack gets lost in their thoughts. No one is sure what to say, and is still concerned about the fate of the severely beaten man on the cot. Spencer attempts to break the uncomfortable silence.

"Any idea what the hand signals and that symbol means?" Twin Bears attempts to explain but is interrupted by a soft, frail voice coming from the darkness.

"It's the eye of the Great Spirit and it watches over his pack tonight, the hand signals simply mean brave wolf." The Chief walks slowly and joins the others. Henry stands up and is quick to give the leader his chair, who graciously accepts, "he will protect you and heal his injured *tala*." The elderly leader looks down at Joshua, "I swore the same oath that my father and grandfathers took to kill the wendigo when they return." He sits quietly for a moment with his son standing quietly behind him, "my son will have a different path when he becomes chief, he will be the one to bring prosperity to our people." The Chief stands up with assistance from his son, Twin Bears looks at the group that is hovering around Joshua.

"Please let us know if you need anything; you are all welcome here."

CHAPTER THIRTEEN

Joshua looks down at the row of newly built homes from the roof of the schoolhouse that has just been renovated. It's been about five years since his fight with John, and all that is left of his wounds are scars, and the memory of how he received them. Sarah and Spencer returned to the diner, and business was good. Lyle stayed for a few weeks and removed the abandoned cars from the reservation before he left. Dawn asked him to help her people, and Lyle was as good as his word. He bought all the supplies needed and also left enough money to help out in the future. Joshua turned to Henry, who remained with him at Lyle's request. "That's the last of it."

"And not a bad job considering we had to figure it out as we went," The two werewolves laugh briefly before descending to the ground on the aluminum ladder. They walk up the dirt path, stopping to talk to the Native American's that approach them as they stroll up the small hill, and soon reach the top of the slope. The two construction workers enter the grand hall through the new wood door, and walk proudly past the freshly painted drywall. Cement slabs were poured for most of the construction, but the great hall required a wood floor to be built on top of footers, so the floor creaks a bit. The two werewolves join Twin Bears at the long wood table that sits in the center of the large room. Joshua looks up from his chair at the recently appointed leader.

"Chief Twin Bears, we just finished, and all the houses are built, including the outhouses" Twin Bears nods at the two men that have become a member of his tribe.

"Everything except your home on the hill" the red-eyed werewolf looks around the large room and sighs.

"It didn't seem right to change anything up there" The Chief smiles and agrees with the two men that he considers family. Twin Bears shakes his head and points to the almond-colored phone that sits at the far corner of the building.

"Why did you insist on putting a phone in the great hall that no one will use?" Joshua sits and laughs with Henry and the newly appointed leader. Chief Grey wolf died a few months ago, and Twin Bears was soon appointed as the Chief.

"In case I need to call you, so please pick up the phone when it rings." The three men sit and stare at the large stone fireplace, quietly, until the chief turns to the werewolves.

"You gave my people and my father the greatest gift anyone could give," Twin Bears looks to the large war staff that his father used to fight John Bennett's pack, hanging proudly on the wall. "This is your home, and you are always welcome here, but I think the time has come for you to return to Virginia." Joshua looks to Henry, who nods in agreement with Twin Bears. He walks to the phone but hesitates to pick up the receiver as a flood of thoughts rush through his head. His mother has Spencer, and Lyle shows up anytime he wants. Every woman he meets never ends well, so maybe he is destined to be alone. Henry has been as loyal a friend as anyone could be, but he deserves someone to love, and maybe all that Joshua can hope for, is a lifetime of loneliness. The black werewolf turns and looks at his friends, who are still seated. Twin Bears sat with him as he healed and is a trusted friend. Joshua and Henry officiated at his father's burial, guarding the fallen warrior;

both stood guard at the gravesite for weeks until Chief Grey wolf's spirit soared, the gesture was ceremonial, but the two werewolves did this with pride. Henry has fought with Joshua and is the only person he can talk to about the events of the past, Henry is also one of the few people that can talk openly to the red eyed wolf. He walks over to his friend and hands the phone to a struggling Joshua.

"It's time" Joshua takes the phone from his friend's hand and calls the restaurant. A familiar voice comes over the phone, Joshua stammers a bit before speaking.

"Hello mama, could someone come to get Henry and me?" Sarah stands behind the counter of the renovated restaurant. She and Spencer purchased the building next to the restaurant and expanded. The new and improved Spencer's offered a separate bar area, additional seating, and a much-needed makeover, with off-white walls and blue table cloths that cover the new tables and chairs. Word of the down-home cooking spread and business is good. When news of John's pack being eliminated reached the east coast, the werewolves returned to the establishment. The new and improved restaurant offers a hidden room for vampires, and any other supernatural creatures that do not mesh well with mortals. This was Lyle's idea, and considering he paid for the improvements, including the upstairs apartment that Spencer and Sarah share, no one refused his request, and given who he is, no one wanted to dispute him. The blonde woman smiles softly.

"Of course honey, someone will come and get you" Sarah motions for Spencer to join her at the register, as she returns the receiver to its home on top of the phone. She reaches up and kisses her man. "He wants to come home" Spencer looks down with a concerned look.

"Is his head right? No one was allowed to disturb him until he wanted to come back to us" Sarah nods as her lover kisses her forehead.

"I'll do whatever it takes for him," the blonde co-owner of Spencer's does nothing to hide her excitement. "But the main thing is he's coming back to me," Spencer motions for Rodney to join them from behind the bar. The clean-shaven, well-dressed bartender comes over and joins his employers at the front of the restaurant. The three werewolves stand briefly as Sarah reaches out and hugs Rodney.

"He wants to come home Rodney, he just called" Spencer reaches under the counter and hands Rodney a set of keys.

"We're swamped here with the addition and training the staff. Could you go to Montana and get him? It will take a few days" the bartender grabs the keys and nods.

"It would be an honor boss." Spencer walks outside with Rodney, pointing to the modest Chevrolet car parked behind the restaurant. Staying inconspicuous is a way of life for werewolves, and this will never change. Rodney takes his place behind the wheel of the medium blue four-door Impala. Spencer leans in and tells his employee about the pistol under the seat with a clip for mortals, and a clip for not so mortal enemies. " I got this boss, I'll get him home" Spencer gives some additional instructions, before handing Rodney a roll of money, then steps back and watches as his car leaves the parking lot.

Joshua and Henry sit outside the building that he and his mother called home for a few years. The two sit outside the shack and enjoy sitting in the shade that the building provides from the sun. Most of their time was spent building homes with little time to dwell on the past. Over the years, Henry has become extremely good at reading people. He looks at his friend, who sits quietly on the wooden chairs that used to sit in front of the great hall, staring at the ground in front of him.

"You do not look like a man who is going to see his family in a few days, my friend," Joshua snaps out of his trance and looks to his closest friend.

"It'll be nice to see mama and Spencer, but what then? Work at the restaurant or try to find work under the table?" Henry scans the area around him, as he has done this for many years and does it frequently. He speaks to his friend as he looks around the area, and the beautiful valley that the two men have called home for the past five years.

"It has been said the path of the righteous man is not an easy one, my brother" Henry turns his attention to his friend. "Love is out there for us, we just need to have faith" Joshua sits upright and stretches, but returns to staring at the ground.

"I found love Henry, and watched it die while I was tied to a tree." Nothing more is said as the two werewolves sit quietly for the rest of the day.

The next day Joshua and Henry walk to the tears of the river for one last time, stopping to admire the beauty of the picturesque setting. The two men eventually enter the cavern, Joshua picks up a piece of silver and watches it smoke in his hand. He looks to Henry, who is struggling to remain in the cave, and soon asks him to drop the silver. Joshua turns to his friend "It really doesn't hurt since I turned into a red-eye."

"Well, it's painful for those of us that are not as fortunate as you" Joshua tosses the silver nugget back into the water at his friend's request. The pair walks slowly back to the cabin, but stops at a small clearing off the water's edge, where the deceased chief is buried. The two men look up at the wooden platform, suspended on poles that hold the fallen warrior.

"He stuck it out until he took care of John and the rest of that bunch, didn't he?" Henry nods but is silent for several minutes before responding.

"And he died leaving the world a little better, something we should all be doing" Joshua looks to his friend with a somber look.

"Let's go home Henry," the two men walk slowly back to the small cabin and look up to see Dawn sitting on a chair waiting for their return. Joshua approaches the doctor, who looks up at his large frame.

"Little A.J. is down with his granddaddy and uncle" Henry looks at the dirt path and smiles.

"I think I'll go see little Andrew Joshua," leaving the two at the cabin. Joshua sits down beside Dawn, struggling to find words until his former lover looks at him.

"Andrew was happy about his son sharing his first name, but when I told him I wanted his son's middle name to be named after an Amish guy that's living on the reservation." The attractive doctor pats the werewolf's leg. "Well that took a bit of convincing" Joshua looks to the attractive doctor.

"We're leaving soon, and heading back to Virginia" Dawn looks up and strokes Joshua's face.

"When Daddy told me, I knew I had to come," she leans in and kisses him. "We haven't spoken that much since you healed up" Joshua kisses his former lover for several minutes before answering.

"I never knew what to say, so I said nothing" he leans back in his chair, no longer holding her in his arms. Dawn looks to the ground, and her long black hair falls down on both sides of her face.

"I sometimes question if I made the right choice with Andrew." The attractive doctor looks up from the ground and pushes her hair to one side. "He never lights up at the sound of my name, like you do when you talk about Anna." Joshua sits silently as she continues "but I can't compete with a ghost and a memory" Joshua looks to the woman who is obviously waiting for a response.

"Dawn, I will never be the man that you deserve. I can barely read, and my head is a mess." Dawn shakes her head, disagreeing with Joshua.

"He may be a doctor, but he could never survive like you have all these years" Dawn smiles, and tilts her head slightly. "He also never saved an entire race of people" Dawn rises and steps directly in front of the werewolf, she places his head in her hands and tilts it until her lips meet his. She kisses him passionately for a second time and holds her forehead to his, "I hope you find peace and someone to love; a girl could do a lot worse." She releases Joshua's head and begins walking slowly away from him, but turns to look at him with tears in her eyes. "You were never an animal, and I would have been proud to have your children" Joshua gets up, and walks down the path to the great hall, holding Dawn's hand. A very young boy in overalls runs out to him, falling a few times before reaching the large man. He picks up the small child and smiles as his eyes turn red. The little boy laughs as he leans in and hugs the werewolf, unafraid of what he has just seen. Joshua hands the boy to his mother and smiles softly at her.

"For what it's worth, you were never second best, and I would have been lucky to have you." Dawn smiles back and waves at the three men standing on the porch. Kajika walks briskly to his sister and helps her strap little Andrew in the simple car seat. Joshua stands and watches the Ford Bronco drive off. Kajika playfully slaps the werewolf on his stomach as he walks past. Twin Bears and Henry join Joshua as he stands looking down the road.

"Are you okay?" Twin Bears said, but doesn't expect an answer and simply stands with his friends. Joshua spends that night, and most of the next day, staring at the grass-covered spot where John and his pack are buried, all members of the pack were buried face down, and all that remains of them are painful memories. Henry is silent, as nothing is left to say that hasn't been said countless times. The next day, Chief Twin Bears returns to the two wolves and asks them to walk with him. The three men enter the great hall to find the large wooden table covered with food. Henry and Joshua are visibly stunned at the food, and how many people are able to fit in the large room. Chief Twin Bears turns to the two men standing silently. "This is for you; we all have better homes because of what the both of you have done," Snow Bird walks up and hands them a plate loaded with roasted deer and hugs the two men tightly.

"And we all sleep safer after what you did for us" most of the day is spent eating and celebrating, and everyone has a chance to speak with the departing warriors, that are now family. Living on the reservation has allowed the two wolves the opportunity to learn the language of the Blackfoot nation, but both are unsure of what is being said from the departing members of the community. Henry looks to the Chief and his wife, and asks what everyone is saying. Twin Bears laughs as he leans into his two guests.

"I asked that everyone said good journey" Snow Bird rubs her husband's shoulder and joins the conversation.

"Good-Bye is what is said to people that leave and don't come back." The Chief looks at his wife and nods before turning to the two guests.

"But a good journey mean that you will return to us one day" Kajika waits silently, as everyone takes there turn speaking to the guests of honor, before walking in front of the two werewolves and places his forearm across his chest, and nods. Both werewolves stand up and respond, by respectfully mimicking the mute Indian.

"Thanks Kajika, for everything" the only son of the chief leaves and goes back to his home at the edge of the sacred land. The two men sit down and realize that most have left, leaving them with the Chief and his wife. Joshua looks to the Indian couple.

"Kajika will do well as caretaker of the sacred land," Chief Twin Bears nods with a look of pride.

"He has walked those lands since he was a baby" the Chief looks to his wife and nods. Snowbird leaves but soon returns with two items wrapped in the simple brown paper giving them to the two werewolves. The two men graciously accept the gifts and open them. Joshua lifts up the deerskin shirt with a red-eyed black wolf staring back at him. He looks over at Henry, who has the same shirt but with a grey wolf. "They're war shirts, my father wanted everyone that fought the wendigo to have one, and we also have some for the others in your pack." Henry and Joshua are visibly stunned at the detail on the garments, and thank the Indian Chief, but are interrupted by an unfamiliar voice.

"Is it okay if I eat some of this food?" The four individuals seated at the table look up to see an unfamiliar man loading a plate with food. The man sits his plate down and licks his fingers before approaching the two werewolves, who looks the man up and down, noticing his wrinkled tuxedo shirt and uncombed hair. "I'm Rodney, the boss told me to come and get you" the man sits down and begins to devour the meat. "I was hoping that one of you could help drive back, I drove straight here" Henry looks to Rodney and points to the Chief and his wife.

"You should probably introduce yourself to the Chief and his wife properly." Rodney stands up and wipes his hands on his pants before extending his hand. The Chief smiles and points to the plate.

"Please rest and eat; you are welcome to anything here" the newcomer smiles and nods as he sits back down and begins to eat. He stops and swallows hard, pointing to the black man sitting across from him.

"You're Henry" Rodney then turns to the large brown-haired man sitting beside Henry, "and you're Joshua" another bite is taken as the youngest werewolf of the three continues. "It's an honor, a lot of people are happy about what happened to John and his pack, but you two are legends" Joshua leans back as curiosity overtakes him.

"Why are we legends? No one knows we're alive, and no one here talks to outsiders," Rodney stops and looks at the two senior werewolves.

"I'm like you guys, but I'm only a medium grey, and I haven't been changed for very long, but you guys don't get it to do you?" Everyone is silent and doesn't answer the question. Hence, Rodney continues. "It's a hell of a story, left for dead but came back and avenged your lady by taking on one of the largest packs that anyone has ever seen," the awestruck werewolf points his fork at the others sitting with him. "No one liked John, but everyone likes Spencer and your mother, the word is your gonna take over for Lyle." Rodney dives into the plate and takes another bite before he continues. "Word is there's a new sheriff in town, and he's a really big fucking red-eyed dog" Joshua's facial expression changes.

"Lyle is our leader, and that will not change; I have no plans on taking over anything." No one responds to Joshua's statement, as the tone in his voice reminds everyone of who he is.

CHAPTER FOURTEEN

Joshua stares out the window of the Chevy Impala, at the crowd of Native Americans that he lived with for years, as Henry begins driving to the main road. After everyone is settled in the car, Rodney leans up between the two men sitting in the front seat.

"Thank you for driving first Henry, If Joshua drives next; I'll drive the rest of the way, after we reach Chicago." Henry doesn't say anything as he begins to merge onto the interstate. Joshua looks at the large I-94E sign but remains silent. Henry and Joshua have been together for years and, at times, are silent as they know everything about each other, but Rodney is new to this crew and tries very hard to fit in. He mentions how he stayed behind and took care of the restaurant, how Mama Nell was one of John's people, and his past as a soldier in world war two. Rodney was obviously a good person, and a good friend to the family, but didn't need to try so hard to fit in. Joshua turns and looks at the man sitting in the back seat.

"I have no problem with that, but why don't we just stop when we get past Chicago?" Rodney shrugs his shoulders but nods in agreement.

"That's no problem big dog, but I have no problem driving, I know you want to get back home." Joshua turns and continues staring out the window.

"Get back to what Rodney? Mama is happy with Spencer, and God knows she deserves it." He shifts his gaze to the floorboard of the car, "and Henry deserves to be happy." Henry looks in the rearview mirror, to his passenger in the back seat, and tilts his head toward Joshua. Rodney nods and places his hand on the other passenger's shoulder.

"Don't forget about your happiness too, big dog" Joshua hears Rodney, but doesn't say anything. His happiness died years ago with Anna, and Dawn found happiness with Andrew. Everyone close to him either finds happiness when he's gone, or dies if they stay with him for too long. His mother found happiness when he wasn't around, and Henry will need to leave at some point if he is to be happy. As far as Joshua is concerned, a life of loneliness is all that is waiting for him. Henry, who has remained silent for most of the trip, speaks up.

"I know you think happiness will never find you my brother, but everyone deserves to be happy, including you." Henry has known Joshua most of his life, he and Anna were the ones that trained him on how to be a werewolf, and is one of the few people that can speak openly to him about Anna. "I have never lost hope that I will find love, but the only way you will find someone is to get over Anna," Joshua looks up from the floorboard, emotionless, at his friend's statement. "I realize that Dawn was carrying another man's child, Still, that woman was in love with you," Henry reaches out and places his free hand on his friend's shoulder. "But no one can compete with a memory, promise me that you find a place for Anna and open your heart for someone else." Joshua nods as he knows that his friends are speaking the truth. The three men spend the rest of the trip telling tall tales, Joshua tells Rodney about life as a Mennonite when he was a boy and his travels with the pack. Henry speaks up from time to time, speaking about his brother and life as a slave. No one speaks about John as his time has passed. Henry pulls into the small motel parking lot and turns to the others. "This looks like a clean place, look good to you guys?" Rodney begins pulling money out of his pocket and counting it.

"Spencer gave me a lot more money than I needed" after counting the money, he looks up at the two men in the front seat. "We can sleep and eat good tonight, boys" everyone laughs as Rodney walks to get a room and returns half an hour later. He points to the small office at the center of motel rooms. "The owner just got back from Vietnam" the younger werewolf opens the door and steps aside to let the others in. "Sorry, I lost track of time talking to a fellow G.I." No one was upset, and nothing was said as the three entered the room. There was enough money for each man to have his own room, but werewolves are pack animals, so they sleep close to each other whenever possible. The room was like most of the rooms they have all been in. Light blue walls with a television sitting in front of two twin beds and a cheap painting above the nightstand, with a chair sitting in front of a large window with a view of the parking lot. The three men find a small restaurant to eat but soon find themselves fighting sleep, all but Joshua.

Joshua sits in the chair watching the sunrise, it was Sunday, and images of his family going to church fill his head. Each church family would take turns cooking, which meant going to someone's house and having a large plate of fried chicken waiting. Sometimes a pig would be roasted outside if the weather was nice. Someone would bring green beans, and another family would bake bread, but everyone brought something. Sarah tried to keep the services going and would read the Bible to Joshua. She frequently prayed and always asked him to join, but the bible reading and the prayers stopped after a while. Keeping the faith is hard when life keeps throwing so much at you. It's even harder when you're all but immortal, and no end appears to be in sight. Next year will be 1970, and Joshua will technically be 77 years old but still looks like a 20-year-old man, granted some life experience shows on his face, but that will only get you a few more years. Joshua walks over to the single bed where Henry is sleeping. He opens the drawer and pulls out the Bible, which can be found in any motel. The sleeping werewolf looks up at Joshua, as you will never sneak up on a sleeping wolf, especially an experienced one like Henry. The red eyed werewolf picks up the Bible and looks down at his friend, "it's early, go back to sleep" he returns to the chair at the window but checks on Rodney, who is sound asleep, before flipping through the pages, stopping at Proverbs, pausing at chapter 10 verse 28 *"The hope of the righteous brings joy, but the expectation of the wicked will perish."* Joshua reads the passage a few times and thinks about what he has just read, by werewolf standards he is young, so maybe he will find joy, or perish at some point, as his journey has just started. The werewolf flips to some other passages before being interrupted by Henry.

"You okay "Henry said, Rodney wakes up and struggles to join in.

"Is who okay? I'm okay" he looks to Joshua, who smiles at the two men.

"Everything's fine" Joshua places the Bible on the small table before standing up. "I was just catching up on some reading."

Rodney calls the restaurant, telling everyone when they will arrive, before returning to the car where Joshua and Henry are waiting. "Spencer wanted me to call when we got closer to Richmond," no one questions Rodney as this made perfect sense. The youngest member of the small pack begins driving, while the returning werewolves look at the scenery. It's been years since Henry or Joshua has been in Virginia, and things have grown since they were last here. Rodney yawns while his passengers continue to look around, and they soon find themselves getting close to their destination. Everyone is awake, but quiet, as everyone is lost in their own thoughts. The vehicle exits in Harrisonburg, confusing the two passengers.

"Where are we going?" Rodney doesn't answer, and becomes visibly nervous at Joshua's question. "Is the car okay?" Henry looks around but is silent and Rodney finally looks up from the road.

"The boss told me to take you to Elkton, but that's all I know" both Henry and Joshua look at each other, wondering what's waiting for them, Henry shrugs.

"I guess we'll see why we're going to Elkton in a few minutes" Rodney turns off the main road, and continues to drive until the asphalt turns to dirt. He keeps driving until the road ends at a fence with the gate opened. The car tops the large hill and reveals a yellow house that is very well maintained. The three men pull up in front of the house; Joshua gets out of the car and looks at the large farmhouse, before turning to the large red barn on the other side of the wide driveway. Henry and Rodney join him, and the three wait for something to happen. Henry's nose begins to twitch as he raises his head. "Do you smell that?" Joshua looks to the other two men standing with him.

"Chicken! And I also smell hamburger" Joshua said, all three men walk to the corner of the building, to find picnic tables loaded with food. Joshua looks at the red and white tablecloths flowing in the breeze. A stranger appears from the opposite corner of the building and approaches the three men. The three men recognize one of their own kind and Joshua grabs the overweight black haired man by the neck, lifting him off the ground with his eyes turning red. The well-dressed man lifts his hands up.

"I am sorry to startle you, my name is Harry, and you're in no danger. I represent someone who gave me specific instructions, when you guys show up today." Joshua sits the man down and waits as the gentleman adjusts his hair and tucks his shirt in. "I was turned after the stock market crashed back in 29, I was a banker." The man smiles back at the pair after composing himself, "a family of Romanians banknote came due, and one of them bit me as payment." Harry laughs nervously at the three men "or cursed me, I'm still trying to figure that out" the banker goes on to explain how he fell on hard times as a result of his curse, eventually ending up homeless, before Lyle found him and got him back on his feet. The well spoken banker reaches in the pocket of his tailored shirt. "That reminds me, you'll need these" the two returning pack members are given a driver's license and social security card. "I take care of things like this, I also change precious stones and gold to currency, sell antiquities, and make sure no questions are ever asked." The middle aged banker reaches in his dress coat and pulls out a manila envelope, "I also have a birth certificate for each of you that will work for a few years" Joshua looks up and grins as he sees a familiar face.

"Mama!" Sarah looks up as she sits a large bowl on the table and rushes to embrace her son. Sarah looks up at Joshua then turns her attention to the other two men standing with her son.

"Henry, thank you for staying with him" she reaches out and pats the black man on the shoulder, then turns to Rodney. "Thank you too, Rodney, and we'll pay you for your time," the bartender looks at his blonde boss and nods his head, assuring her that no payment was needed. Sarah motions for Harry to join them, who eagerly approaches the four werewolves. "Harry was the one that made all this possible" the newest member of the pack approaches and nods.

"It's an honor to finally meet you both, I've grown very fond of your family as I tend to everyone's business affairs, but you're a bit of a legend for the little nobody wolves like me." Henry looks around with a lost look on his face and points to the house. He gets ready to say something, but is interrupted by the businessman. "And yes, this was John Bennett's old house; I got it at auction when the taxes weren't paid about a year ago." Harry walks out to the edge of the yard and points to the barn. "We completely remodeled the house and tore down the barn" the banker points to the pristine wood floor of the barn "and added a basement before rebuilding, come on, let me show you around." The crew walks over to the very pristine barn and Joshua looks at the neatly painted boards that separate the stalls, before pointing to a door that leads upstairs to the enclosed loft.

"What's up there?" Harry is quick to answer Joshua, as if he is trying to sell him the property.

"That is a fully functional apartment with a full bath, kitchen, and two bedrooms, no expense was spared, and the apartment is very nice." Harry rubs his hands and grins, "but the best is downstairs." The well-dressed businessman escorts Joshua and Henry downstairs, flipping

293

a light switch before descending. The two newcomers look at the tall ceilings and concrete stalls, pointing at the large newly painted steel rings, each holding a large log chain. "A place for people like ourselves to change and not worry, we also purchased the adjoining property." The three men emerge from the basement to join Sarah and Spencer, who walked over. Everyone remains silent while Harry continues his sales pitch "over 300 acres that join the national forest, on a dead-end dirt road, this is as isolated as it gets." Henry looks to Spencer and Sarah, standing beside each other.

"I thought you two had an apartment above the restaurant?" Sarah smiles at the two men and starts to answer but is interrupted by another familiar voice.

"They don't live here, this is for you two" Joshua looks up to see Lyle standing in the large opening of the barn. Everything was pristine and newly painted, but Lyle is the one constant in this world, and still wore the same button topped hat and bulky sweater, despite the weather. His stubble was a bit shorter but not by much. The senior wolf instructs everyone to leave, except Sarah. "This is your home Joshua; it just seemed to be your kind of place" Sarah steps between Lyle and her son.

"You needed time to heal before we said anything about this." The three family members walk slowly back to the house where the others have started eating. Lyle grabs Joshua's arm and stops at the edge of the yard while Sarah joins the others.

"I made a choice some time ago son," the senior red-eyed wolf raises his hand, displaying a ring, shining in the sunlight. "This is all that's left of my kingdom, but it's also a reminder of the lousy husband and father I was, all I have left, is the hope that I'll see my wife and family one day." Lyle releases his arm and sighs."I have tried for years to make amends, then something happened, and I knew this was my chance to set things right." Joshua nods; he trusts Lyle with his life but is still unsure what's going on, so he remains silent. The senior red-eyed alpha is aware of the confusion on the young man's face, but continues. "There was too much at stake, and I had to know you're the man I need you to be." Joshua remains confused, still unsure of what is being told to him. Both men stand at the edge of the yard, just out of sight from the others, the former king rubs the stubble on his face before finishing his statement. "A man needs to decide when it's time to drop to his knees and pray or when to grab a sword and protect what's his, and I needed to know if you could make the right decision." The elder black wolf assures his protégé how proud he is of the new red eyed Alpha, but finishes the conversation with a concerning remark. "So if you want to get pissed off at someone, get upset with me," Joshua walks with Lyle and joins the others, who are eating, still unsure what the senior Alpha disclosed to him. He reaches down to grab a plate but stops as he looks at the attractive black woman sitting at the table.

"Jayde?" the young woman stands up and hugs the absentee homeowner, and Joshua continues to speak with the woman who was a child the last time he saw her. Jayde goes on to tell him that Mama Nell had passed a few years ago. Nothing more was said, but Joshua would later learn that someone shot the woman shortly after she revealed she was working for John. She goes on to tell the former Mennonite that she has a degree in psychology and is currently attending law school. Joshua turns to Henry, while Jayde continues to speak about Martin Luther King being assassinated the previous year, and how she changed her major to criminal law after hearing the news. Joshua looks at Henry and Jayde standing beside each other.

"I like how this looks, you two make a good-looking couple" Jayde turns to the former slave, who is staring in the distance with a confused look. The stunning black woman attempts to console the black man standing beside her, as tears fill his eyes. Joshua remains unsure of what is happening and is confused at his friend's reaction. Henry looks to the former Mennonite and swallows hard before speaking.

"Oh my God, It's not possible" the black man looks to his friend, and points to the house. "I heard her heart stop, I know she was dead when we left," Joshua starts to turn but freezes at what he hears.

"Joshua" The former Mennonite looks to his friends, confused at what he has just heard. He continues to stand with his mouth open, unsure what he should do. Jayde turns and gets in front of the nervous werewolf, and places her hands on his midsection. Joshua was sure that he lost the love of his life years ago, and refuses to turn around.

"She's gone, and I can't, I just can't turn around and lose her again" Joshua said, as the beautiful black woman smiles at the distraught werewolf.

"Turn around sweetie and welcome home" Jayde said.

Joshua turns to see Anna standing a few feet behind him. Time seems to stop for a few moments as a flood of emotions overtakes him. For years the Alpha convinced himself that a life of loneliness was all this life had to offer, and that it was all he deserved. Time has a way of mixing up memories of the past, and can leave a grieving individual with nothing but bitterness and despair. Joshua struggles to breathe but is still unsure if what he is seeing is real. He reaches out, grasping the love of his life's arm, and looks into her deep blue eyes, that always seem to see into his soul, finally realizing that she is real. "I saw you die, you're not real, I couldn't save you, and you died" is the only words that a shocked Joshua can say. The attractive dark-haired woman steps closer to him, stroking his stomach, feeling the scares inflicted by John, before looking up at him.

"It's me honey" Joshua's knees begin to buckle, and he falls into Anna, who catches him. "I got you," She kisses his neck gently," and I'll never let go this time." Joshua regains his footing and kisses her passionately, and continues to hold her as she falls into his chest, wrapping her arms around him. The red-eyed wolf looks down at the only woman he has ever loved. Nothing is said as family and friends quietly witness the reunion.

"I thought I lost you" Joshua laughs for the first time in years and hugs his beloved, who continues to stroke his hair, as the two stares lovingly at each other. Joshua picks up his soul mate, who melts into him, placing her head on his shoulder, and glances at Sarah, who has been sitting quietly witnessing everything. The two have made efforts to get along, but Sarah blames Anna for the death of her family and being on the run for so many years. Sarah looks to Anna and nods as she smiles softly at her; any issues she has with this woman vanished at the sound of her son's laughter. She looks to the woman holding her son and without making a sound whisper's

"Thank you" Anna rubs her man's back and smiles back at her future mother-in-law. The two lovers stand beside each other as the others crowd around them, hugging and expressing how happy they are. Joshua and Anna take a seat at a wooden picnic table, but nothing is said for several minutes until he finally asks how she survived. The stunning werewolf explains to Joshua that Lyle took her to a motel just down the road, and tried to heal her. Joshua looks to Anna, confused.

"But he stabbed you in the heart?" Anna pauses and collects her thoughts before leaning in and kissing him gently. She has gone through this conversation in her mind a thousand times but is still struggling to say the words.

"Our baby saved me" Joshua nods as he attempts to console her before turning to Lyle, who explains that he came back for him at her request, but saw Sarah dragging him to the cabin and that his first priority was saving Anna, so he went back to help her. Joshua turns and continues to look into the eyes of the woman he loves.

"I would have gladly died if it meant saving her life" he leans in and kisses her passionately, "the important thing is we're together and we can try to have another baby." Everyone attending the reunion is quiet, as Anna places her hands on both sides of her man's face, and lovingly looks into his eyes.

"I didn't lose the baby" Joshua leans back, not quite sure what to say but soon notices his mother approaching with a dark-haired girl in a simple dress, covered in flowers. The young girl nervously looks up at her father. Joshua looks at the child and smiles as he sees his own eyes looking back at him. The young girl walks up and stands beside her mother, who adjusts the strap that is holding her daughter's hair back. "Selene, this is your father" the young girl looks to her father, and the two are silent as they take a moment to look at each other. Joshua looks at his daughter lovingly, unsure what to say.

"It's a pleasure to meet you, Selene" Joshua said, the fourteen-year-old stays close to her mother as she looks at the large man sitting in front of her.

"Mama and Papou said you were off fighting some bad people. Are you finished fighting?" The new father looks to his daughter, who looks just like her mother, and assures her that he is finished and is home to stay. The young girl steps forward and hugs her father. "Is it okay if I call you papa?" Joshua reaches out and hugs his daughter tightly.

"You can call me papa or anything you want, sweetie" the young girl steps back and looks at the man she now calls papa.

"Did you eat any potato salad yet? Me and mama made the potato salad, and it tastes just like grandmas" Joshua rises and gets a plate of food, including a very large helping of potato salad. He takes a seat across from Anna and begins to eat with his daughter sitting beside him. His eyes begin to turn red, and a small growl escapes his lips as he devours the chicken. The werewolf's face turns red from embarrassment, and he turns his head, attempting to hide his eyes from his daughter. Anna lovingly reaches out and grabs Joshua's hand.

"She knows all about our family and what we are" Joshua holds Anna's hand as he looks down at the young girl staring back at him.

"It's okay Papa, Papou's eyes turn red, and mama's eyes turn yellow when they eat sometimes." The black werewolf looks up at Anna, realizing what Lyle meant earlier about what was at stake.

"The white wolf?" Anna nods slightly as Selene encourages her father to eat some potato salad. A rush of both worry and excitement overtakes him.

"She doesn't know yet, and we haven't told her" The couple sit and talk for a moment as Anna explains that they want her to have a normal life, proudly proclaiming how smart she is, and how she has a lot of friends. The new father kisses his daughter's forehead, and returns to eating, unconcerned about his eyes or his growling. After finishing, he looks to his lover.

"So she's happy?" Joshua said, Anna smiles.

"Very happy" Lyle approaches the new family and hugs Selene, who affectionately calls him Papou. He looks down at the young girl and instructs her to go see her grandmother, before taking a seat.

"I wanted to tell you for a long time Joshua, but after John started chasing you, I decided not to say anything, in case something went wrong." Lyle said, as Joshua looks to the senior werewolf and nods, but his facial expression soon changes.

"But why didn't anyone say anything after John died?" Anna speaks up and explains to Joshua that it was her decision not to call.

"Everyone agreed, including your mother, but she took some convincing." The dark haired beauty looks to the man she loves, and tells him about the guilt she felt about not telling him about her or their daughter, and about all the sleepless nights, worried to hear that he died, never knowing she survived. "I wanted the man I fell in love with to return to me, and I couldn't take the chance of another version of you coming home to us." Joshua pauses and looks down at the tablecloth in front of him. He nods his head slightly before looking up at her.

"I'm not the same man" Joshua goes on to tell Anna how close he came to killing John, and how all he's done is question his beliefs, and is unsure if he's a good man. Anna reaches across the table and grabs her man's hand. She leans toward him and smiles.

"I never worried about the choices you would need to make, but if you knew about us, you wouldn't have made it, and John would have used it against you." The beautiful werewolf kisses his hand. "The minute I looked into your eyes, I knew you're the same man I fell in love with," Joshua tells her about working at the mill, the reservation, and Master Chang. Anna nods at Lyle and listens to Joshua's story. She kept a close eye on him for years with everyone's help, and asked about him frequently while he was away, but remains silent, as he tells her his story. Lyle looks at the happy couple and smiles.

"Too much is at stake here guys, and when word gets out about her, it could be dangerous." Everyone's attention turns to the elder wolf, who goes on to tell the history of the white wolf. "I have been around long enough to see a lot of false emissaries, and when word gets out, a lot of people will be coming to see for themselves," Lyle ponders a bit before continuing. "Most will not be anything to worry about, but some may want to cause trouble," the senior wolf doesn't say anything else, and an uncomfortable silence fills the air, until Joshua speaks to the crowd around him.

"I've spent most of my life questioning my faith, my life, and the choices that I've made, but everything was clear the moment my Anna and my child came back to me. Sometimes we all wonder if it's our human side or our wolf side that controls the choices we make, but we are a family and a pack. The things that bind us together are primal and have nothing to do with being a werewolf, it's who we are. If someone comes to harm any of us, they will not like what is waiting for them, and I'll be waiting" Pride can be seen on everyone's face at the Alpha's statement, and everyone nods in agreement. Lyle looks at his fellow red eye with a stern look.

"No Joshua, we'll be waiting" Lyle said.

Everyone turns their attention to Selene, carrying a large chocolate sheet cake out of the side door. Joshua smiles at the sight of his daughter struggling to place the cake, and realizes he is happy and that his mind is at rest for the first time in several years. The future will take care of itself, but for now, he's home with his family, and whatever path he took that led him to this moment was worth every step. He looks to Anna, who smiles back at him quietly, but is interrupted by the sound of his daughter's voice.

"Do you want cake, papa?" Joshua attempts to answer but is presented with a rather large piece of cake before he can answer. Selene smiles at her father as she presents him with a fork. The red-eyed wolf pauses to pray before eating, something that he hasn't done for years. Joshua opens his eyes to see Anna staring lovingly at him.

"Welcome home, honey."

ABOUT THE AUTHOR

Dwight Tusing lives in the Shenandoah Valley in Virginia where he resides with his wife Dawn and there dog George. He is a fan of Comic Books, Stephen King and enjoys writing stories that originates in the Shenandoah Valley, where he finds his inspiration. Dwight is also an avid animal lover.